ON WINGS OF SONG

ROBERTA GRIEVE

ISIS
LARGE PRINT
Oxford

First published in Great Britain 2009
by
Robert Hale Limited

Published in Large Print 2010 by ISIS Publishing Ltd.,
7 Centremead, Osney Mead, Oxford OX2 0ES
by arrangement with
Robert Hale Limited

British Library Cataloguing in Publication Data
Grieve, Roberta.
    On wings of song.
    1. Women singers - - Family relationships - - Fiction.
    2. Mothers and daughters - - Fiction.
    3. Upper class - - Fiction.
    4. Large type books.
    I. Title
    823.9'2–dc22

ISBN 978–0–7531–8660–2 (hb)
ISBN 978–0–7531–8661–9 (pb)

Printed and bound in Great Britain by
T. J. International Ltd., Padstow, Cornwall

CHAPTER
ONE

A burst of raucous shouts and laughter erupted from the auditorium as Arabella Raynsford hurried from her dressing room and stood waiting in the wings. Her heart beat faster as a drum roll and a clash of cymbals signalled the end of the previous act.

"Two minutes, Miss," the stage manager whispered. "Good crowd in tonight."

Arabella nodded. She had already seen the soldiers thronging the foyer as she hurried to her dressing room to get ready for her performance. They were not boisterously drunk as they sometimes were, but they were determined to have a good time. Understandable, she thought, when they were waiting to be shipped off to the Crimea where there was already news of a huge naval battle. She listened to the catcalls and jeers directed at the juggler and his assistant as they left the stage, hoping they would quieten down when she went on.

She clasped her hands in front of her abdomen, just below the diaphragm, breathing deeply and evenly as she had learned to do before a performance. Maisie, her maid, made a final adjustment to her bonnet and gave her an encouraging smile.

Gradually, the butterflies in her stomach stopped their frantic struggle and eased to a gentle flutter.

It wasn't vanity that told her the rowdy theatregoers would fall under her spell as soon as the first notes of the song left her mouth. She had been bewitching her audiences as long as she could remember, including the officers in her brother's regiment, who often attended soirees at her parents' large Georgian townhouse in exclusive Essex Square.

She didn't blame the young men in the auditorium for wanting to let off steam before facing battle with the Russians and the fearful experiences that awaited them — experiences she could only imagine, for they were not a fit subject for discussion when ladies were present. There was always trouble somewhere in the world and the British soldiery was always ready to do its bit in preserving the might of the rapidly expanding British Empire. Not that Arabella took much notice of what went on outside her own little empire — top of the bill at the Half Moon Theatre, Capon Street, not far from Covent Garden.

The juggler and his assistant stumbled off the stage to a smattering of applause and the curtain came down. There was another loud drum roll and Sam Fenton, owner of the Half Moon, who also acted as master of ceremonies, banged his gavel on the lectern at the side of the stage. "Ladies and gentleme-en," he bellowed, "I now give you your own — your very own — Miss Bella-a-a Fo-orde."

There was a burst of applause, a few whistles, feet stamping.

Arabella tripped onto the stage, the hoops of her crinoline swaying to reveal enticing glimpses of slim ankles encased in satin slippers. She stood in the centre, hands clasped beneath her bosom, eyes downcast, a picture of innocence in her cream satin dress, its flounces edged with lace, trimmed with pale blue bows and pink silk rosebuds. She wore a little bonnet, adorned with flowers and ribbons to match the dress. A cascade of golden ringlets descended from beneath the bonnet to brush her shoulders.

The pianist played a few bars and she lifted her head, took a deep breath, opened her mouth and began to sing.

An unusual hush descended and even the most hardened cynics in the audience stopped fidgeting and listened, entranced, as the pure liquid notes poured from Bella's throat.

A hack from the *London Reporter*, sent along to find out what all the fuss was about, stopped scribbling and held his breath. A talent spotter for a rival theatre, who had slept through the first half of the entertainment, sat up and leaned forward open-mouthed. At least three subalterns in the Hussars fell instantly and irrevocably in love.

Arabella was oblivious to them all. She finished her first song — a heart-rending ballad of lost love — and launched immediately into another. This time it was a slightly saucy music hall song. As she sang, she leaned forward, her finger on her chin, a dimpled smile curving her mouth, a completely different Bella from the heart-broken lass she had been a few moments before.

When the audience cheered and shouted for more, she lowered her eyes demurely and started to sing softly, her voice swelling as she reached the final bars. "In the Gloaming" had become her signature song and the audience held its breath until she reached the end before bursting into applause once more.

Ever since she was a small girl Arabella had loved to sing. At the age of four she had stood on a chair in the drawing room of Essex House, the Raynsfords' London residence, as her mother accompanied her on the piano. She had glowed in the applause of her parents' friends. But as she grew older and the determination to make a career as a singer took hold, she'd had to accept that it was never going to happen. Nice girls did not go on the stage. Yet here she was — top of the bill. Sometimes she wondered how it had happened — and what the consequences would be if her oh-so-respectable family ever found out what she was up to.

Maisie stood in the wings listening enchantedly as the pure notes of the song rose to the rafters. There was none of the cat-calling and whistling that usually accompanied a music hall performance. The audience had come to hear Miss Bella Forde who was fast becoming the sensation of the London theatre.

Maisie wondered how much longer her mistress could keep up this double life. She knew that she would lose her position when the deception was inevitably discovered. They had run many risks so that Miss

Arabella could achieve her ambition but Maisie didn't care so long as her mistress had no regrets when it eventually had to end — as it surely must before long.

She thought back to that day six months ago. It had been her day off and, much as she loved her young mistress, she'd been eager to get away from Essex House. She couldn't wait to see her sister and find out how the new theatre, due to open any day now, was progressing.

She turned the corner into Capon Street and saw with pleasure that the scaffolding had come down and the painters had finished the façade. A sign writer perched on a ladder added a final flourish to the gilded lettering over the entrance — *Half Moon Theatre.* What a difference from the dingy tavern and adjoining music house that Violet and her husband had taken over a few years ago, Maisie thought. Sam Fenton might be a bit rough and ready, not exactly respectable according to the standards that the sisters had been brought up to, but he was a hard-working man. And he had a determination to succeed. He had turned the Half Moon Tavern round until it was no longer a dingy, noisome hangout for drunks and doxies. By securing the very best of entertainers and publicizing them in the penny broadsheets, he had brought in a different clientele. It had taken time but now, here he was, about to open a brand new theatre which he boasted would be the talk of London.

Maisie pushed open the door in the alley at the side of the new building and hurried along the corridor to the auditorium. Her sister and brother-in-law were on the stage, talking to a large florid man in a loud suit. Sam was waving his hands around as he always did when agitated, while Violet tapped a tiny foot against the newly installed footlights.

As Maisie approached, the man threw up his hands and said, "Well, there's nothing I can do about it." He stormed off, pushing past her as if she were not there.

"Well, that's put paid to our grand opening," Sam said.

"Don't worry, Sam. We'll find someone else," Violet said.

"Not at such short notice — and no one as good." Sam turned and saw Maisie. He gave a short laugh. "What you doin' here? Don't s'pose you can sing by any chance?" He strode away, calling to one of the workmen.

Violet kissed her sister's cheek. "Take no notice. He's in a bad mood." She sighed. "Can't say as I blame him."

"What's up, sis? I thought everything was going all right for the opening."

"It was — till Kitty let us down. Got a better offer, she says — one o' them posh theatres up west."

"Oh, no. What you gonna do, Vi?" Kitty Tyler was the singing sensation of the decade and had been engaged to top the bill at the grand opening of the Half Moon as well as to give one performance a week until further notice.

"We'll have to try and find someone to take her place." Violet kicked the edge of the stage. "How could she do this to us?"

"Did she sign anything? Can you hold her to her promise?"

"No — it was a friendly agreement. Some friend she turned out to be." Violet and Kitty had known each other since the days they'd belonged to a travelling theatrical party. Kitty's superb voice had taken her on to higher things while Violet had married Sam and settled down to run the tavern.

Maisie didn't know how to comfort her sister. She knew how much this new venture meant to her and Sam. "You've got a couple of weeks yet," she said.

"Something'll turn up. Not your worry anyway. Come and have a cuppa tea before we open up. I want to hear what the nobs have been up to." She took Maisie's arm and led her through a door at the back of the theatre which linked the old tavern to the new building.

From the front came the shouts of the workmen, the rumble of a barrel being rolled into the tavern's cellar, the clop of horses' hooves. But here in the kitchen where a kettle simmered on the black-leaded range it was quiet and cosy. Maisie sat at the scrubbed table while Violet made the tea.

They sipped in silence, enjoying this interlude when just for a few minutes they were free of the demands of others.

"So what's the news from Essex House? Has that handsome Captain been making eyes at you?" Violet asked.

Maisie giggled. "Don't be daft. He don't even notice I'm there. Oh, but he is 'andsome though. Not that he's there much — he'll be off again soon — God knows where. They say the Turks and Russians are at it and our boys will be dragged in before long. Don't know why they has to go off fighting in foreign places meself, but there you are."

"We had a lot of them hussars in the other night — ordinary soldiers, not officers. What a racket — banging their pots on the tables and stampin' their feet." Violet sighed and stirred her tea. "I was hopin' we'd be done with all that — get a better class of customer with the new place opening up. It's all gone wrong though with Kitty letting us down. She's billed as the main attraction and you know how ugly it can get when the customers ain't satisfied."

"Sam knows lots of people in the game — he'll come up with something."

"I surely 'ope so," Violet said.

The kitchen door opened and Sam came in looking thoroughly dejected. "Just popped up the road to see old Grimes — thought he might help out, but all the singers he knows are booked up." He threw himself into a chair beside Violet and drummed his fingers on the table.

Violet took hold of his hand and squeezed his fingers but she did not say anything.

Maisie spoke up. "My mistress has a lovely voice — sings like an angel," she said.

Sam snorted. "Drawing room singing. Pretty little tunes with soppy words. These society lasses sing and play the piano just to show off their dainty white hands and their latest fashionable dresses."

8

"Miss Arabella's not like that," Maisie protested. "I reckon she could be a professional."

Violet laughed. "Don't be daft, Maisie. You're surely not thinking your Miss Arabella could top the bill at the Half Moon? Even if she sings as good as you say, can you see your mistress allowing her to do it?"

And of course, she never would have — if she'd known about it. But they had found a way. For the past few months on two nights a week, the two girls had slipped out of the house and taken a cab to the Half Moon where Maisie, using her skills with make-up and needle and thread had transformed her mistress into the sensational Bella Forde. But how much longer could they get away with it? Maisie wondered.

Arabella came off the stage and rushed into the dressing room, a tiny cubbyhole at the end of a corridor. Maisie was waiting and pulled out a chair for her mistress.

"Did it go well, Maisie?"

"You don't have to ask, Miss. You were a sensation — as usual."

Arabella laughed. "Did you hear the applause — I haven't come down to earth yet."

"Well, forgive me for saying so, Miss, but it's time you did — and quick, if you want to get away before them fellers come round beggin' to take you out to supper."

She leaned over and removed Arabella's bonnet with the fringe of false blonde ringlets attached, then took the pins from her hair. She brushed the long straight strands until they shone like polished mahogany and, a few minutes later, had it pinned up in its usual smooth chignon.

While her maid brushed, Arabella rubbed cold cream into her skin to remove the thick stage make-up, the rouge on her cheeks and the bright blue paint on her eyelids which had the effect under the stage lights of making her grey eyes look almost blue.

That done, Maisie helped her to step out of the wire-framed crinoline overlaid with flounces of cream satin, revealing beneath it a skirt of deep green velvet. A matching jacket faced with pale green satin and a bonnet with ribbons of the same colour completed the transformation.

Maisie flung a shawl round her mistress's shoulders and opened the door, peeping into the corridor. Arabella could hear a clamour of voices but the maid whispered, "All clear" and beckoned her outside.

As she slipped through a side door and hurried down the alley, she heard Maisie say, "I'm sorry, gentlemen. Miss Forde is exhausted and regrets she cannot see anyone tonight."

Caroline Raynsford was annoyed. She had arranged this dinner party specifically in order to introduce her daughter to a couple of candidates more suitable for her hand than the rather dull Captain Wilson, who had been making sheep's eyes at Arabella since her coming out ball a year ago. As far as her husband was concerned, their son's friend would be an ideal match. But Caroline had higher ambitions for her daughter.

She tried to forget that the Raynsfords owed their prosperity to trade and that her own father had been a small farmer in the north of England. She had fostered the impression among their London acquaintances that her family had been landowners on a slightly larger scale and that it had been a bit of a comedown for her when she had met and married Henry. In fact, her parents had seen Henry Raynsford as a good match, despite his being in trade. His fleet of colliers based on the north Kent coast and a copperas smelting plant had brought him sufficient wealth to extend his country house just outside Whitstable as well as to purchase the lease on Essex House. Caroline was more than satisfied with her life. But she wanted even more for Arabella and did her best to see that her daughter was introduced to the best of London society.

She had high hopes of this evening's gathering — the younger son of Lord Barfield and an eager young politician who, although not quite out of the top drawer, looked set to rise quickly to a high position. Caroline would be immensely satisfied to see her daughter the wife of a future prime minister of England.

And where was the spoilt miss at this moment? Shut up in a dark room suffering from a migraine. It was almost as if she did it on purpose, she thought. How many more times must she plan these introductions, only to have Arabella retire to her room? She bit her lip and forced a smile for Mr Delaney, a friend of her husband, and another contender for Arabella's hand.

"And how is your charming daughter?" he asked. "I hope her indisposition is not too serious."

Caroline managed to repress another flicker of annoyance at her wayward daughter's behaviour and forced a smile. "It is just a headache. Rest in a darkened room is the best remedy, I find."

"I hear she sings like a nightingale. What a pity she cannot join us tonight. I had been so looking forward to hearing her," he said.

"Perhaps another time, Oswald," Henry Raynsford said, wiping his moustache on his napkin and throwing it down beside his plate. A footman stepped forward and removed it, the signal for the ladies to rise and for Jennings, the butler to place the decanter of port in front of his master.

In the drawing room, Caroline dismissed the maid and served the coffee herself. She sipped from her own cup, idly listening to the other ladies' gossip, wondering how she could get her daughter to take an interest in her future — and marriage was the only future open to a girl of her class. At the same time she was worried about the girl. These migraines seemed to be occurring with alarming frequency.

She roused herself when one of the guests addressed her directly. "I'm so sorry Arabella could not sing for us tonight. That reminds me — my servants have been gossiping about this new theatre and the singer they have engaged. Apparently she is a sensation. Such a pity we are prevented by convention from going to hear her for ourselves."

12

Caroline was shocked. "How can you think of even going near such a place?" she asked.

"I was not suggesting we should, my dear Mrs Raynsford. Of course, those places are for the entertainment of the lower classes." The woman took a sip of her coffee. "It is a pity though — I hear she has the voice of an angel."

"But nothing to compare with our dear Arabella, surely," said another guest.

Caroline stood up. "Maybe she will come down and join us, if she is sufficiently rested. I will send a maid to enquire." She pulled at the bell rope beside the fireplace.

CHAPTER
TWO

Arabella had been back in her room just long enough to remove her outer clothing and to throw herself down on the bed, not forgetting to clasp a lavender-soaked handkerchief in her hand, when a knock sounded at the door.

Maisie came through from the dressing room where she had been tidying her mistress's clothes and opened the door quietly, indicating that Arabella was resting.

It was no use. If she didn't respond, her mother would come up to see for herself if she was really ill. She lifted her head from the pillow and listened to the low-voiced exchange.

"It's all right, Maisie. I'll go down," she said, swinging her legs over the side of the bed. "Just give me a moment to tidy myself."

Maisie passed on the message to the maid and closed the door. "Are you sure, Miss? You must be worn out. You should rest."

"I must. I can't keep avoiding Mama's guests. If I have a migraine every time she has a dinner party she'll guess something's up." Arabella laughed and bent to peer at herself in the mirror, looking for telltale signs of the stage make-up she had hurriedly removed only an

14

hour before. Satisfied, she patted her hair and crossed the room.

"Suppose they ask you to sing, Miss?"

"Then I'll sing."

"You should save your voice. You don't want to go gettin' a sore throat."

"You worry too much, Maisie. I'll only sing one song — a short one — then plead fatigue."

Maisie grinned. "You should be an actress, not a singer."

Arabella forgave the familiarity. Sometimes she felt closer to her maid than to the daughters of her parents' friends, the young ladies who were deemed fit companions for the Raynsfords's daughter. But she had more in common with the quick-witted cockney girl who had been with the family since she was twelve years old and worked her way up from tweeny to ladies' maid. And she owed her a lot. How could she have kept up this deception for so long without the loyalty of little Maisie?

She took a deep breath and opened the drawing room door. Her brother Harry and a group of his fellow officers, resplendent in their dress uniforms, were gathered round the piano. She recognized most of them and, smiling, she crossed the room to join them, noting how Captain Wilson's eyes lit up.

She had known James Wilson since he had been at school with Harry and knew that her father would be only too pleased if they made a match of it. Until Robert Wilson's death two years ago the families had been linked through their businesses and a marriage would have strengthened those ties. Despite wanting to please her father, Arabella sided with her mother — though for different reasons. Caroline Raynsford had high ambitions for her only daughter and would not let her make the mistake of marrying into trade as she herself had done.

Arabella had no wish to marry at all. Besides, fond as she was of James, he was far too conventional for her — kind but dull. She could just picture his reaction if he discovered what she'd been up to earlier this evening. His sister Charlotte, who was engaged to Harry, would no doubt be just as shocked. Although the girls had been friends since childhood, Arabella sometimes grew impatient with Charlotte's wish to conform. Still, seeing her friend's adoring gaze lingering on Harry, she couldn't help being slightly envious that she had found true love — and what's more would be allowed to follow her heart. Whereas she, Arabella, was expected to marry whomever her mother decided was suitable.

A bubble of laughter rose in her throat at the thought of their horrified expressions if any of them ever discovered her secret. She turned her face away to hide her smile and found herself looking up into the face of a stranger. The smile faded as his dark eyes bored into hers, one eyebrow lifted in a sardonic grimace. She felt a blush rising up her neck but before she could turn away again her brother stepped forward and said, "Allow me to introduce Mr Delaney, a business acquaintance of Father's. Oswald, my sister, Arabella."

The stranger took her hand and bowed over it. "Charmed, Miss Raynsford. I hope we shall have the pleasure of hearing you sing for us — if you are quite recovered from your migraine. I hear they can be quite debilitating."

"I am much better, sir. They come on so suddenly but they go as quickly as they arrive."

Henry Raynsford appeared at their side. "I see you have met my daughter, Oswald. But, I beg you, do not try to persuade her to sing tonight. These attacks leave her quite weak, you know." He turned to his daughter. "Go and sit with your mother, my dear. Mr Delaney and I wish to discuss business."

Arabella smiled. "Do not let Mama hear you say so. You know how she feels about such talk at social gatherings."

Her father laughed and patted her hand. "I know I can trust you not to tell her." She laughed with him and crossed the room to join her mother and other ladies.

"My dear, I do hope you are feeling better." Caroline patted the seat beside her. "Come and sit down. You still look a little pale. Charlotte is going to sing for us instead of you this evening."

Seated beside her mother Arabella let the music and the other guests' chatter wash over her. James's sister had a pleasant voice and Arabella was pleased that for once, the attention was directed away from herself.

"Don't they make a charming couple?" Charlotte's mother said. She smiled and nodded in time with the music as her daughter sang, accompanied by Harry at the piano. When the song ended, she applauded politely, then turned and tapped Arabella's hand playfully with her fan. "If it were not for you, my dear, my daughter's voice would be the talk of London," she said. "Are you going to give us a duet this evening?"

Before she could reply, her mother said, "Arabella has been unwell. She must rest for a while."

Arabella wasn't a bit tired but it was easier to keep up the pretence a little longer. She wondered how she would get through the next hour before the guests began to leave. To stave off her boredom, she looked across at the group of men now engaged in a heated discussion and tried to work out which of them had been earmarked as a potential suitor.

She didn't want to think about it. Sometimes she wished she were more like Charlotte. Her future was all mapped out for her and she seemed quite content with the prospect of marriage, apart from her distress that her wedding would have to be postponed because Harry's regiment would soon be embarking for the Crimea.

Arabella's singing career was far more important to her than any thoughts of marriage. Realistically, she acknowledged it would have to end some day but that would be time enough to think about a husband.

As if he had read her thoughts Oswald Delaney appeared in front of them. He bowed over Caroline's hand as he made his farewells then turned to Arabella. "I am so sorry you could not sing tonight. Maybe I will have that pleasure another time." His eyes bored into hers and she felt herself flushing.

When he had gone her mother turned to her, eyes glittering with unusual animation. "I do believe Mr Delaney was quite taken with you, my dear. He's Irish, you know — but from a very good family. They have a large estate in County Cork and he has factories in Kent." Her mouth twisted in a grimace and she lowered her voice. "Of course, although it is vulgar to mention it, he is very rich."

"And why should that interest me, Mother?" Arabella asked, smiling and tapping her mother's arm with her fan.

"Oh, you little tease. What girl wouldn't be interested in a handsome man of good family — and with a fortune as well?"

Not me, Arabella thought. But she kept the teasing smile in place. Maybe it wouldn't hurt to let Mother think her match-making plans were working. She stood up. "May I be excused, Mother? I really am very tired," she said.

"Of course, my dear. I'm pleased you were able to join us for a little while at least."

Back in the sanctuary of her room, Arabella undressed and sat at her dressing table to allow Maisie to brush her hair. She sighed. Those few moments making polite conversation with her mother's guests had taken all the fun out of the evening. It was hard to recapture that feeling of euphoria as she'd left the stage earlier, the applause ringing in her ears. She had to face up to reality — Bella Forde didn't really exist. The face that looked back at her from the mirror was that of Arabella Raynsford, respectable daughter and, before long, she suspected, respectable wife of some boring, pompous son of an equally respectable family.

"Tired, Miss?" Maisie said, wielding the hairbrush with long soothing strokes.

"A little." Not even to Maisie could she confess how the thought of the future, its boring emptiness and restrictions, frightened her. But did it have to be like that? As she got into bed an image of Oswald Delaney's dark eyes and sardonic smile came into her head. His dark good looks both fascinated and repelled — there had been a cruel twist to those lips even as he smiled. She shivered and pulled the blankets over her head. No, whatever Mother might think, Mr Delaney was not a suitable candidate for her hand. Still, it might be fun to flirt a little, to let him think . . .

Arabella was a little disappointed that there was no sign of the mysterious Oswald Delaney over the following weeks. She had been looking forward to sparring with him in order to relieve the tedium of her mother's interminable round of social engagements. Her only relief was her twice-weekly appearance at the Half Moon Theatre but it was getting harder to manufacture excuses to leave the house alone — or to pretend to be indisposed, especially as her so-called migraines seemed to occur with such regularity.

"I'm sure Mama is becoming suspicious," she told Maisie. She had barely made it home from the theatre that evening before her mother swept into the room demanding why she had once more kept to her room.

"You do not look ill," she said. "You cannot keep avoiding my guests. People are beginning to talk."

20

"They must have something to gossip about, I suppose," Arabella said.

"Don't be impertinent, miss," her mother snapped. She sat down on the side of the bed and took her daughter's hand. Her voice softened. "What has happened to you, Arabella? You used to be so gay, so vivacious. But now, you sulk in corners and —" She sighed. "I don't know what I'm to do with you."

"I'm sorry, Mama. I know these social occasions are important to you. But I find them so tedious."

"Nonsense. You used to love showing off to our guests with your lovely singing. But you don't even seem to enjoy that any more."

How could she explain that after a couple of evenings a week, singing her heart out on the stage of the Half Moon, her voice was ready to give out? The smoky atmosphere of the music hall made her cough and she was frightened she would lose her voice altogether. If she could not sing, she would die. The melodramatic thought was accompanied by a heartfelt sigh and her mother patted her hand again.

"Sometimes one has to do things one does not enjoy" she said, "but I think I have brought you up to do your duty. You must marry well — it is expected. And how can that be when you avoid every young man who comes your way?" She paused. "Mr Delaney was asking after you this evening."

"I'm not interested in Mr Delaney," Arabella said.

Caroline frowned. "He is a man of property even if he does also own factories. You know how I feel about trade and I did so hope that you would make a better match. But Mr Delaney is from a good family — even if he is Irish."

Arabella forced a light laugh. "I'll bear that in mind, Mama."

"Well, make sure that you do — and next time he comes to call, have the courtesy to join us, please."

"Very well, Mama."

Her mother bade her goodnight and left the room, seeming satisfied with her reluctant acquiescence. But she wasn't really ready to give in so easily. Mr Delaney might be good-looking and possessed of a certain charm, but there was something in the way he looked at her that made her uneasy.

It was a beautiful evening and Arabella, having escaped her mother's eagle eye, had slipped out into the garden. She leaned against the lilac tree, breathing in the scents of early summer — the blossom, the freshly cut grass and, mingled with them, the not unpleasant smell from the stables in the next street. It reminded her of Mill House on the North Downs above Whitstable Bay where they spent every summer. She used to look forward to their yearly exodus from the city, enjoying the relative freedom of the countryside. When Harry was home from school, they had loved to ride over the Downs or take the pony and trap down to the harbour to watch her father's ships unloading at the quayside. How much happier and more carefree she had been then. But that was before her life got so complicated.

And it was about to get even more so. She had to tell Sam and Violet that she was about to let them down and she did not relish the prospect. The Raynsfords were due to leave for the country in two weeks time and she would have to give up her double life. She had tried to persuade her mother to let her stay in London but it just wasn't done, especially as her brother would not be there to chaperone her. He and James were due to re-join the regiment any day and would soon be embarking for Constantinople.

Her mother had jumped to the wrong conclusion. "I know you want to stay until the regiment departs but I cannot have you seeing too much of Captain Wilson every day. I know you are fond of him but he is not for you. Best to get away and leave him in no doubt. He will soon tire of mooning after you and find another, more suitable, girl."

Arabella was happy to let her mother think that was why she wanted to remain behind. But now, as she made her reluctant way back to the house, she was racking her brains to think of another excuse. It was no good, she would have to let the Fentons down. And while she was away in the country, they would find another singer to take her place. By the time she returned to town, everyone would have forgotten about Bella Forde.

Lost in thought, she jumped as her mother's voice spoke from the French windows leading on to the terrace. "Oh, there you are. Why did you not come inside to say goodbye to our guests? And what on earth are you doing out here all alone in the dark?"

"I came out for a breath of air. It is so hot inside."

Her mother drew her into the light. "You do look rather pale. Thank goodness we are leaving town next week — you'll soon feel better after a few days in the country."

"Next week. Oh, no —"

"What's wrong now? I told you, you may not stay behind. It is not seemly."

Arabella thought quickly. "Oh, no, Mother, I agree. It's just that I wanted to do some more shopping before we go. Charlotte and I had planned —"

"Well, there's plenty of time before we leave. Besides, I have invited Charlotte to accompany us. Mrs Wilson has gone to Norfolk to visit a sick friend."

"Charlotte will miss Harry if she comes with us."

"He'll be gone in a couple of weeks. She'll have to get used to him being away. It won't be easy for her when she is married to a soldier." She took Arabella's arm. "Come, dear, it is time we retired for the night." She nodded to Jennings to close the French doors and turn out the lamps.

Upstairs in her room, Maisie had turned the bed down and was waiting to brush her hair. Sitting at the dressing table, she gave a huge sigh and the maid looked at her sympathetically. "Has the mistress been on at you about getting married again?"

"Not tonight, thank goodness. No, it's worse than that. She just told me we are going to the country next week instead of in a fortnight. That means I shan't be able to do my usual two nights at the Half Moon." She shook her head. "I don't know how I'm going to tell Sam. I thought I had plenty of time to break it to him."

"Oh, Miss. What a shame. He'll be so disappointed — and so will his patrons. What are we going to do?"

"I'm sorry about letting Sam down, of course. But I'm more disappointed for myself. What on earth am I going to do with myself in the country?" She stood up abruptly, almost wrenching the hairbrush from Maisie's hand. "I'll be so bored. It's not fair. I'm twenty years old. Why can't I lead my own life?"

Maisie put a gentle hand on her shoulder, easing her back onto the stool. She began brushing again. "I know how you feel, Miss. But you always knew it wouldn't last for ever. You've had a good run for your money. And it's been fun, hasn't it?"

"But I don't want it to end. Singing's my life now, Maisie. For the first time in my life I'm doing something I really love."

"But you can still sing, Miss. Your friends and family love to hear you —"

"It's not the same thing at all," Arabella snapped.

Maisie carried on brushing, without replying. The rhythmic strokes were soothing and she began to calm down. With a resigned sigh, she acknowledged that her maid was right. Deep down, she had always known the adventure would have to end sooner or later.

But, she vowed, she would have one last fling. Her final performance would be one to remember and leave her the talk of the town.

CHAPTER
THREE

Essex House was in an uproar of packing and planning for the household's annual visit to their country house in Kent. Usually, after the months in town, with its shopping and boring dinner parties and balls, Arabella looked forward to being at Mill House. But not this year.

As a child she had loved the countryside and the rambling old house that had been in her father's family for three generations. It had started off as a substantial farmhouse but over the years new wings had been built and the original house was now the servants' quarters. Recently, a whole new façade had been added with a terrace looking down over the fields and orchards to the distant waters of the bay.

Much as she loved the place, Arabella wished she could stay in town this summer. Her secret life as a singer had given meaning to her life. She knew that within a couple of weeks, the round of visits to people her mother deemed suitable friends for people of their station, the provincial dances and entertainments, would begin to pall and she would be bored to distraction.

There wasn't even the prospect of going down to the harbour to watch the ships and seamen at work, for her mother would no longer allow her to mix with what she called the common people without her brother to chaperone her. But Harry and James were due to leave any day to join their regiment at Dover where they were awaiting a ship to take them to the Crimea.

Arabella would have been able to bear the enforced exodus from London if it were not for letting the Fentons down — and the fact that her singing career had become the most important thing in her life now.

It wouldn't be fair to Sam to wait till Saturday to let him know that this would probably be her last performance as Bella Forde. She could have sent Maisie with a message but she felt she ought to tell him herself.

Taking advantage of the chaos of servants and trades people preparing for the move, she and Maisie managed to slip out and get a cab at the corner of Essex Square. At the haberdashery a few streets away she told the cabbie to stop and Maisie jumped out and bought a length of ribbon, their excuse for the outing.

As Arabella tucked it into her reticule, she said, "I know Sam is going to be upset." She sighed, "I'm not looking forward to telling him."

Violet welcomed them with a beaming smile and the usual offer of tea. "Sam's not here at the moment but he'll be back shortly." She busied herself at the range. "It's not often you manage to visit us when you're not singing. What brings you here today?"

Her smile faded as she came to the table and set the teapot down. "Oh, no — have they found out?" She had never been comfortable with the idea of deceiving her sister's employers.

Arabella shook her head. "I wanted to tell Sam in person, but we can't stay long. My parents are taking me to the country and —"

"Don't worry, I'm sure we can spare you for one or two performances. We'll find someone to fill in for you. Sam says they're queuing up for a spot here now that the Half Moon is so popular."

Arabella twisted her hands together. "That's it, Violet. It won't be just for one or two performances. We'll be away for at least three months. My mother hates London in the summer."

"Three months. Sam won't be happy about that." Violet pursed her lips as she refilled their cups.

"I'm sorry, Violet. I hate letting you down."

"Not your fault, ducks. Sam was saying only the other day we must make the most of you. He knew it wouldn't last — too good to be true." She patted Arabella's hand. "Maybe it's for the best. At least you're quitting before you're found out. There would have been a terrible scandal if your real identity was discovered — and trouble for you too. Your family would never forgive you."

"Mama certainly wouldn't," Arabella said with a rueful smile. She finished her tea and stood up. "We must go. Tell Sam I'm truly sorry for letting him down. But we're not leaving till Monday so I'll be here on

28

Saturday as usual and I promise I'll give a performance to remember me by."

Back at the house no one seemed to have noticed Arabella's absence. She left the new length of ribbon in her reticule. It would provide an excuse should she need to slip out of the house again.

As she passed through the hall, her mother came towards her with a list in her hand, a harassed expression on her usually calm face. "Oh, there you are. Is your trunk packed? Hayes will be bringing the boxes down shortly."

Maisie, who was holding Arabella's cloak, bobbed a curtsey. "It's all done, Ma'am."

"But we're not going till Monday," Arabella protested with an inward groan. Surely Mother hadn't changed their plans at the last minute. She had promised faithfully that she would be at the theatre on Saturday.

"The trunks and boxes are going down by train in the morning. That will give the servants time to unpack and have everything ready for us when we arrive." Caroline turned to Maisie. "You will go down with the luggage, girl. Miss Arabella's dresses will be creased. I shall expect to see everything in order by the time we get there."

"Yes, Ma'am." Maisie bobbed another curtsey and hurried away to hang up Arabella's cloak.

"Come along, dear. Luncheon will be served in a moment." Caroline took Arabella's arm and led her towards the dining room. "You haven't forgotten we are going to the theatre tonight? The Wilsons will join us there."

Normally Arabella would have been excited at the thought of seeing the famous actor Charles Kean striding across the stage of the Princess's Theatre in Oxford Street, declaiming his lines in that rich mellifluous voice. But their imminent departure for Kent weighed on her mind and she couldn't summon up any enthusiasm for sitting through three hours of Shakespeare. She had hardly been able to hide her surprise when Mother had announced that they had taken a box at the theatre. A few years ago the very idea of attending a public performance of any kind would have been anathema to the haughty Caroline Raynsford. But since Her Majesty and Prince Albert had become ardent theatre-goers, it was now deemed quite respectable, and those in high society dressed in their best and made a night of it.

As Arabella picked at her food, she scarcely listened to her mother's chatter about the forthcoming evening's entertainment, speculating on whether the Queen or any of the royal family would be there and whether Charles Kean's performance would match that of his famous father Edmund.

When the maid arrived to clear the plates, Caroline looked sharply at her daughter. "Really, child, you haven't been listening to a word. What's got into you lately? I thought you liked the theatre."

"I'm sorry, Mother. I do. I'm looking forward to it, really I am."

Arabella couldn't concentrate on the performance, excellent as it was. Her mind was on how she would manage to hide her absence the following evening without the connivance of her faithful maid. Whatever happened, she was determined not to let the Fentons down. Besides, tomorrow's performance could well be her very last as Bella Forde, and she was determined to go out on the very highest note possible.

The final curtain came as a welcome relief and she followed her parents downstairs, smiling and managing to respond to Charlotte's comments about the play as if she had nothing else to think about.

While they waited for their carriage, the Raynsfords greeted friends and acquaintances. They were going on to Simpson's in the Strand for supper and Arabella glanced up as her father spoke to a young man she had never seen before. "We'll no doubt run across each other while we're down in Kent, living so close and having business interests in common," Henry said. "Why don't you join us for supper?"

Arabella noticed her mother's expression of distaste at the word "business" and suppressed a smile. Wherever they went, her father seemed to run into someone with the same interests.

He turned and smiled. "I believe you already know my son, Harry, and Captain Wilson. Let me introduce my wife and my daughter, Arabella. And this is Mrs Wilson and her daughter."

Arabella smiled up at the stranger, liking what she saw. He was not as handsome as Oswald Delaney but he was taller, with broad shoulders and a tanned skin that spoke of an outdoor life. He was clean-shaven, unlike most of the young men of her acquaintance, and smartly but not overfashionably dressed, his jacket well cut to accommodate his muscular frame, his cravat neatly tied.

"Nathaniel Sloane — at your service, Miss Arabella." He inclined his head and she returned his warm smile. He seemed not to notice that her father had also introduced Charlotte.

It did not matter to Charlotte — she was gazing adoringly at Harry, hanging on his every word. But Arabella was aware of James's glowering stare and she felt a flicker of annoyance. She had made it plain that she did not share his feelings. The four of them had grown up together and she had always thought of James as a brother. Why should he assume that now they were grown up her feelings would change? Just because it had happened with Charlotte and Harry . . .

The carriage arrived and the Raynsfords and Wilsons climbed in, leaving Nat Sloane on the pavement.

"Why did you ask that man to supper?" Caroline demanded. "Have you forgotten Mr Delaney is joining us?"

"I'm sure they can put another seat at our table," Henry said mildly.

At the restaurant, Arabella was pleased to find Nat Sloane seated beside her. To her relief Oswald was at the other end of the table beside her mother. She knew that her mother hoped for a match with the rich Irishman. And she had looked forward to him being a member of their party in the country — if only as a relief from the inevitable boredom. But she did not feel up to making polite conversation with so much on her mind.

The food was served, the wine poured and conversation centred on the evening's entertainment and Charles Kean's interpretation of the part of Hamlet.

Arabella, who had scarcely heard a word of the play, turned to Nat. "So, you are in the copperas business, Mr Sloane? I was not aware there were other factories besides ours in the vicinity."

"You are mistaken, Miss Arabella. I do not mine the copperas myself. I am an engineer —"

Caroline interrupted. "Why should you assume my daughter knows anything at all about her father's business? It is not a fit subject for a young lady to discuss. As for engineering —"

"I beg your pardon, Mrs Raynsford. Sometimes my enthusiasm carries me away." He turned to Arabella. "Maybe I should ask your opinion of the play?" His tone was serious, but she saw the twinkle in his blue eyes and smiled back at him.

"You are fond of Mr Shakespeare?"

"Not really," he said in a low voice. "But when you're alone in town you tend to find some way of filling the hours."

Arabella glanced across to where her mother was now engaged in animated conversation with Oswald. "I really am interested in the smelting plant," she said. "When I was small my father took me there a few times, but mother said it was dangerous and not a fit place for me. He will not tell me anything these days."

Nat nodded. "I would have thought he'd be pleased you take an interest in where your wealth comes from." He glanced across at Harry. "With your brother in the army and no other sons —"

"When Harry returns from the Crimea he will leave the army and join my father. They certainly would not want me there, even if my mother would allow it."

"So, why are you so interested?"

"I have a confession to make, Mr Sloane," Arabella said with a smile. "I find the life of a young lady of society too stifling. I am expected to conduct myself properly, to take an interest in ladylike pursuits — I sing, I play the piano, I paint a little, embroider a little —"

"What is wrong with that?" Nat asked.

"It is so boring. I have a brain — I want to use it. My brother had a good education, went to university, and now he is to go off soldiering, while I —"

"Things will change, you know. It is not unheard of for a woman to conduct a business, to take charge of her own affairs."

At least he understood, Arabella thought. But he did not know her mother.

"What would you really like to do?" Nat asked.

"I don't know," she replied. How could she tell him about her secret career and her fear of the empty life which stretched before her once it came to its inevitable end?

★ ★ ★

34

Back at Essex House, where Charlotte was to stay with them until their departure for Kent, Arabella tried to put Nat Sloane out of her mind. As she and her friend prepared for bed, she feigned an interest in the other girl's chatter.

"I'm so pleased your parents invited me to stay with you. It would have been so boring in Norfolk with Mama." Charlotte sighed. "I'll miss Harry though. Oh, I do wish he wasn't in the army. Goodness knows how long he'll be away this time."

"You would fall in love with a soldier," Arabella said with a smile.

As she settled down to sleep, she wasn't thinking of Charlotte's problems. With her friend in the house and no Maisie to create a diversion, how on earth was she going to fulfil her obligation to Sam Fenton at the Half Moon tomorrow night?

Nat stood in the pool of lamplight, staring after the carriage until long after it had disappeared round the corner. When would he see her again? He wished the evening could have gone on forever. Knowing it was hopeless, he acknowledged that he had been completely captivated, not only by Arabella's beauty but by her refreshing candour. It was so unusual to meet a society lady who was not afraid to voice her opinions.

He sighed and began the long walk back to his lodgings, hoping the fresh air would dispel the foolish notions he had started to entertain. He had almost reached home when a cab pulled up alongside him and Oswald Delaney leaned out.

The Irishman gave a low chuckle. "I thought you'd be safely tucked up in bed by now and dreaming of the lovely Miss Raynsford," he said.

"Don't talk such nonsense, Delaney," Nat said, hoping that the darkness concealed his blushes.

"Well, she's a beauty, all right — and she has spirit. But don't get your hopes up, Sloane. She's not for the likes of you." Oswald laughed again.

Nat clenched his fists at his side and took a step towards the cab. "Not for the likes of you either," he said.

"I wouldn't be too sure about that."

"What do you mean?"

"Let's say I have plans for the lovely Arabella."

"You mean to ask for her hand?" Nat was incredulous. He knew Delaney was rich and had an estate in Ireland but he was no gentleman and, from what he knew of the Raynsfords, he felt sure that they wanted better for their only daughter. Although he knew he stood no chance for himself, he couldn't bear the thought of Arabella in the arms of this odious man. "Caroline Raynsford will never allow it," he said.

Again that low menacing chuckle. "It is not Mrs Raynsford's decision to make. It is her father who has to give his consent and — well, let's say I can be very persuasive."

The desire to raise his clenched fist and punch Delaney's smirking face almost overwhelmed him and he took a step forward.

As if he had guessed the other man's intention, Oswald rapped his cane on the cab roof. "Drive on," he snapped.

Back at his lodgings, Nat went over the encounter in his mind, wondering what Oswald Delaney had meant by "persuasion". As he prepared for bed he sighed, having a pretty good idea what means the Irishman would use. He'd heard rumours that Henry Raynsford was in financial difficulties and money was a powerful incentive for someone in his position. Who could blame him for wanting to ensure that his daughter was well provided for?

Thumping his pillow, Nat desperately tried to tell himself it was not his concern. The Raynsfords might be on the verge of losing their fortune but whatever happened Caroline Raynsford would never countenance her daughter being courted by a poor engineer.

Determined to put disturbing thoughts of Arabella out of his head, Nat conjured up the blue eyes and blonde curls of the singer at the Half Moon Theatre. She was due to appear again tomorrow night. Maybe he'd go along and hear her, ask her out to supper afterwards. But, as he drifted off to sleep, the faces of Bella Forde and Miss Arabella merged and in his dreams the lovely Miss Raynsford was singing just for him alone.

When he woke next morning the encounter with Oswald Delaney was still playing on his mind and, despite telling himself that he should not interfere, he resolved to speak to Arabella's brother. Harry was not a close friend but they got on well and he was sure the other man would listen to him. Surely if he knew the true nature of the man who wanted to marry his sister he would not allow it to proceed.

But when he opened his morning paper it was to read that Harry's regiment were to embark for the Crimea any day now and were at that moment on their way to Dover. And, when a messenger arrived telling him that there were some difficulties with a railway bridge he had designed which was being built across the River Orwell in Suffolk, he knew he could do nothing more. By mid morning he was on his way to Ipswich, wondering if he would ever see Arabella Raynsford again.

Half the servants had gone and the trunks were on their way to Whitstable. Arabella was worried, wishing her mother had not sent Maisie with them. How would she manage to slip out this evening without her maid's help, and with Charlotte staying in the house too?

To her relief, they spent a quiet evening, retiring early, almost as soon as supper was over. But Charlotte was already missing Harry and was anxious to talk, lingering in Arabella's room until she was ready to scream in frustration.

"They're probably in Dover by now. Harry said they'll be billeted overnight in the castle and embark early tomorrow. How long do you think it will be before they arrive at Balaclava?" Without waiting for a reply she went on, "Do you think he will write before they leave England? He promised to write every day. Will he remember to send his letters to Mill House?"

"Charlotte, you must wait and see. You know that army routine does not give much time for writing. I expect he will send a letter when he is able. You must just be patient and pray that he will not be gone too long. I am sure our army will run those Russians out of Turkey in no time."

"Do you really think so? Oh, I do hope Harry is all right."

She would have gone on but Arabella could stand her friend's chatter no longer. Biting her lip and striving to remain calm she said, "We should have an early night if we are to rise early for the journey tomorrow. Besides, I have a headache — all this fuss and rushing around just for a few weeks in the country. Anyone would think we were emigrating to Australia." She gave a little laugh.

Charlotte managed a smile too. "I suppose you are right. But I'm sure I will not sleep for thinking about Harry."

Arabella held a lavender-soaked handkerchief up to her forehead and sighed. "Well, I for one am ready for my bed."

"Will you manage all right without Maisie or shall I send Tilly along to you when she has finished with me?"

Arabella managed to stop herself snapping that she was quite capable of undressing without the aid of a ladies' maid. "I'll manage," she said, sighing with relief when Charlotte said goodnight and at last closed the door.

Quickly arranging her pillows under the coverlet so that a quick glance would show someone sleeping, she snuffed out the candle, grabbed her cloak and reticule and quietly opened the door.

A lamp burned at the end of the corridor but all was quiet. As she crept to the bottom of the sweeping staircase she heard the clink of glass from the library where her father was indulging in a late nightcap.

She slipped past the half-open door into the drawing room. Jennings had already bolted and locked the French windows onto the terrace but Arabella had perfected the art of opening them without noise.

Along the terrace and across the lawn, holding her breath as a gleam of light shone out from an upstairs window. Then through the side gate and along the lane to the busy main road where, with a bit of luck, she would be able to get a cabriolet to the theatre. There were sufficient coins in her reticule to buy the cabby's discretion.

Violet was waiting for her by the stage door. "You're late. Where's Maisie?" She hurried Arabella along the passage to the dressing room without waiting for a reply. "You'll have to hurry — the patrons are getting restless. The juggler's doing another encore and I don't think it's going down too well."

"I'm sorry — my mother has sent Maisie to the country to get ready for our arrival there and I had difficulty getting away," Arabella said as she threw off her cloak and grabbed the hooped skirt off the rail.

"Never mind, you're here now." Violet fastened the skirt and arranged the lace shawl over Arabella's shoulders. She placed the little bonnet on her head, making sure that no thread of brown hair showed beneath the fringe of golden curls. "No time for proper make-up," she said, busying herself with the little pots

40

on the dressing table. "Never mind, they've had enough to drink out there, maybe they won't notice you're not your usual self. Besides, it's your voice they've come for."

Arabella touched her lips with red and rubbed a little of the rouge into her cheeks. Her head began to throb and the lie she had told earlier came true. But there was no time to think about herself, no time for the usual butterflies in her stomach either.

The pianist was playing the introduction to her song and before she knew it she was tripping lightly onto the stage and launching into her first number. Her appearance was greeted with the rapturous applause she had come to expect but, as the liquid notes soared up to the smoky ceiling, the noise died down and it was as if everyone in the theatre held their breath.

One song followed another and Arabella was transported into another world, far away from the petty restrictions of a young lady of society. This was what she had been born for and she never wanted it to end.

The last notes of her signature song, "In the Gloaming", a wistful air which suited her look of youthful innocence, died away and the audience gave a collective sigh before breaking into thunderous applause. It was as if they knew that Bella Forde had probably given her last performance.

Well, I've gone out on a high note, she thought, as she curtsied and smiled after her third encore. But it was hard to hold back the tears as she hurried offstage and realized that she might never be back. Sam would find some excuse for her abrupt withdrawal from the theatre — probably ill health — and he would soon find someone to take her place.

The thought hurt more than she would have thought possible and, blinded by tears, she pushed open the door to her dressing room and threw herself into the chair in front of the mirror.

It was some seconds before she became aware that someone was in the room with her. A flash of movement in the mirror, a discreet cough.

She whirled round, gasping as she recognized Oswald Delaney. But had he recognized her?

"Miss Forde, I'm sorry to startle you but I had to congratulate you personally on your excellent performance — as always. Oswald Delaney at your service." He took her hand, raising it to his lips. As he kissed it, he glanced round the room. "Where is your maid? I've been trying to get past her for weeks. She is most zealous in guarding your privacy — quite understandable with those drunken stage door johnnies hanging around." He smiled and stroked his moustache. "I can assure you, my dear, that my intentions are entirely honourable. I merely wish to take you to supper."

Arabella shook her head. If only Maisie was here. "I'm sorry, sir. I have a prior engagement."

"Surely not, Miss? I hear you have no truck with your many admirers — that you scuttle off home as soon as your performance is over. Surely it would not hurt to accompany me to supper? I would make sure you got home safely afterwards."

He was still holding on to her hand and Arabella tried to pull away. "No, sir. I really must go."

"Then if you will not dine with me at least let me have a little kiss." He gripped her hand more firmly and pulled her towards him.

Terrified that at any moment he must realize her deception, Arabella screamed and stamped on his foot. "Let me go, you beast," she yelled.

He swore and released her just as the door flew open. Sam Fenton strode into the room and seized Delaney by the collar. "Get your hands off her," he snarled. "Call yourself a gentleman, forcing yourself on a lady?"

Delaney shrugged and straightened his coat. He looked Arabella up and down, a sneer on his handsome face. "Lady?" he spat, and left the room.

"I'll have you know, Miss Forde is more of a lady than you'll ever know," Sam shouted at his retreating back. Turning to Arabella, he wrung his hands. "Are you all right, Miss? I swear I don't know how he got in."

Arabella sank into a chair. "It's all right, Sam. He's gone now. But I wish you hadn't shouted after him. He is a frequent guest at Essex House — suppose he sees a resemblance between Bella Forde and Arabella Raynsford and begins to think —"

"Don't worry Miss. You pass muster with your false curls and the make-up. No one would guess —" He ran his hands through his sparse hair. "Violet told me you're off to the country. I wish you didn't have to go. God knows how I'm going to tell my regulars. There'll be a riot."

"I'm so sorry, Sam. But you must see how impossible it is to carry on."

"We're lucky to have got away with it so long." Sam looked up and grinned. "Who'd have thought it, eh? Miss Arabella — the talk of the town."

Arabella couldn't help smiling. "I do hope not, Sam," she said.

His grin faded and he sighed. "Oh well, I knew it couldn't last."

While they were talking, Arabella had been removing her make-up and tidying her hair. With no Maisie to cover for her she was anxious to get home before her absence was discovered.

"I've called a cab for you, Miss," Sam said. "And I've paid the driver well. He'll drop you on the corner of the Square." He took her hand, squeezing it painfully. "I don't know how to thank you — it's all down to you, the Half Moon doing so well. I bless the day our Maisie brought you to us."

The suspicion of a tear gleamed in his eye and Arabella had to swallow a lump in her own throat. Impulsively, she leaned forward and kissed his cheek. "I should be thanking you — it's been the most exciting time of my life." She grabbed her reticule and hurried out of the dressing room.

Outside, the crowds which usually lingered by the door had dispersed, except for a couple of men who were arguing under a flickering street lamp. Their shadows danced on the pavement as they gesticulated and Arabella winced as she recognized Oswald Delaney's distinctive voice, the Irish brogue more apparent as his temper rose.

44

"It is none of your business, man." He shook his fist under the other man's nose. "Besides, the old man has made a bargain. He's a gentleman and will not go back on his word."

As Arabella climbed into the waiting cab, she heard the other man say, "A gentleman would not make such a bargain in the first place. Believe me, you have not heard the last of this."

Oswald's laugh sent a shiver down Arabella's spine and, as the cabbie whipped up the horses, she leaned back in case he should glimpse her through the window. But not before she had seen that the other man was Nat Sloane, the man who had intrigued her by his unconventional views.

As the horse clopped through the quiet streets, Arabella, instead of dwelling on her sadness at having to give up her singing career, found herself thinking about the two men who had so recently come into her life. She wondered what they had been arguing about and if it had anything to do with the business they had been discussing with her father earlier.

Arabella was woken early next morning by Tilly, Charlotte's maid, drawing back the curtains and placing a tray on the table by the window.

"Miss Charlotte is up and dressed already," Tilly said. "You were sleeping so soundly, she told me to leave you. But Mrs Raynsford is anxious to be on her way and says if you don't come down within the next half hour you will get no breakfast."

Arabella had slept badly and wished she could stay in bed a bit longer. But her mother demanded obedience and she reluctantly swung her legs over the side of the bed.

"I've laid your travelling clothes out, Miss," Tilly said. "Maisie showed me what you wanted before she left."

"Thank you, Tilly. I can manage by myself if Miss Charlotte needs you —"

"She's gone down, Miss. She said I must look after you as if I were your own maid." She poured hot water from the jug into the china basin and laid a soft fluffy towel alongside it.

"I really can manage," said Arabella. How she missed Maisie at this moment. Her own maid knew when to speak and when to keep quiet. Besides, if Maisie were here they'd be talking and giggling over her performance last night and planning their next escapade.

But she mustn't think about it. It was too depressing. All she had to look forward to now was a boring three months in the country. She couldn't even look forward to wandering around the quaint narrow streets of the busy little harbour town. With the coming of the railway and the steam packet services from London, the number of day trippers to Whitstable had increased and her mother had declared it was becoming far too vulgar.

Arabella thought she should have more regard for the place that was the source of the family's wealth. As a child she had loved watching the oyster boats unloading their haul at the horse bridge, walking along the harbour wall hearing the shouts of the workers loading copperas onto the barges for their journey up the Thames to the gunpowder mills situated on the creeks and estuaries along each side of the river. But Caroline declared that Canterbury was more refined and their social life for the next three months would be limited to shopping trips in the cathedral city five miles away, as well as visits to other landed families in the area.

With a sigh, Arabella finished dressing and went downstairs to the dining room. Her mother and Charlotte were discussing the coming journey. "It is so tiresome having to hire a coach," said Caroline. "Why we do not have our own conveyance I do not know."

"Father says it is a nuisance having to find stabling for so many horses in town. And the chaise is hardly fit for such a long journey."

"I know what your father says," Caroline said with a sniff, throwing down her napkin and rising from the breakfast table.

"Where is Papa?"

"He's left already — he has taken the train, would you believe?"

"The train? How exciting. Why could we not do that, Mama?"

"What a stupid question — of course we could not. It is hardly a suitable mode of travel for ladies — so noisy and dirty."

"Papa says it is the best way to travel. He says in fifty years, no one will go by coach or chaise. You will be able to visit the farthest parts of the country by train."

"Nonsense, child." Her mother silenced her with a glare. "It is all very well for the lower classes."

Arabella knew better than to argue and silently helped herself to scrambled eggs from one of the dishes on the sideboard.

"Hurry up, Arabella. The coach will be here soon and we do not want to be late starting. It is a long enough journey as it is." Caroline swept out of the room.

Charlotte smiled. "Your mother is anxious to be off," she said.

"She looks forward to our time in Kent. But she hates the journey and the preparation."

"I know how she feels, the prospect of sitting in a swaying, bumpy coach all day is not pleasant."

"If only we'd have gone by train with Papa, we'd have been there in time for luncheon. The journey takes half the time." Arabella sighed. "Instead, we have to endure the heat and discomfort, not to mention hanging around at those roadside inns while they change horses."

CHAPTER
FOUR

The long, tiring journey was almost over, but it had not been quite as tedious as Arabella had feared. To her surprise, and she had to admit, delight, Nat Sloane had accompanied them on the journey.

Caroline Raynsford accepted that her husband had arranged this so that the ladies would not have to travel alone. But, although she was polite, her displeasure was thinly veiled.

They talked about the play they had seen and of mutual acquaintances they would see in Kent. Soon, the conversation petered out and Caroline began to doze. Arabella seized the opportunity to ask what business brought Mr Sloane to Kent.

"As I told you, I am an engineer," he said. "I am presently engaged in plans to extend the railway. To do so we must blast a tunnel through the hills and for that we need explosives."

"How exciting," Arabella said. "Now I see why you and my father have so much to talk about."

"I am to visit the gunpowder works at Faversham to negotiate supplies. It is not really part of my work but I like to make sure that all the materials we use are of high standard. Too many of these enterprises use inferior stuff and this causes accidents. Only last year several men were killed while working on a tunnel in the north. I would not have that happen on any project I am connected with."

"My father feels the same," Arabella said. "The mining and refining of copperas has its dangers too but he is very careful of the safety of his workers."

Charlotte appeared bored and had been looking out of the carriage window but she turned now and said, "Harry tells me that Mr Delaney is engaged in gunpowder manufacture among his many business interests. I do not understand why men are so interested in fighting and blowing things up."

"That is not what we were talking about, Charlotte," said Arabella.

"I'm sorry. I was thinking about Harry going off to fight, my brother too. I don't know why we have to interfere in Turkey. It is nothing to do with us."

Nat leaned forward and spoke gently. "I am afraid it is, Miss Charlotte. We must protect our interests — and the Russians are preparing to attack."

Charlotte gave a little sob and Arabella patted her hand. "It will all be over by the time Harry and James get there," she said. But a little chill went through her. Nat had spoken quietly but with authority. And hadn't she sensed her mother's worry, her father's conversations in lowered tones, quickly ceasing as she entered the room. How she wished they would not try to protect her from the harsh realities of life. There was so much she wanted to ask Nat — he did not seem to mind engaging in serious conversation with a mere girl.

But the carriage bumped over a rut in the road and her mother's eyes flew open.

Arabella smiled. "We are almost there, Mama."

"Thank goodness. I could not endure this lurching a moment longer."

The house was set on a hill at the end of a long drive about a mile from the village. In the distance the spars and sails of the ships in the harbour towered over the little cottages clustered along the seashore and beyond them the open waters of the bay gleamed in the summer sunshine.

Nat helped Arabella's mother out of the carriage and turned to give his hand to her. But she had already leapt down, oblivious to her mother's "tut" of disapproval for her unladylike behaviour.

Despite her reluctance to leave London and her burgeoning singing career, it was good to be in the fresh country air, away from the heat and smells of the capital.

Maisie was waiting for her in her room with hot water and a change of clothes. Arabella was pleased to see the little maid, whom she also regarded as a friend. As she freshened herself after the journey she answered Maisie's eager questions about her last performance at the Half Moon Theatre.

"I managed, but only just," she said. "Struggling out of that crinoline made me realize how much I depend on you. And I nearly got found out."

"Ooh, Miss, what happened?"

Arabella told her about Mr Delaney being in her dressing room and how Sam had managed to get rid of him before he could suspect anything. "But I think he guessed there was something going on. He commented on the fact that I was so reclusive and did not wish to meet the public who adore me. Such nonsense." She tried to shake off the uneasy feeling that Oswald Delaney might cause trouble for her in the future.

By the time she returned downstairs Nat was preparing to leave. He had taken lodgings in Canterbury and was anxious to start work.

Braving her mother's displeasure she said, "I do hope we shall see something of you when your business permits, Mr Sloane. We get few visitors here and country life can be rather dull."

"I am sure Mr Sloane has better things to do with his valuable time," Caroline said tartly.

Nat smiled. "It is true I have much to do over the coming weeks but I do hope you will permit me to call. I must see Mr Raynsford some time anyway — a matter of business."

"Surely you can see my husband at the harbour office," Caroline said, her mouth tightening in distaste. "The housekeeper told me he scarcely stopped for a bite to eat before saddling his horse and rushing down to the town. I fear we shall see little of him over the coming weeks."

Nat bowed and took his leave. When he had gone Arabella went to the window, hoping to catch a glimpse of him as he strode away.

★ ★ ★

52

The lazy days of that long hot summer settled into a routine of visits to neighbouring county families, picnics and shopping trips to Canterbury. Arabella's fears were soon realized as the novelty of being in the country wore off, although she tried not to let her boredom show.

It was hard to hide her impatience with Charlotte too. Fond as she was of the girl who would soon be her sister-in-law, her constant chatter began to get on her nerves. When she wasn't discussing frivolous subjects such as fashion, she was speculating on where she and Harry would live once they were married, and asking if Arabella thought Harry and James would be all right.

Finally her patience snapped. "How do I know? They're soldiers, aren't they — and soldiers fight."

Charlotte's eyes filled with tears and Arabella immediately regretted her outburst. "I'm sorry. I'm just as worried as you are — really, I am." She kissed her friend's cheek. "Now cheer up — it may all be over before they arrive. When they return we will have a big welcome home party. You and I will sing and Harry will play for us."

But Charlotte would not be comforted and Arabella knew in her heart that her friend was right to be worried. Who knew when, if ever, they would be home again? And, only the day before, she had heard her father talking about the increase in production that was needed in order to supply the gunpowder mills which in turn supplied the Arsenal at Woolwich.

Arabella could not be downcast for long, though. Nat Sloane would be among tonight's supper party and she looked forward to more interesting conversation than she'd had to endure lately. A small voice told her that it was not only his conversation she was interested in.

She had so far managed to resist her mother's efforts to find her a suitable partner. But she was now almost twenty-one and wouldn't be able to hold out much longer. She would rather remain an old maid than marry without love but her mother had impressed upon her she must make a good match — and as far as Caroline Raynsford was concerned, Oswald Delaney was perfect for the role.

If Nat Sloane had been as rich as Oswald, Caroline might have been persuaded to overlook his lowly origins. For, although it was never openly spoken of in her presence, Arabella knew that her father's business was in trouble. The copperas deposits on their land down on the coast had almost been worked out and the gunpowder mills were looking for sources elsewhere. Henry had already laid off some of his workers, causing some hardship in the little coastal town.

Arabella would have known nothing of this if Nat Sloane had not arrived at the house one summer afternoon. Her mother had been lying down, nursing a headache, and her heart had lifted with joy at the thought of an exciting hour in his company, even if she had to endure Charlotte's presence as chaperone. She had already rung for tea when her father came out of the library and invited Nat inside.

Disappointed, Arabella hovered outside the door, hoping for an opportunity to speak to him when their business was finished. When she heard them discussing the closing of the copperas works and the consequent unemployment it would cause, her heart sank. Were they going to be poor? Was that why her mother was desperate for her to marry a rich man? She was somewhat comforted when she heard her father say, "At least I still have my ships. There will still be plenty of work around the harbour."

And Nat replied, "The extension of the railway will also need labourers. I shall make it my business to see that we employ local men."

Arabella felt a twinge of guilt that she was so discontented when she had every material thing she could wish for. She could not imagine what it must be like to go without new clothes, or to feel hungry. She stepped away from the half-open door when she heard footsteps in the hall. Charlotte came in from the garden.

"It is so hot out there," she said, running a hand over her forehead.

"I'll ring for some lemonade," said Arabella, leading her friend into the morning room. "You should not have gone out in this heat," she said. She was worried about her friend, who looked pale and listless. Despite often feeling irritated with her, she sympathized with Charlotte's worries about Harry and James. But the regiment couldn't have reached Sebastopol yet. Besides, there had so far been no reports of any real battles.

Arabella was worried about her brother too, but her emotions were more complex. She was fond of him and of his friend James and hoped no harm would come to either of them. But they had chosen to join the army. However, she did feel a little guilty at the thought that the man she was beginning to fall in love with was safe at home.

The maid came in with glasses and a jug of lemonade, followed by Caroline holding a card in her hand. "I think you girls should rest until dinner as we are going out this evening." she said.

"Are you sure you feel well enough to go out, Mama?"

"My headache has gone and I need a little distraction," Caroline said.

Arabella hadn't been looking forward to the recital in the Assembly Rooms in Canterbury but she needed distraction too. And now that Nat was here, she hoped the evening would prove more entertaining than she had anticipated. Her hopes were dashed when her mother told her that Oswald Delaney would be a guest at dinner and would escort them to the recital.

As the girls went up to their rooms to change for dinner, Arabella said, "At least it will pass the time. We might even enjoy it."

"I can't enjoy anything," Charlotte said. "How can I think about having fun when Harry might —" Her voice broke on a sob.

"You mustn't think like that." Arabella touched her friend's arm, helpless to know how to comfort her.

Charlotte shook her off. "It's all right for you. You have Mr Sloane and Mr Delaney falling over themselves to gain your attention. While your brother and poor James are off to war. You don't care for him at all —"

"Of course I care. I'm very fond of James — we've been friends since childhood. But I don't love him, I don't love anybody." It wasn't true, but Arabella couldn't tell her friend that the thought of spending an evening with Oswald made her feel sick while Nat Sloane crept into her thoughts far more often than he should.

Arabella's love of music meant that she did manage to take pleasure in the recital after all, although the presence of Oswald Delaney sitting beside her almost spoilt the evening.

During the interval he leaned across and indicated a name in the programme. "The best is yet to come," he said. "Are you enjoying the music, Miss Raynsford?"

"Very much, Mr Delaney." She turned away, craning her neck to see who else was in the audience, disappointed that there was no sign of Nat. He had left earlier, refusing an invitation to join them for dinner and Arabella hadn't dared to ask her mother if he would be at tonight's concert.

Oswald laid a hand on her arm. "I take it amiss that you should look elsewhere when you have a devoted admirer right beside you," he said.

"I am sorry, Mr Delaney. I did not mean to be discourteous." Arabella forced a smile. She knew her mother was watching, nodding her approval of his attentions.

The music started up again and she sighed with relief. The last performer was the singer whose name Oswald had pointed out. She had a rich contralto voice and held the audience spellbound. It was not the sort of song Arabella would have sung but she murmured the words under her breath, wishing she were in the other woman's place.

During a lull in the thunderous applause that followed, Oswald leaned over and whispered. "A wonderful performance. But her voice doesn't hold a candle to someone I heard in London recently. Have you heard of Bella Forde, the singer who performs at the Half Moon Theatre? She is the talk of the town. Sadly, she is no longer in London — a serious illness I hear."

Arabella's heart began to pound. Surely he wasn't hinting that he knew her secret? How could he have found out? But he had turned to speak to Charlotte and she convinced herself he was just making conversation — until he turned back to her.

"You did not answer my question, Miss Raynsford — have you heard of the Half Moon's star performer?"

She steadied her breath and answered calmly. "I believe my brother has spoken of her. But you must know, Mr Delaney, that the Half Moon is not the sort of theatre a lady would patronize."

He gave a low chuckle and a most ungentlemanly wink. But his words were courtesy itself. "Of course not, Miss Raynsford. I should not have mentioned it."

The audience began to disperse and Arabella hoped he would not be included in their supper party. She hoped in vain and he manoeuvred himself next to her once more. He did not return to their previous conversation, mainly speaking to her parents.

As the interminable evening came to a close and they were making their farewells, Oswald said, "I'm afraid this will be my last social engagement for some time. I have to return to Ireland — some business with the estate." He bowed over Caroline's hand. "I hope I will not be gone long. May I call on you and Mr Raynsford when I return? I have an important matter to discuss."

She smiled warmly. "You will be very welcome in our home, Mr Delaney — whether here or in London."

Arabella went cold. She knew what they would be discussing.

CHAPTER
FIVE

The rest of their time in the country passed in a blur, enlivened only by Nat's occasional visits. Arabella was discouraged from speaking to him more than politeness dictated and besides, he usually spent most of the time closeted in her father's study.

Charlotte moped around, waiting for the post to arrive and lapsing into depression when there was no news of Harry, much to Arabella's irritation.

Soon after their return to London the first letter from her brother arrived but it was small comfort, although there was no mention of any fighting. "*Most of the troops have not even disembarked,*" he wrote, "*but the Russians are massing for attack. Do not fear — we have almost twice as many men and our vast numbers will soon push them back.*"

Caroline almost swooned with relief as her husband read the letter out at the breakfast table. But Arabella saw the thinly veiled disquiet in her father's eyes. And she knew why. Braving her mother's disapproval, she often sneaked into the library after her father had left the house, retrieving the newspapers from the waste basket. The news in the *Times* was not weeks old as it had been before the invention of the telegraph, and the daily reports from the Crimea painted a vivid picture of what was going on in that far-off country. Arabella eagerly devoured the news but she never told Charlotte what she'd learned. Her friend would have been even more depressed if she'd known how dreadful things were.

Harry's letter was some weeks old whereas yesterday's paper had carried news of the recent Battle of the Alma in which 3,000 of the allied troops had been lost. It was small comfort to know that nearly twice as many Russians had perished on the same day.

Maybe she should stop reading the papers, Arabella thought, as she pushed her plate away. But she could not agree with her mother that such things were not for ladies to worry about. Surely they had a duty to their loved ones to keep up with what was going on, even if they could do nothing to help. She did not count knitting and sewing comforts for soldiers or rolling bandages for the wounded, although a little voice told her it was really the only practical thing she could do. Charlotte had joined in the sewing circle with enthusiasm and Arabella knew it would please her mother if she did likewise.

As she dutifully stitched, stifling her yawns, she thought back to the heady days of her singing career when life had held some excitement. How she longed to go back to it, but her experience after that last performance when she was sure she had been caught out had made her cautious.

But a week after their return to London, when Maisie returned from visiting her sister on her day off she was bubbling with excitement. "They want you back, Miss," she said. "That girl who filled in for you is all right — but she's not in your league, they say."

Arabella hesitated. "I don't know, Maisie. You know I'd love to — I really miss it. Drawing room music isn't the same. Besides, it's too risky."

"We could manage it, Miss. I'll cover for you like I always do."

Arabella was tempted. But if she started having "headaches" again her mother would become suspicious. She had already commented on the fact that the migraines had disappeared while they were in the country. And the hints dropped by Oswald Delaney at the concert in Canterbury had really rattled her.

She shook her head. "No — I can't do it," she said.

"I'll tell Violet next time I see her then. She'll be disappointed — so will Sam. He's banking on you coming back — even had some posters printed."

"All right — tell him one night a week only." Even as she made the decision, butterflies began to flutter in her stomach. But it was from anticipation, not apprehension. With Maisie's help no one would find out. She told herself it was only her maid's absence that had caused the problem last time. Besides, Oswald Delaney was still in Ireland.

She'd have to learn some new songs and get new costumes made. A secret smile curved her lips as she bent her head to her sewing. In a few days she would be back on stage, doing what she most loved.

It was easy to slip back into the routine of pleading fatigue or a headache and retiring early. Several times during the next week she went to her room straight after supper, setting up the excuse that she would need for the coming Saturday evening.

Now that she seemed to have accepted that Oswald Delaney would begin his courtship when he returned from Ireland, her mother was prepared to be more indulgent and readily gave permission for a shopping trip. Arabella held her breath, hoping she would not offer to come too. But she merely said that if Charlotte could not accompany her, she must take her maid instead.

Arabella had no intention of asking Charlotte to come and, after an early luncheon, slipped out of the house attended by Maisie carrying her basket.

At the Half Moon she was greeted like a long-lost relative. Violet pressed tea and cakes on her and Sam couldn't wait to take her through to the theatre to show off the improvements that had been made in her absence. There were new stage curtains and a railing had been erected around the orchestra pit in an effort to stop the audience from throwing things on to the stage.

"Not that they throw anything at you, Miss," he said. "But if they're not happy with the show, well —" He sighed, then beamed at her. "Still, now you're back we'll be packing them in. A better class of clientele too."

"But Sam, it's only one night a week. I'm sorry I can't manage more but you know how difficult it is."

"Of course, me dear. I'd have you up on that stage every night of the week if I could but —" He sighed. "I do understand. I'm just grateful you're prepared to take such risks."

"I'm doing it for myself as much as for you, Sam," Arabella said.

He laughed. "I know. But I don't blame you — you're a natural." He dashed across the stage to the piano. "I've got some new music in," he said, scrabbling through the pile of papers on top. "I think you'll like this one." He handed her a printed song sheet.

Arabella skimmed through it, picking up the tune in her head. She began to hum softly. 'On Wings of Song —' She turned to Sam. "It's lovely. I needed a new one — I think they were getting tired of "In the Gloaming". They do like the old favourites though."

Sam sat down at the piano and played a few bars. "Quick rehearsal, Miss? I know you practise at home but I want to hear your lovely voice."

Arabella hastily did a few breathing exercises. It was weeks since she'd sung properly. When she was ready, she turned and nodded to Sam. The liquid notes flew up to the high ceiling and in seconds she had forgotten where she was as the music took over. Such lovely words too. She sighed as the song came to an end. If only she could be borne away to the beautiful land of the song.

As the last note died away she became aware of applause from the stalls. She hadn't realized that Violet and Maisie had followed them into the theatre. Still slightly dazed, she descended from the stage.

"Haven't lost your touch then," Violet said, smiling.

"I am out of practice though. Since the boys went away we haven't had so many soirees and when I do sing it's usually in company with Charlotte."

Maisie tugged on her sleeve. "I think we should go, Miss. The mistress will be wondering where we've got to."

Arabella was reluctant. She wanted to carry on singing but she knew it would not be wise to make her mother angry.

The cabriolet dropped them outside Essex House and a footman opened the door. As they started up the wide staircase, Jennings appeared. "Miss Arabella, the mistress wishes you to join her in the drawing room as soon as you return. She has a visitor."

Arabella handed her cloak and bag to her maid. "I suppose I'd better go and act the dutiful daughter," she whispered.

Maisie giggled and the butler frowned. "Run along, girl," he said.

She bobbed a curtsey and disappeared in the direction of the back stairs.

Arabella sighed and, still clutching the song sheet, opened the drawing room door.

Her mother was seated, straight-backed, her lips tight. "Where have you been, Miss? It does not take all day to buy a few fripperies. And I heard you laughing and talking with that girl. She is getting far too familiar. You must not allow her to take liberties."

"I'm sorry, Mother. Jennings said there was a visitor." She looked round and only then noticed the figure standing by the window, silhouetted by the sun streaming in. Her heart leapt — until he turned round and she recognized Oswald Delaney.

He gave a small bow and said, "Miss Raynsford, my business was completed sooner than I thought. So I took the liberty of calling unannounced."

She glanced at her mother, who was now smiling. She swallowed and forced a smile to her own face. "It is a pleasure to see you, Mr Delaney," she said. "Won't you sit down?"

She gestured to a chair and hastily took her place on the sofa beside her mother. She laid the sheet music on the small table between them. After a few moments exchanging pleasantries and small talk, with Arabella feeling increasingly uncomfortable, Oswald leaned forward and picked up the music. "A new song, Miss Raynsford. I do hope you will give us the pleasure of hearing it."

She blushed. "I cannot sing it yet. I have not had time to learn the words or the tune."

"You seem to have a feel for music. I feel sure I'll be hearing it quite soon."

His lips twisted and his eyes gleamed and Arabella wondered how she could ever have thought him attractive. There was an underlying cruelty in that smile. She realized that, as he had hinted in Canterbury, he had guessed at her secret life and was now toying with her. He had said "I", not "we", and she had a feeling he was not referring to a future visit as a guest of the Raynsfords. He was sure to be in the audience at the Half Moon next Saturday night. Why had he not exposed her?

The desire to run out of the room almost overwhelmed her and she half-rose from her seat.

Her mother's hand on her arm stopped her. "I have asked Mr Delaney to dine with us," she said. "I must go and tell Cook there will be one more for dinner." She stood up and swept out of the room.

It was unlike her to go in search of a servant. Why had she not rung the bell and given directions to a maid? Arabella wondered. She was not left in doubt long.

Oswald rose from his chair and came to sit beside her. He took her hand. "I think you have guessed what I am going to say," he said, that disconcerting gleam back in his eyes. "I have spoken to your father —"

Panic-stricken, Arabella snatched her hand away. He knew and he had revealed her secret. Too late to beg him to say nothing. As she searched for something to say, his next words penetrated her confusion.

"He has given me permission to ask for your hand. Arabella, I wish to marry you."

"What? Marry? Oh, no, I couldn't possibly —"

"I'm sorry, I spoke hastily. But surely you guessed my intentions? Ever since I first saw you, I have not been able to get you out of my mind."

"You must give me time, sir."

He took her hand again, squeezing her fingers painfully. "Not too much time, Miss. My mind is set on making you my wife. And I always get what I want."

Arabella shook her head. "I can't —"

"You can and you will." His voice became gentler. "Arabella — I may call you Arabella, mayn't I? It is what your parents want too. Maybe you do not realize that your father's business is in trouble. And your mother would not want to give up her lavish lifestyle. I can help them, Arabella." He put a finger under her chin and forced her to look at him. "Would it be such a bad bargain? I am rich, I have connections, and" — he smiled — "I am not such a bad-looking fellow."

He had not mentioned her singing and Arabella felt a flicker of hope. Maybe he hadn't guessed after all. But did it really matter in the face of this disaster? Of course, she had known her parents' plans for her but she had thought there was time to find a way out of the dilemma. Now he was talking of taking her off to his estate in Ireland. And, twisting the knife still further, telling her of his plans to help her father out of his current difficulties by investing in the business.

When her mother returned to the drawing room, Oswald was still holding Arabella's hand. She smiled and gave a nod of satisfaction when he said, "Your daughter has done me the honour of agreeing to be my wife."

His fingers tightened painfully and tears welled in Arabella's eyes. As she dabbed at them with a lace handkerchief, her mother leaned over and kissed her cheek. "Congratulations, my dear. I am sure you and Mr Delaney will be very happy."

She forced a smile. Does she think these are tears of joy? she wondered.

Excusing herself to go and dress for dinner, she rushed upstairs to her room and threw herself on the bed, sobbing.

Maisie entered from the dressing room and sat beside her, putting her arms round her and patting her back. "What's the matter, Miss?" She gave a gasp of horror. "Oh, Miss, they've found out where we've been, haven't they? What are we going to do?"

Arabella sat up and shook her head. "No, Maisie, it's worse than that. I am to be married."

"But that's good news, isn't it. I like Mr Sloane — you do too, don't you? It's nothing to cry about."

"It's not Nat Sloane — my parents want me to marry Mr Delaney." She threw herself down on the bed again. "I hate him. I won't marry him. I'll run away. I'll be Bella Forde and make my living singing."

"Oh, Miss." Maisie carried on soothing and rubbing Arabella's back.

Suddenly the door flew open. "What is going on here?" Caroline Raynsford took in her daughter's blotched face, the sodden handkerchief clutched in her hand. "There is nothing to cry about. Pull yourself together and come down to dinner." She turned to Maisie. "You, girl, fetch some water, then lay Miss Arabella's clothes out."

When Maisie had gone, she snapped. "I have already berated you for being too familiar with the servants. You give that girl far too much latitude. If it does not stop, I will have to dismiss her."

"I'm sorry, Mother. I was just upset and she was trying to help."

"Nothing to be upset about. Girls of your station must make good marriages — you will get used to the idea in time."

"Yes, Mother." Arabella knew that an appearance of meek compliance would calm her mother down. She had enough problems without risking the loss of the little maid she had come to regard as a friend.

CHAPTER
SIX

Arabella looked at herself in the mirror and turned to Maisie. "More eye shadow do you think?" she asked.

"Stop worrying, Miss. You look fine."

Arabella picked up the powder puff and dabbed at her cheeks. "I'm not usually this nervous."

"Is it the new song? I know you haven't had time to practise properly."

"It's not that — I just have an awful feeling something will go wrong. I have a feeling Mr Delaney has guessed my secret."

"What did he say?"

"It wasn't what he said but the way he looked at me when he was speaking. He seemed to be taunting me." She clutched Maisie's arm. "Suppose he's here tonight?"

"I've been looking out for him and so far he hasn't turned up. Besides, no one would dream it was you under all that make-up. And the blonde curls too — they just make you look so different."

Someone tapped on the dressing room door and Arabella leapt up, her heart racing. It wasn't really her looks she was concerned about. She knew that "Bella Forde" looked nothing like the Raynsfords's eligible daughter. But when she began to sing it was a different story.

The day before, Oswald Delaney had come in to the drawing room while she was seated at the piano practising "On Wings of Song". As soon as he entered the room she stopped but he smiled his wolfish smile.

"Don't let me interrupt you," he said.

She gathered up her music and stood up. "I was about to go and change for dinner," she said.

He came towards her and took the sheet music from her trembling hand. "Your new song, I see. And when shall we have the pleasure of hearing you perform it?"

"I'm not sure, sir. I have not yet learned all the notes. I would rather practise a little more before inflicting it on my mother's guests." She coughed. "Besides, I have a slight sore throat so maybe I will not sing tonight. Charlotte will be here — she can entertain us instead."

"I would rather hear you," Oswald said, taking her hand. "When we are married you will sing for me every night."

She had forced a smile and snatched the music away from him. "I must go." She had hurried out of the room, conscious of his eyes boring into her back. How she hated his casual use of the words "when we are married". They were not even formally engaged yet. And if she had her way, they never would be.

Now she wiped her moist hands on her skirt, took a deep breath and hurried down the passage towards the stage. Maisie followed her. "You'll be all right, Miss," she said.

"Have another look, Maisie. Make sure he's not here. If he is, I can't go on — I just can't."

"Don't worry, Miss. I'm sure he's not here."

Arabella just hoped the maid was right. But it was her cue and there was no more time for nerves. She took another deep breath and stepped on to the stage to an enthusiastic burst of applause. Sam was right — they had missed her.

As she began to sing they settled down and a hush descended over the theatre. As usual when she was singing, Arabella forgot where she was. All her doubts and worries fled as she lost herself in the music.

She sang all their old favourites. Then Sam announced the new song and, for a moment, her nervousness returned. Would it go down well? She hadn't had time to practice "On Wings of Song" properly. Would she be able to reach those high notes? And, if Oswald Delaney were in the audience, would he connect the dazzling Bella Forde with the girl he hoped to marry?

She need not have worried about her performance. The song was met with the audience's usual enthusiasm and there were cries of "encore". But Arabella felt drained. She couldn't sing another note and she hurried off stage only to stop short as she heard Delaney's voice.

"Surely she will not refuse to have supper with such a devoted admirer," he protested.

Sam's voice was firm. "Miss Forde doesn't accept invitations from her so-called admirers. She's here to sing only. Besides, as you've no doubt heard, she's recently been ill and I fear this evening's performance has exhausted her."

Arabella sank into the shadows, her heart racing. Thank goodness for Sam, who stood no nonsense from his clientele whatever their class or station in life.

Delaney was persistent. "Another time, then. Tell Miss Forde I won't give up. I am determined to meet the lady in person."

Arabella bit her knuckles. Had there been some emphasis on the word "lady" or was her guilt causing her to read too much into his words?

Another voice joined in. "Didn't you hear what he said — Miss Forde does not accept supper invitations. Now, sir, the theatre is about to close, so if you'd kindly leave —"

There was the sound of a brief scuffle and then, to her relief, the footsteps died away. She stepped out from her hiding place to be confronted by a tall figure in a dark coat, the brass buttons gleaming in the lamplight. She gasped but the man put out a hand. "Don't be alarmed, Miss. He's gone."

Sam returned from locking the door. "Thanks, Davie. I was beginning to think I'd never be rid of him." He turned to Arabella. "This is Constable Keen. It doesn't hurt to have a Peeler around to keep the troublemakers in order."

She shook the policeman's hand. "Thank you," she said and then slipped into the dressing room.

Maisie was waiting for her. "Did I hear Mr Delaney out there?" she asked. "He didn't see you, did he?"

"No — thanks to Sam and that policeman."

Maisie coloured slightly. "I thought that was Davie . . . Constable Keen's voice I heard out there."

"Do you know him?"

"He's an old pal of Sam's," Maisie said with a feigned air of nonchalance. Arabella wasn't fooled. She could tell that her maid was more than interested in the tall young policeman. She smiled as Maisie helped her out of the hooped skirt, cleaned off the thick make-up and smoothed her hair, teasing a few strands from the chignon to fall over her forehead.

"There, that's my Miss Arabella back again," Maisie said, surveying her work in the mirror. "Be sure, Miss — no one could tell." She put down the hairbrush. "Now, let's get you home before anyone sees you." She opened the door and looked up and down the corridor. "All clear," she whispered.

Sam had called a cab. He laid a hand on her arm. "He's gone, Miss. I think I fobbed him off." He frowned. "Maisie tells us that's the man you are to marry. Do you think it's wise to carry on performing now that you are engaged?" He coughed and mumbled. "I shouldn't say this but you must know from what you've seen here that men of his class do have liaisons with people they think beneath them — singers, actresses and such. I mean no disrespect, Miss, but he seems very taken with Bella Forde. If he persists in trying to meet you after your performance he will eventually discover your secret."

"I believe he already guesses and he delights in tormenting me. For myself, I do not care. A scandal would probably send him packing. But for the sake of my family I must keep these two lives separate."

Sam opened the cab door and helped first Maisie, then Arabella, inside. He leaned into the cab. "I know I've said this before but, much as it pains me, Miss, I think this really must be your last performance, don't you."

With a little sob, Arabella nodded. But she couldn't believe it really was the last time she'd sing on stage. Surely there must be a way.

Back at Essex House, the two girls slipped through the side gate, crept across the lawn and in at the glass door which gave on to the terrace. Arabella always held her breath at this point, fearful that Jennings might have noticed the unlocked door. But it opened at her touch. The house was in darkness but they had no need of lamps. From long experience, they felt their way across the hall to the back stairs.

Safely back in her room, Arabella quickly undressed and slipped into bed burying her face in her pillow as at last she let the tears flow. She wasn't sure if she was crying for the loss of her singing career or the prospect of marriage to a man she did not love. Unbidden, the image of Nat Sloane popped into her mind. Now there was a man she'd have no hesitation in giving up her singing for.

The next day Arabella went down to breakfast, her heart heavy. She couldn't even console herself with the memory of the rapturous reception her new song had received — for she was forced to acknowledge that she'd probably never sing on stage again. Not only that, she knew that Oswald would soon insist on them announcing their formal engagement.

Her first thought when she entered the dining room and saw her mother crying was that she had been found out. But there was no anger in her father's face when he turned from trying to console his wife. His face was grey, a suspicion of tears glinting in his eyes. Arabella gasped when she saw the flimsy piece of paper in his hand. News from the battlefields travelled fast these days.

"Harry," she gasped.

"It says wounded, not killed," her father said.

Her mother's sobs grew louder and Arabella took a hesitant step towards her. It wasn't like her to show her feelings so plainly and she didn't know how to comfort her.

"Does Charlotte know?" she asked, shaking her head as she realized that the next of kin would have been informed first. "We must tell her. Poor Charlotte."

"I have sent a footman round with a message," Henry said.

"I must go to her."

"My dear, have some breakfast first. It is far too early to call on the Wilsons."

"But Papa —"

Caroline wiped her eyes with a slip of handkerchief. "Your father is right. Sit down and calm yourself." She made a visible effort to control herself. "We should not be so distressed — he is merely wounded. He will be home with us before long."

Arabella wasn't so sure. She remembered overhearing a friend of her mother's talking about conditions in the hospital at Scutari. The wounded were often left unattended for long periods and there were too few doctors and surgeons. Still, she managed to force a smile and sat down beside her mother. "I'm sure you're right, Mama." She couldn't eat but she drank a little coffee and crumbled a slice of toast on her plate.

As soon as she could escape she returned to her room where Maisie had already laid out her cloak and bonnet. The news of Harry's wounding had spread through the servants' quarters and Maisie offered a sympathetic word. "I expect you'll be wanting to call on Miss Charlotte — she'll need a friend," she said.

"She dotes on Harry, as you know — she'll be inconsolable. I don't know what I can say to comfort her."

"You'll find the words, Miss."

Arabella shook her head. "I haven't given a thought to Charlotte's brother. James could have been wounded too. They would have been together." She gasped. "Suppose it's worse than that —"

"You would have heard, Miss. Now, don't upset yourself before there's any need. You must be strong for Miss Charlotte."

Before she could don her outdoor clothes there was a tap at the door and a maid informed Arabella that Mrs and Miss Wilson had called and she was to join them in the morning room.

78

Her mother had composed herself and there was no sign of her earlier distress. She sat straight in her chair, offering refreshments to her guests.

Charlotte's eyes were puffy, her face blotched from weeping. "I know he's going to die," she sobbed.

Caroline spoke sharply. "You know no such thing. The message said wounded — it does not even say how badly. You must hope and pray that he will be all right." She turned to Charlotte's mother. "One feels so helpless in these situations," she said. "I just cling to the knowledge that my son is out of the fighting and will be shipped home before long." She bit her lip. "I'm sorry. I should not have said that when poor James is still out there."

"I try not to think about it," said Mrs Wilson. "I just wish there was something we could do, besides praying and rolling bandages."

"So do I," Charlotte said.

Arabella took her friend's hand. "There is something," she said. She turned eagerly to her mother. "You remember — when we were at Lady Masterson's the other day. She was speaking of Miss Nightingale and her plan to train nurses for the hospitals out there."

Caroline Raynsford gasped. "Don't talk such nonsense, child. It is a ridiculous notion — taking girls from respectable families to work in such conditions."

"I don't think it's nonsense," said Arabella. Before her mother could speak, she went on, "Why shouldn't we do what we can? I, for one, would feel privileged to help in such a way."

"Do you really think we could?" Charlotte asked.

"Why not? Miss Nightingale is a respectable woman who has connections in high places. She would not be allowed to do it if those in power wanted to stop her."

Mrs Wilson spoke up. "I have met Miss Nightingale. She seems a very sensible person, if a little advanced in her views."

Caroline was horrified. "You surely don't condone her actions?"

"I feel as Arabella does — we women so often have to sit at home and wait for news. If we can do something practical, why not?"

"But it is not done."

"You forget. I too have a son in the army. He could be languishing in some filthy barracks hospital as we speak. We should be pleased that there are people like Miss Nightingale who are willing to do something about it."

Arabella and her mother were both lost for words. Such an outburst was quite unlike the normally quiet Mrs Wilson. But concern for her son had made her bold.

Caroline quickly recovered. "That's as may be. But surely, the girls she is training are not *ladies*."

"I don't see why not — and what's more I'm going to find out more about it," Arabella said.

"I absolutely forbid it. Your father will agree with me, I'm sure. Besides, you are to be married. Mr Delaney will not —"

"It is nothing to with Mr Delaney — we are not yet formally engaged. Besides, I don't care what he or anyone else thinks." Ignoring the shocked expressions on their faces, Arabella rushed from the room without even saying goodbye to her friend.

"Why is life so difficult?" she muttered, slamming the door. Why couldn't she take an interest in business, marry who she wished, sing in public, join Miss Nightingale's band of nurses? It seemed that everything she wanted to do was simply not done — at least by someone brought up to be a lady.

When Maisie came in to the bedroom, Arabella was sitting by the window gazing out at the square. She rubbed her eyes and stood up.

"What's wrong, Miss? Not more news about Master Harry?"

"No. We haven't heard anything more. And there's no news of James either." She gave a little laugh. "It's worse than that — I've just embarrassed my mother — and in front of guests too. Poor Mrs Wilson — she didn't know where to look."

"What on earth did you do, Miss?"

"I contradicted her, shouted at her —" Arabella sighed. "I don't know what got into me."

Maisie smiled sympathetically. "I know you find it hard, Miss — conforming to what is expected of you. But it *is* your station in life — just as it's mine to bend my knee and obey orders and pretend to be all meek and mild."

"Oh, Maisie, you're the only one who understands," Arabella gave a little sob. "Maybe I will run away."

"Well, you could certainly earn your own living on the stage. But think what it would do to your family. In spite of everything, they love you, Miss. Your mother only wants what she thinks is right for you."

Arabella sniffed. "I know." She straightened her shoulders and smiled. "I can't run away. But there is something I can do." She told Maisie about the nurses who were going out to the Crimea with Miss Nightingale. "That's what the argument was about. My mother said ladies couldn't go and I said I didn't see why not." She drew herself up and put on a haughty expression in imitation of her mother. "Don't talk such nonsense, child."

As they collapsed on the bed in a fit of giggles, the door opened and Arabella's mother stood framed in the opening, her eyes cold, her lips tight. "What is going on here?" She strode across the room and pulled Maisie to her feet, shaking her roughly. "I have spoken to you before about your familiar behaviour. You are dismissed."

"No, Mama, please — it was my fault. Don't punish Maisie."

"I did warn you." She turned to Maisie who was shaking her head, tears trickling down her face. "Pack your things, girl. I want you out of here tonight."

"Mama, please don't send Maisie away. I'm sorry I behaved so badly —"

"My mind is made up. I am convinced she has been a bad influence on you. From now on — until your marriage at least — my maid Burton will attend to you."

She swept out of the room, shooing Maisie in front of her.

82

As the door closed, rebellion hardened Arabella's heart. She had always known that eventually she would have to do what her parents wanted. And, despite her aversion to Oswald Delaney, she had been prepared to go through with the marriage in order to save her family from penury. Now, she was determined not to give in without a fight. She had already accepted that her career in the music hall was over. Besides, without Maisie's help she would never have been able to keep it up. But now, a new adventure beckoned. After today she would have a hard task getting her mother to agree. But she was determined to go to the Crimea with Florence Nightingale. Afterwards, she would settle down and marry whomever her parents wished.

CHAPTER
SEVEN

The following day, Arabella submitted to having her hair done by her mother's maid. She missed Maisie already and Burton's dour looks made her even more depressed. When the older woman tried to fasten her bodice for her, she pushed the hand away. "I can manage, thank you," she snapped.

Burton looked even more sour but her strict training forbade her to answer. She merely gathered up the scattered clothes and prepared to tidy the room.

As Arabella went down to breakfast she wished she hadn't been so sharp. Her bad mood was not poor Burton's fault. She wondered how Maisie was faring. At least she didn't have to worry about getting another job straight away. She had sent a note round to say that Sam and Violet were happy to let her stay for a while. Now that the theatre was so successful there was plenty she could do to earn her keep. Arabella felt a pang of envy.

Still, if things went according to plan, she wouldn't be able to complain of being bored for much longer. She and Charlotte were to call on Lady Masterson. To her surprise, Mrs Wilson had agreed that her daughter could find out more about Miss Nightingale's plan to take a party of nurses to the Crimea. Charlotte was determined to be with Harry. And if she were allowed to go, Arabella's mother could hardly refuse permission too.

Lady Masterson's drawing room was crowded with young ladies. Arabella smiled. It seemed she wasn't the only one longing for adventure.

When they were all seated and the maid had passed round refreshment, Lady Masterson stood up. She was an imposing figure and there was an immediate hush as the girls waited for her to speak.

"Miss Nightingale has already left with her party of nurses. They should reach Constantinople any day now. But more will be needed, I'm sure. Unfortunately, she has refused to have any ladies in her party — they must be trained hospital nurses or sisters from religious houses."

There was a collective groan from the assembled girls. Most of them, like Arabella and Charlotte, had loved ones fighting in the war against the Russians and wanted to do something to help.

Lady Masterson smiled. "I cannot doubt your enthusiasm, my dears, but Miss Nightingale is right. The hospital at Scutari is no place for ladies. From what I hear the conditions in the hospitals out there cannot be imagined."

Arabella spoke up. "What can we do then? Is it possible to train at a hospital and then go out?"

"Some of you may obtain places at the Institute for the Care of Sick Gentlewomen in Harley Street. Miss Nightingale has connections there. If, after a period of training, you prove suitable, you will travel out with the next party." She paused and looked at the serious faces. "I am not going to pretend that this will be fun for you girls — that is, if your parents allow you to proceed. Frankly, I would not blame them if they refused."

She paused to let her words sink in and spoke more quietly. "You are all gently brought up young ladies. You will not have seen such sights as I have already seen. But, if these young men who have gone out to fight and die for their country can endure it, why should not we — their sisters, mothers, sweethearts — also endure it? I feel we have a duty to do what we can."

She went on to tell them that she had recently returned from the hospital at Scutari, where already her friend Miss Nightingale was beginning to make a difference with her nursing methods. She had also demanded more equipment and better food for the wounded.

"Miss Nightingale is very persuasive and she has the ear of those in power. By the time you reach the Crimea, things will have improved even more. But it will not be easy," said Lady Masterson, looking round at the eager faces.

Arabella listened avidly. Thank goodness her engagement had not been formally announced yet. If it had been, Oswald would be within his rights to forbid her to go. And, despite Lady Masterson's grim picture of what they would find when they arrived at the hospital, she was determined. Her singing had already brought pleasure to soldiers on leave from the Army. Now, she would bring comfort to them in another way.

At last she would be doing something useful with her life.

But first she had to persuade her parents.

It was easier than she had anticipated. She could hardly believe that her father seemed to be on her side. When her mother protested, he quietly remonstrated with her.

"You have said yourself, my dear, how helpless you feel to help poor Harry. Surely you can understand our daughter feels the same. And here is her chance to do something that may make a difference to him."

"But Mrs Wilson said it really is dreadful — no place for ladies."

Arabella sat quietly during this exchange. It was best to say nothing until she knew what the outcome would be.

Henry spoke soothingly. "I am sure neither Mrs Wilson nor Lady Masterson would allow their daughters to go if it were really so bad. Rest assured, they will be well chaperoned."

"But Arabella is to be married. What will Mr Delaney think if we allow her to do this?"

"I have already spoken to him. He did not seem too put out by the idea."

Arabella gasped. But before she could say anything, her mother sighed and dabbed at her eyes. "How did I come to have such a headstrong daughter?"

"It is precisely because of her temperament that I feel she should be allowed to have her way in this. Both Oswald and I agree that if Arabella does go to the

Crimea, she will come back ready to settle down and be the dutiful wife he demands."

How I wish they wouldn't talk about me as if I were not here, Arabella thought. And how dare that man discuss me behind my back. The thought of submitting to him and becoming a dutiful wife was even more abhorrent now.

But still she said nothing. Her mother was almost persuaded and she would not jeopardize her chances of such an adventure by saying the wrong thing. Besides, she had to get through her training first.

She and Charlotte had been accepted by the Institute for the Care of Sick Gentlewomen in Harley Street which Florence Nightingale had recently taken over and completely reorganized. Arabella soon found that, far from bathing fevered brows and murmuring words of comfort to the sick, she was expected to do far more practical tasks. And, to her surprise, she found she enjoyed the work. How good it was to feel useful, to go home tired at the end of the day, instead of feeling listless and bored.

Charlotte did not agree. Her initial enthusiasm soon faded and when Harry was well enough to be shipped home, she left the Institute, using the excuse that her fiancé needed her and that she must plan for their forthcoming wedding.

Pleased as she was that her brother was making a good recovery from his injuries and that her friend was happy to be able to spend more time with him, Arabella couldn't help feeling disappointed at her friend's desertion. She also worried that, because her brother would soon be home, her mother would change her mind about letting her go.

One day, when she had spent a long day on the wards and was anxious to get home to a hot bath and bed, she found Maisie waiting outside on the pavement.

"What are you doing here? Is everything all right?" she asked, her first thought that Sam or Violet had been taken ill. Cholera had been reported in the poorer parts of the city and the death toll was mounting.

"I just wanted to see you, Miss," Maisie said. "I couldn't believe it when I heard what you were up to. How on earth did you persuade the mistress to allow it?"

"It wasn't easy," Arabella said with a laugh. "But how did you hear?"

"I bumped into Mr Sloane at the theatre — I was on the door selling tickets and he turned up with some of his friends. I think he was just as surprised to see me — wanted to know why I wasn't working at Essex House any more. Then he mentioned that you were determined to learn nursing and go out with Miss Nightingale to that dreadful place where there's all the fighting —"

Maisie paused for breath and Arabella seized her friend's arm. "You spoke to Nat? How was he?"

"I knew you were sweet on him, Miss." Maisie grinned. "He looked fine — handsome as ever. But I thought you were engaged to Mr Delaney."

"It hasn't been officially announced yet. And I hope it never will be. I can't stand the man but my parents think he is a good match. It is only by promising to do my duty when I return that they have allowed me to take part in this venture."

Maisie nodded thoughtfully. "Who knows what will happen in the meantime."

They had been walking in the direction of Essex House and, on reaching the corner, they stopped. "I'd better not come any further, Miss. I don't want you getting into trouble with Mrs Raynsford."

"I'll say goodbye now then. Our party is to leave next week. Unfortunately, although I have been allowed to work at the Institute, Miss Nightingale has said she will not allow ladies to work in the hospital at Scutari. However, there are other ways in which we can be useful and maybe things will have changed by the time we arrive. Mrs Wilson has arranged for me to go as a companion to Lady Masterson and her daughter. I need not tell you that my mother is happier with that arrangement."

"I wish I could come with you," Maisie said.

"I do too," said Arabella.

Maisie's eyes widened. "Why can't I? You'll need a maid, won't you?"

Arabella didn't think she would, but the idea appealed to her. She had not admitted to herself before how much she had been relying on Charlotte's company — a familiar face among so many strangers.

"Are you sure? I thought you were happy at the theatre. And what about Constable Keen? I had hoped you and he —"

90

Maisie blushed. "I admit I'm sweet on him, Miss. But he's only a constable. He says he won't commit himself until he's made up to sergeant."

"Will he mind you leaving London?"

"It's not up to him, is it? We're not engaged yet. Besides, if he misses me, it might make him think again."

Arabella smiled. "And your sister — will she and Sam be upset? Don't they need you at the theatre?"

"They'll manage. After all, they only gave me a job because I was out of work."

"Well, if you're sure you really want to come I'll speak to Lady Masterson and make the arrangements. I'm sure she'll allow you to accompany me."

Maisie's eyes lit up. "It'll be like old times, Miss."

Two weeks later, after travelling from London to Paris and on to Marseilles, the girls boarded a fast mail boat, joining a group of ladies and their maids on their way to join diplomats and officer husbands stationed in Constantinople. With them were a party of nurses sent for by Miss Nightingale, who was already making her presence felt since she had arrived in Constantinople with her original group of nurses two months earlier. How Arabella wished she would be joining them in the barracks hospital. She didn't care how hard she had to work — anything to put off the day when she would have to submit to Oswald Delaney and become his wife.

Just before she had left Essex House, her parents had allowed her a few minutes alone with him to say goodbye. She had cringed as his lips brushed her cheek and his hands tightened on her shoulders. "I shall miss you, my dear. I will be counting the days till you return," he said.

"If you are so eager for my company, I am surprised that you agreed to let me go," Arabella said sharply.

"Ah, well." He stroked his moustache and looked her up and down. "I can't deny that I would prefer you to remain. But the thought of you in my bed one day will sustain me in your absence."

Arabella felt her face redden and she tried to push him away. But his grip remained firm. He laughed. "I can't tell you how much I am looking forward to taming this little wildcat." He pulled her to him. "Now, my dear, there is something I wish you to do for me."

When she struggled more wildly, he laughed again. "No, it's not what you think. It is a matter of business." He released her and felt in the pocket of his waistcoat, withdrawing a sealed envelope. "When you reach Constantinople, you will be contacted by a business acquaintance of mine. Give him this letter — it is very important."

"Why not send it by the regular mail?" Arabella asked, her curiosity aroused.

"I do not wish it to fall into the wrong hands." He gripped her shoulders again, thrusting his face near hers. "If you value your reputation, you will speak to no one of this. Do you understand?"

Arabella felt a quiver of fear. The threat was unmistakable. He knew her secret and would not hesitate to make it public if she did not obey him.

92

Somehow, she managed to keep her composure, injecting just the right amount of indignation into her voice. "I don't know what you mean, sir," she said.

"I think you do."

She stared at him for a moment, finally tossing her head and summoning a teasing smile. "Why is it so secret — are you perhaps a spy?" she asked.

As Oswald threw back his head and laughed aloud, the door opened and her father entered smiling. "I see you are keeping your fiancé entertained," he said.

"Indeed she is," said Oswald. "I shall miss this young lady while she is away. But when she has had enough of adventuring, I look forward to her entertaining me once more." He bent and kissed Arabella's hand. "You will not forget what I said, my dear?"

Now, as rain lashed the deck and the cold wind whipped her hair across her eyes, Arabella recalled Oswald Delaney's words and his threatening posture. Clinging to the ship's rail, she thought of the letter secreted at the bottom of her trunk and wondered when the mysterious person would contact her. The sooner it was out of her possession the better. She had no wish to become involved in Oswald's business — whatever it was.

She peered through the grey murk towards the shore. "That's it — Constantinople," she said.

"Thank god — we've arrived at last," Maisie said, smiling weakly. Like most of the passengers on this stormy voyage, she had succumbed to seasickness.

Arabella pointed. "And that's the hospital over there." She pointed to the opposite shore where the huge bulk of the barracks with its fortress-like towers loomed out of the mist.

The ship tied up at the harbour and the nurses were the first to disembark, rowed across the still choppy waters of the Bosporus in small boats that looked like Venetian gondolas. Arabella watched enviously, wondering if she'd done the right thing in coming here. Acting as companion to Lady Masterson and her insipid daughter wasn't her idea of adventure. Still, at least she was away from her mother's stifling rule and she had her beloved Maisie with her. Who knew what would happen before she had to return to the life she hated — and would hate even more once she was the wife of the noxious Oswald Delaney.

Arabella shivered at the thought. Would she be able to do what he'd demanded? And, if she didn't, would he carry out his threat to ruin her and bring scandal to her family?

CHAPTER
EIGHT

Over the next few weeks there were many times when
Arabella wished she had not come. She stood at the
bedroom window, hugging her robe round her, gazing
out at the heaving grey waters of the harbour below.

"They say it's the worst winter in living memory,"
she said, turning as Maisie entered with her washing
water.

"Better be quick, Miss, before it freezes," the maid
said with an attempt at humour as she set the jug down
on the washstand.

She bustled around the room, getting Arabella's
clothes out of the trunk where most of them had lain
since their arrival. Arabella had refused to let her
unpack properly. She still had not given up hope that
soon she would be allowed to cross the Bosporus to
help in the hospital. From her window she had seen
boatloads of sick and wounded being taken off the
ships and landed at Scutari and she hated feeling so
useless.

"What will you wear today, Miss?" Maisie interrupted her sombre thoughts.

Arabella shrugged; feeling so depressed, she didn't
care. It wasn't the bitter cold, the biting wind and the

overall greyness souring her mood. It was her usual affliction — boredom. Being a companion to the colourless Lavinia Masterson had turned out to be just as tedious as she'd anticipated, a round of afternoon visits to the dull wives of the ambassador's staff, sewing circles and boring dinner parties. Even worse, Lavinia had not completely recovered from the seasickness and spent a lot of time in her room. Arabella was expected to keep her company, but she was bored with the religious tracts that Lavinia deemed suitable for reading aloud.

She completed her washing and donned the clothes Maisie had laid out for her. As she sat at her dressing table and allowed the maid to brush her hair, she listened to the girl's description of the below stairs preparations for Christmas. But nothing could cheer her up. A wave of homesickness swept over her. Essex House would be ablaze with candles to supplement the recently installed gas light, fires would be lit in all the rooms, the Christmas tree would have been brought in to stand it the hall, reaching almost to the ceiling. She pictured Harry and Charlotte decorating the tree as they had done each year since her mother had insisted on copying the fashion brought to England by Prince Albert.

Where had her impulsive nature led her this time? For the first time, she regretted leaving her home and family. She gazed at her listless reflection in the mirror as the maid pinned her hair into its elaborate chignon. "We shouldn't have come, Maisie," she said.

"Oh, Miss, it's not like you to be so down. It's an adventure, like you said. Who'd have dreamed I'd have crossed the sea to this strange place? I'd never have seen those wonderful buildings with all those gold domes if it weren't for you. And that place with the blue tiles. It's better than anything in a picture book." Maisie's eyes glowed with excitement.

Arabella couldn't help smiling. "It was rather splendid, wasn't it?" she said. The smile quickly turned to a frown. "But that's not why we came, is it?"

Despite her maid's enjoyment of their excursion to explore the old city, she was conscious of the sombre atmosphere here in Constantinople. The stench from the harbour, which was littered with refuse, including dead horses, reminded everyone of the war. Although the actual fighting had ceased for a time, the armies bogged down by mud and bitter weather, the siege went on and with it, death and disease.

The thought of all those fine young men being needlessly slaughtered frightened her. Her brother might be safely at home now, but her childhood friend James and others she'd grown up with were still here. She'd seen for herself how bad things were. Every day more sick soldiers arrived at the hospital across the water, tattered and weary, helping each other up the steep muddy slope.

Arabella sighed. She shouldn't be here, leading the leisurely life of a lady. She should be over there in the barracks hospital, helping Miss Nightingale and the other nurses. She resolved once more to ask permission to join them. Surely even so inexperienced hands as hers would be welcome, especially as she was so willing.

Maisie pushed the last hairpin into place and stepped back. "There, Miss, you look a treat. What are your plans for today then?"

"I must get out of this house," Arabella said.

"But it's still bitterly cold out," the maid protested.

"Never mind. I have a warm cloak. We shall go to the grand bazaar. I have heard you can buy anything there and it is better than staying here and listening to Miss Lavinia's complaints about her health."

Maisie stifled a giggle. "But, Miss, what about her ladyship — surely she won't allow you to go."

"We shall not tell her." Arabella put a hand to her brow. "Oh, Maisie, I am feeling rather faint. Perhaps I will keep to my room this morning. Will you please inform her ladyship that I shall not be down to breakfast."

The giggle became a loud laugh. "You are naughty, Miss." She straightened her face and bobbed a curtsey. "Yes, Miss, anything you say, Miss,"

She left the room and Arabella took the opportunity to make sure the letter she had concealed in her muff was still in place. She had not even confided in her maid about the mission Oswald Delaney had thrust upon her.

Since their arrival in Constantinople she had been on the alert for an approach from his business contact. Whenever a visitor was announced at the Masterson house she would look up expectantly, anxious to get the errand over with. But so far, no one had approached her.

Maisie came back and announced that everyone was in the dining room. "Her ladyship wanted to come up and see how you were, but I said you were sleeping," she said.

"Good. We'd better slip out while they are all otherwise engaged." Arabella fastened her cloak, pulling the hood up to hide her hair. She tucked her little purse into her muff alongside the letter and beckoned Maisie to open the door and check that there was no one in the corridor outside.

Heads down against the cold wind, the two girls hurried towards the bazaar, clutching each other's arms and giggling at their escape. For a while, as they wandered the narrow streets, marvelling at the sheer *foreign-ness* of their surroundings, Arabella was able to mask her discontent with the narrowness of her life.

As they entered the bazaar, the spicy smell of food cooking on a brazier wafted towards them, reminding her that she'd eaten no breakfast. She pulled Maisie to a halt outside a booth where colourful sweetmeats were displayed. An old woman in black gabbled some words, pointing to her wares and smiling through broken teeth.

"Let's try some," Arabella said, picking up a small cake dusted with sugar. She held up four fingers. The old woman nodded vigorously and wrapped the cakes in paper as Arabella took some coins from her purse. The girls walked away, nibbling at them and exclaiming at their sweetness.

The tightly packed booths were a feast for the nose and eye; mingled smells of perfumes and spices almost overwhelmed them as they wandered along, brushing their hands against exotically coloured silk hangings and intricately woven carpets, all the while listening to the garbled shouts of the vendors.

There were few women about and most of them were swathed in long black robes. Arabella knew that women here were expected to be self-effacing and she made sure to keep her cloak pulled closely round her, the hood obscuring most of her face.

They had seen a few soldiers and one or two men in European dress but most of the street traders wore long white robes, their heads swathed in turbans. As they ventured further into the market, Arabella began to feel apprehensive. Adventurous as she was, she began to realize that they should have asked one of Lady Masterson's servants to escort them.

She could see that Maisie, too, was becoming nervous. "Perhaps we'd better turn back," she said, finishing the last of her cake and brushing the sugar from her hands.

"A wise decision, ladies," said a voice from behind them.

Arabella whirled round, clutching Maisie's hand. An unshaven, shabbily dressed man confronted them. But although he spoke with a foreign accent, his voice was cultured and she noticed that his fingernails were clean. "What do you want?" she asked, proud that she had managed to keep her voice even.

100

"It's what you want, ladies," he said, smiling. "A protector, an escort. This is no place for two English ladies alone."

He took Arabella's arm and began to lead her back the way they had come. She pulled away. "How dare you? We have no need of an escort," she protested.

"I think you had better come with me," he said. The smile had gone and his fingers dug into her arm. He pulled her into a space between two booths. "Now, Miss Arabella Raynsford, I believe you have something for me."

By now, she was terrified. But she managed to find her voice. "Run, Maisie, fetch help," she said.

But before the frightened maid could move, the stranger's other hand shot out and grabbed her too. "Do not be so foolish, Miss. I mean you no harm." He turned to Arabella. "The letter — you have it?"

In her terror, Arabella had quite forgotten the letter. With trembling fingers she retrieved it from her muff and handed it over. He let go of her but still kept his grip on Maisie, whose face was white, her eyes wide with fear. He snatched the paper, nodding with satisfaction.

"May we go now?" Arabella asked, regaining some of her composure. "I will inform Mr Delaney that I have completed his errand."

The man's lips curled in a snarl. "No names, Miss." He gave her a final shake and nodded. "You can go — for now. But I will need to contact you again with a reply to this message. Be here at the same time in two days."

"Why not come to the house and state your business like a respectable caller?"

"It would not be wise." He pushed her away and seemed about to say more when he turned abruptly as a shadow loomed over him.

"What's going on here?"

Arabella sagged against the wall and closed her eyes as, with one final push, the man barged past her and disappeared into the alley between the booths.

"Miss Raynsford. Are you all right? Have you been robbed?"

Arabella's eyes flew open in disbelief. "Mr Sloane. What are you doing here?" she asked.

"I was about to call on the Mastersons when I spotted you going into the bazaar," he said.

"And you followed us?" Arabella's fright had turned to indignation. "As I said to that other fellow — we have no need of a protector."

"It seems you are wrong about that." Nat Sloane's lips tightened. "What did he want?"

"Nothing." Arabella almost confessed. But, although she told herself that passing on the letter was purely a matter of business, Oswald's threatening manner and his insistence on the need for secrecy had made her suspicious. And much as she liked Nat Sloane, she hadn't forgotten that a few months ago she had witnessed an argument between Nat and Oswald outside the Half Moon Theatre. Now she was sure that the letter contained some secret to do with the war and she couldn't shake off the suspicion that Nat might be involved too.

She put her arm round Maisie, who was still shaking. "Maybe you're right — he did mean to rob us. It is fortunate you came along, Mr Sloane."

"Fortunate indeed, Miss Raynsford." Nat pursed his lips and Arabella knew he did not believe her. "Perhaps you will allow me to escort you home." He held out his arm and Arabella took it.

With Maisie following closely behind, they made their way back to the Masterson's harbourside mansion.

As they turned the corner, Arabella let go his arm — reluctantly. She had, despite her suspicions, been enjoying the warmth of his hand on hers, the faint fragrance of the cologne he wore. She would have liked to keep on walking with him at her side. Pushing such unseemly thoughts aside she said, "I think it better we should part here."

"But I meant to call on Lady Masterson," said Nat.

"I cannot stop you making a social call. However, it is not seemly for us to arrive at the house together."

"Was it seemly for you to be wandering the souks alone?" Nat said, smiling. He raised an eyebrow and nodded his head. "I see — you and your maid have slipped out without her ladyship's knowledge. Well, as I pointed out earlier, it was a foolish thing to do. However, no harm was done on this occasion. If you promise me not to put yourself in danger again, I will hold my tongue for now."

Arabella flushed and tried to protest.

Nat laughed. "Go along — you'd better slip indoors the way you slipped out. I will wait a few minutes before announcing my presence."

Grabbing Maisie's hand, Arabella flounced away. "How dare he speak to me like that," she muttered, her face burning.

They crept through the servants' entrance and up the back stairs, to her relief encountering no one on their way. Safe in her room, she threw her muff onto the bed and swept off her cloak.

Maisie automatically picked up Arabella's things and began to tidy them away. "What a blessing we met Mr Sloane," she said. "I was that frightened, Miss. That other man seemed to know you but —"

"I've never seen him before," Arabella snapped.

"But, Miss, the letter —"

"Maisie, you must forget about that. Mr Delaney entrusted me with the letter — a matter of business." She sighed, the urge to confide in her maid almost overwhelming. "I must confess I was frightened too. But the letter is delivered. We can forget all about it now."

Maisie carried on methodically tidying the room, while Arabella changed her walking shoes for a pair of dainty embroidered silk slippers. As the maid was about to speak again, a knock came at the door.

Swiftly remembering that she was supposed to be unwell, Arabella lay down on the bed and pulled the counterpane over herself. "Who is it?" she called.

"It's Lavinia. I wondered if you were recovered sufficiently to come downstairs. We have a visitor."

Nodding to Maisie to open the door, Arabella got up from the bed and went to the dressing table. "I feel much better. I'm just dressing," she said as Lavinia came into the room. "Who has come to call?" she asked.

"It is a Mr Sloane. He said he knew you in England." Lavinia's usual lacklustre manner had brightened with curiosity.

Arabella felt the telltale flush creeping up her cheeks but she managed a careless tone. "He is a business acquaintance of my father's," she said. "Maybe he has brought news from home."

Downstairs she found Nat deep in conversation with Lady Masterson, seated on a delicate chair and balancing a bone china cup and saucer on his knee. He should have looked awkward and yet he seemed perfectly at home, smiling a welcome as Arabella entered the room.

"Ah, Miss Raynsford, how fortunate I am to find you at home," he said, rising and giving a small bow.

"What a surprise, Mr Sloane," she replied, sitting beside him and helping herself to coffee.

"A surprise and a pleasure, Miss Raynsford," he said, hiding his smile behind a sip from his tea cup.

Stifling the urge to giggle, she said, "What brings you here? Do you have news from home?"

"I have come to Constantinople on a matter of business and thought I would take the opportunity to let you know that your brother is recovering from his wounds. He hopes to be fit enough to return to his regiment shortly."

"I'm pleased Harry is well but I do hope he will not return too soon." From what she had seen from her window as the boats brought the wounded to the hospital, Arabella couldn't bear the thought of her beloved brother returning to this desolate place.

"I believe Miss Charlotte is of the same mind," Nat said.

Lavinia, seated on the other side of Nat, laid a hand on his arm. "I'm sure he will do his duty, as will all you young men. What regiment are you with, Mr Sloane?"

"None, Miss Lavinia. I am an engineer, called out to advise the army on the matter of building a road to make the transport of our big guns easier." He turned to Arabella. "We must blast through solid rock at some point. Your father has been trying to find alternative sources of copperas for the gunpowder factory at Faversham."

"That is where my fiancé, Mr Delaney's factory is situated, I believe. Have you done business with him lately?" Arabella could have kicked herself for using the word fiancé, but perversely she'd had to bring his name into the conversation. She was still a little suspicious of the two men in her life. It couldn't be coincidence, Nat Sloane turning up at this moment.

Nat's lips tightened. "I have not seen Mr Delaney and have no business with him. I only know that he has dealings with your father."

Before Arabella could reply, Lady Masterson leaned forward and tapped Nat's knee. "What is all this talk of business? Young ladies are not interested in such things. Tell us the latest gossip from London."

"I'm sorry, your ladyship. You are right." He finished his drink, leaned forward to place his cup on the tray and stood up. "But, unfortunately it is business that brought me to Constantinople and I must be on my way. Forgive me, ladies. I'll see myself out." He bowed over Lady Masterson's hand and made his farewells. At the door, he paused. "I hope you will allow me to call again."

"Of course," Lady Masterson murmured.

When he had gone, she rang the bell for the maid to clear away the tray.

Lavinia had gone to the window and watched as Nat strode away towards the harbour. She turned to Arabella. "Have you known Mr Sloane long?" she asked.

Arabella nodded.

"A charming young man," Lady Masterson said with a smile in her daughter's direction.

Arabella burned with resentment at the implication that next time he came to call it would be to see Lavinia. After all, wasn't she herself practically engaged to be married?

Later, helping her mistress to change for dinner, Maisie seemed to have forgotten her fright of the morning.

"Have you decided to meet him, Miss?" she asked.

"I dare say he will call again," Arabella said, trying to sound careless.

"Not Mr Sloane, Miss — that man, the one we met in the market."

"Of course not. I hope we never see him again."

"But he said —" Maisie faltered. "Be here in two days, he said."

"My business with him is done. He has the letter. Now I just want to forget about it," Arabella said.

But she couldn't forget. And that night as she lay sleepless, listening to the wind and rain, the waves dashing against the harbour wall, she went over the strange encounter once more. She had imagined that she would be approached by a gentleman, an acquaintance of the Mastersons perhaps. She had not expected to be waylaid by a ruffian in a public place. What was Oswald thinking of, subjecting her to such an ordeal? She was his fiancée, someone he was supposed to love and cherish. And yet he showed her no respect, threatened her and manhandled her. Nat wouldn't treat her like that she thought, as she turned over and tried to get comfortable. She grew hot at the thought. Her feelings for him were still as strong as they'd been last summer. But at the same time there was still that niggle of doubt.

She hated herself for her suspicions. She was already sure that there was something amiss in the way she'd been asked to deliver the letter and she could live with the thought that Oswald might not be altogether honest. But she couldn't forget that furtive meeting outside the theatre and the fact that Nat had turned up just as she was handing over the letter. It was all too confusing. But one thing was certain. As she fell asleep at last, Arabella acknowledged to herself that she loved Nat — whatever he might be up to.

CHAPTER
NINE

The next day passed uneventfully, leaving Arabella with too much time on her hands — time to recall in detail her latest encounter with Nat Sloane. It didn't help that, as she sat at her embroidery under Lady Masterson's eagle eye, Lavinia would persist in asking her questions about him. She was obviously taken with the young man and wanted to know all about him.

"He is a friend of your fiancé, I believe?" she said.

"A business acquaintance merely. He is more a friend of my father's," Arabella said, bending her head over her stitches.

Lavinia was about to say more when Arabella raised her head. "And, if you don't mind my saying so — would you please not refer to Mr Delaney as my fiancé?"

"But surely — I understood you were engaged to be married."

"There has been no formal announcement and will not be until I return home."

She bent her head to her sewing once more, muttering under her breath, "and not even then if I have anything to do with it". Seeing Nat again had made her realize that she could never marry Oswald.

And if Nat called again, she would confront him with her suspicions, praying that there was a reasonable explanation for his involvement with the Irishman. She had now almost managed to convince herself that the letter was nothing to do with him. Surely if he were implicated in what was going on, Oswald would have known he was coming out here. He could have given him the letter. Why ask her to deliver the letter?

While she was trying to puzzle it out, Arabella suddenly remembered where she had seen the roughly dressed man before. A few days earlier he had been leaning on the harbour wall opposite the house, not roughly dressed as he had been in the souk, but smartly turned out and carrying a silver-topped cane. She had assumed he was waiting for a ferryboat to carry him across the Bosporus. Now, she realized he must have been watching for an opportunity to waylay her.

A knock on the drawing room door made her look up sharply. When she saw that Lavinia too was eagerly anticipating a caller, she tried to quell the surge of jealousy. After all, Nat thought she was spoken for. Why shouldn't he call on Lavinia?

Still, she couldn't conceal a little smile at the other girl's disappointed frown when she realized it was only the maid bringing in the tea.

Chiding herself for her pettiness, she turned her thoughts to how she was going to manage a further meeting with the stranger who had taken the letter. For, despite herself, she was intrigued. Maybe he wanted her to pass on a secret message to Oswald.

And, once that's done, she told herself, I'll have nothing more to do with it. She had come here to help nurse the wounded and she would put all her efforts into persuading Miss Nightingale and the authorities to allow her to do so.

The next day she enlisted Maisie's help again.

The maid's eyes grew round. "Surely you're not going into that bazaar place again? It's not safe. I can't let you, Miss."

"I must. If I'm not there at the appointed time, he may come to the house. I can't risk that. You must come with me, Maisie. I can't go alone."

"I won't let you down, you know that. But you can't keep getting away with these scrapes, Miss." Maisie sounded worried.

"You seemed to enjoy our little adventures when we were in London," Arabella said.

"That was different. There weren't all these foreigners around. Besides, we had Sam to look out for us if there was any trouble."

Arabella smiled. "It was fun, wasn't it?" She danced round the room, humming a few bars from "On Wings of Song", grasping Maisie's hands and twirling her round. "Oh, Maisie, I do miss all that, you know. And I must have some excitement in my life. So come on, get my cloak and let's slip down the back stairs while there's no one about."

A few flakes of snow drifted in the wind as the girls hurried towards the bazaar. Arabella was grateful for the bad weather which kept people indoors. Muffled in their cloaks, the hoods drawn close to hide their faces, she felt safe from discovery.

"Look out for the stall where we bought the cakes," Arabella said. "It was near there where we saw that man."

"I hope he doesn't turn up, Miss. We shouldn't be here." Maisie clutched her arm. "What if her ladyship or Miss Lavinia go to your room and find you gone?"

"Stop fretting, Maisie. It will be all right." Arabella tried to sound confident but her teeth were chattering — and not from the cold. Her love of adventure was rapidly fading and she longed to be back in the drawing room at the Mastersons's, listening to Lavinia's inane remarks as she drew her needle through her embroidery.

They passed a narrow alley leading off the main bazaar and Arabella clutched her cloak more closely around her as the keen wind funnelled down from the harbour. Hastening her steps, she did not at first turn round when a voice hailed her. "So, you came then? I was beginning to think you wouldn't show up." A man stepped from behind one of the booths. Arabella almost started to run. She didn't recognize him. This time he was dressed in the long robes of an Arab, his head swathed in a white turban.

He grabbed her arm. "Not so fast. I have not written it down. You must pass on this message in one of your own letters. Tell the Irishman that we must have more. He will not be paid until I have the next consignment."

"Consignment of what?" Arabella asked, meeting his gaze boldly, despite her fear.

"You don't need to know. Just pass on the message. I cannot contact him directly — it is too risky." His fingers tightened on her wrist. "And speak to no one of this — or else . . ."

"I'm not afraid of you."

"Maybe not. But you are not the only one at risk." His eyes went to Maisie who was trembling behind her mistress.

The threat was unmistakeable and Arabella nodded, her bravado evaporating swiftly. "I'll pass on your message — this time." She pulled away from him and took Maisie's hand. "Come along. We have nothing more to say to this *gentleman*." Head held high, she stalked away between the market stalls, unheeding of the sellers crying their wares, the colourful booths and exotic smells.

Back at the house, Arabella hurried into the library to find pen and paper. She must write to Oswald straightaway, making it clear that she had no wish to be involved in his schemes. She wrote rapidly, characteristically saying exactly what she thought. She had filled a page before realizing that such candour might not be wise. She took a fresh sheet, chewing the end of her pen as she wondered how to word the letter. Anyone might read it and she did not wish to implicate herself. For she had finally realized what her so-called fiancé was up to. He was supplying arms — or explosives at least — to the enemy. And he had involved her, knowing she would do anything to protect her father and, not least, her own reputation.

She had learned a lot about subterfuge in her efforts to keep her secret life from discovery and now she found a way to let Oswald know that she had done as he wished. Calling the mysterious man "Mr Smith" was not original but he would know to whom she referred. "He told me he is having trouble with supplies. It is the war, I suppose. But he needs much more if he is to fulfil his obligations to his customers. I wondered if there is anything you could do to help your old friend," she wrote.

It would have to do. As she signed the letter, Lavinia came into the room. "Oh, there you are. Have you been in here all morning?"

Arabella nodded. "I had some letters to write. I wanted to make sure they caught the mail boat today."

"Miss Nightingale has called," Lavinia said. "She and my mother are discussing the problems they are having at the hospital. Why don't you join us?"

When they entered the drawing room, Miss Nightingale was standing by the window. She looked tired but there was fire in her voice as she spoke. "The food was inedible, the men starving. It is as well I brought my own supplies." She sighed. "My dear Lady Masterson, you cannot imagine the trouble I had getting permission to cook extras for the men. But I have installed portable stoves and now we have a proper diet kitchen producing invalid food."

"And have the doctors accepted your presence now?" Lady Masterson inquired.

Florence Nightingale gave a short laugh. "Under protest. But yes — what choice did they have? There were so many sick arriving, the hospital was overwhelmed. My nurses have proved their worth — as I knew they would."

Arabella ventured to speak. "Miss Nightingale, is there any way you would relax your rules and allow me to join you at the hospital?"

"I only employ trained nurses, as you know. It is no place for a refined young lady such as yourself."

"But I have helped at the Institute in Harley Street and would have trained properly had I been allowed. Surely there is something I can do to help. I did not come all this way to sit drinking tea and doing embroidery."

Miss Nightingale smiled. "I cannot fault your eagerness. But what would your family say if I were to expose you to some of the experiences I've had. No, my dear, it is out of the question."

Arabella was not deterred. If she didn't speak up now she might never have another chance. "And what about your family, Miss Nightingale? Were they quick to give their permission for this venture?" She bit her lip at the other woman's frown and quickly tried to apologize.

Florence Nightingale waved her away. "You are right. It took great determination on my part. And I can see you feel the same way. Still, I cannot allow you to nurse the men." Before Arabella could protest, she held up a hand. "However, you may be of some use."

As their visitor made her farewells to the Mastersons, Arabella rushed upstairs to find Maisie. "My cloak, quickly." She was bubbling over with excitement. "I am

115

to accompany Miss Nightingale to Scutari — across the water. She is going to show me round the hospital."

As Maisie helped her on with her outdoor clothing, Arabella said, "I am sure she thinks that I'll be put off. But I am determined not to show my feelings. If those poor men can bear it, so can I."

"Will she let you nurse after all, Miss?"

"No, but she says I might be able to make myself useful in other ways — writing letters, filling in requisition forms and suchlike."

On the rare days of sunshine since her arrival, Arabella had thought the great Turkish barracks with its towers at each corner looked like a magnificent palace, glowing golden in the sun. Close to, it was a different story, but she felt she was prepared for anything as she passed through the great gateway into the square. Far from being a palace, the barracks which housed the hospital were little more than a slum. One side of the quadrangle had been damaged by fire and the rest of the building was not much better, the walls running with damp, the ground a sea of mud and horse manure.

As they entered the hospital Arabella was almost overwhelmed by the smell. She bit her lip, determined not to show her disgust.

Miss Nightingale touched her arm. "You do get used to it in time. Besides, it is not as bad as it was when I first arrived," she said with a grim smile. "At least the place is cleaner and we have established a laundry. But I fear the smell of sickness will always linger."

She led Arabella down a long corridor and into the main ward. Rows of beds were crammed side by side with hardly room to pass between them. Every bed was occupied. Some of the men lay scarcely moving, eyes blank, almost as if they were already dead. Others writhed and moaned in their agony.

Even her experiences at the Institute in London had not prepared her for the reality of an army hospital. There, the beds had been evenly spaced with lockers beside them to hold the patients' belongings, the sheets had been white, the counterpanes neatly tucked in.

Here, some had only a thin blanket, the pillows had no covers, and what sheets there were, were grey and wrinkled. The nurses in their grey tweed uniform dresses and the nuns in their habits moved awkwardly between the crammed rows of beds with their bowls and bundles of bandages. It was a stark and dismal scene — the only splash of colour was the red embroidered words "Scutari Hospital" on the sashes the nurses wore — and the blood.

"We try to change the dressings frequently to keep the wounds clean and free from infection," Miss Nightingale said. At the end of the ward she led Arabella into a small room which was being used as an office. "This is where I do most of my work," she said. "There is so much administration. It is not just about dealing with the men and their wounds. Forms have to be filled in. Every requisition has to go to the right department. A girl of your education and intelligence could be of great help to me."

It wasn't how Arabella had pictured herself. But at least she would be doing something useful. "I'd be delighted to help you," she said. "When can I start?"

"Now, if you wish. I could send a message across to the Mastersons so that they will not worry about you."

"What would you like me to do?" Arabella asked, throwing off her cloak and draping it over a chair.

For the next couple of hours she filled in forms, addressed envelopes and did her best to learn something of how the hospital was run. She soon realized that Florence Nightingale was a very organized and efficient woman.

From time to time a nurse or orderly would put their head round the door with a question and Miss Nightingale would disappear for a few moments, returning with a satisfied smile at yet another problem solved.

Arabella had imagined that she would spend time in the wards, speaking to the soldiers, soothing their worries, fulfilling the roles that were traditionally that of nurses. But the older woman seemed more concerned with seeing that her nurses worked efficiently, that the men were cared for in material ways. She inspected everything from the food they ate to the state of the latrines. Arabella's admiration for her grew and by the end of the day she was ready to do anything Miss Nightingale asked.

When at last she returned to the harbourside house across the water she was exhausted. But she was determined to return to the hospital again the next day.

118

Her determination wavered a little when she heard that Nat had called that afternoon. But she couldn't remain at home just on the chance that he would come again. Besides, Lavinia was aglow as she recounted the details of his visit and Arabella told herself that his visit had nothing to do with her.

She did feel a twinge of satisfaction when Lavinia told her Nat had expressed disappointment to find she was not at home. But it was short-lived.

"He said he had some news from your fiancé," she said.

All her old suspicions of Nat returned. But what could she do about it? If he and Oswald were involved in some business with the enemy she should tell someone. But she still couldn't quite bring herself to believe that Nat was really doing anything wrong. Until she had more evidence she would get on with the job she had come here for and try not to think any more about the men in her life.

CHAPTER
TEN

As the weeks passed Arabella began to enjoy her work. She soon got the hang of the various requisition forms and the masses of other paperwork. As she proved her willingness to work hard, Miss Nightingale began to give her more responsibility. She entrusted her with messages for the surgeon in charge and the army administrators, and even, on occasion, allowed her to carry out the laundry inspection.

Miss Nightingale still refused to let her have any contact with the patients though, no matter how she pleaded. "I have promised Lady Masterson that I will only involve you in tasks fit for a lady," she said. "And she in turn has made a similar promise to your parents — that you will not be exposed to any unpleasantness." Her lips twisted on the word and she gave a wry smile.

It was hard for anyone within the hospital's environs to be completely protected from what was euphemistically called "unpleasantness" and Arabella gave an answering smile.

After the first few days of returning to the Mastersons's each evening, Arabella had asked if she could stay at the hospital. Often, the sea was too rough for the small boats to make the crossing and she dreaded being stranded on the Constantinople side unable to carry on with the work that had come to mean so much to her.

Miss Nightingale reluctantly agreed and allowed her to clear out a small room, little more than a cupboard really, adjacent to her office. She was pleased that she was allowed to have Maisie with her on condition that the girl shared the room with her. "I don't need a maid, of course," she said. "But Maisie can make herself useful in lots of ways."

They settled into a routine. While Arabella worked in the office, Maisie cleaned the room, did their laundry and prepared meals. Sometimes she went into the wards where she unobtrusively helped the orderlies, gathering up soiled linen to be sent to the laundry outside the barracks, fetching and carrying for the nurses.

Watching her little friend bustling around, seemingly very happy in her work, Arabella wondered how they could ever go back to their old lives. She couldn't believe that she had ever needed someone to help her dress and do her hair and, as they got ready for bed one night, Maisie echoed her thoughts.

"What do you reckon the mistress would say if she could see us now, Miss?" she asked.

Arabella laughed. "She'd be horrified. Pray she never finds out or I'd be whisked back home in a flash." She sat on the edge of the bed, hairbrush in hand. "Seriously, Maisie, do you mind? It is not what either of us is used to is it?"

"I don't mind, Miss. Don't get me wrong, I loved being a ladies' maid. It's what I always wanted from when I first went into service. But this —" She waved a hand to encompass the room, the hospital, their whole situation. "It makes more sense doesn't it? I feel I'm really doing something useful."

Arabella nodded. "I feel the same, Maisie. Why should I, a fit and healthy young girl, expect someone to wait on me hand and foot?" She sighed. "I dread going home. And yet it seems wicked to hope the war won't end and that —" Her voice trailed away.

"They say the siege will be raised soon and the fighting will start again in earnest. But it must end some time." Maisie jumped into the narrow bed and pulled the covers up. "You'll feel differently once you're married."

As Arabella turned out the lamp she said, "I don't want to get married." But it wasn't true, was it? The thought of marriage to Oswald Delaney made her shudder, but . . . a picture of Nat Sloane crept into her mind and she thumped the pillow angrily. "I think I'll join a convent," she muttered.

Maisie started to laugh. "You — a nun, Miss?"

Arabella couldn't help laughing too. But the laughter quickly turned to sobs as she thought of what the future held. One day she would have to go home and start leading the conventional life demanded of her.

All through that winter the British army remained marooned on the heights above Sebastopol on the other side of the Black Sea. Despite the siege, the Russians had managed to keep control of the only passable road down to the harbour at Balaclava. But somehow the Allies managed to get the sick men into the boats for the week's journey to Scutari. Most were sick, not wounded, suffering from scurvy, dysentery and starvation, their condition worsened by exposure to the freezing cold and wet.

Thousands poured into the hospital, many to die before they could be attended to. But under Miss Nightingale's administration, the death toll gradually declined.

As they began to realize that her methods were really working, the doctors turned to her for help. Nobody argued when she insisted that the damaged wing of the barracks should be repaired to accommodate the increasing numbers of sick soldiers.

"I knew it was just a question of patience," she said to Arabella as she came into the office one day. "They did not want me here, you know. But now that they can see the difference my methods have made, things will get easier."

She looked tired but she smiled in satisfaction. "Now the real work begins. Thank you for your help, Arabella."

"I am pleased to have been of assistance. But what did you mean about the real work?"

"The winter is almost over. At the slightest improvement in the weather, the fighting will begin again. We must prepare for even more patients in the near future."

★ ★ ★

Since leaving London, Arabella hadn't given a thought to her singing career. It was almost as if her time at the Half Moon Theatre had happened to someone else. She had played and sung a few times at Lady Masterson's — once when the British Ambassador, Lord Stratford, had been a guest. He had complimented her on her singing and asked what had brought her to Constantinople. When she mentioned Miss Nightingale and the hospital over the water, he had waved a hand dismissively and began to talk about the new church he planned to build in the city. He had no time for what he saw as interference in the natural order of things.

One day in early spring as Arabella made her way across the quadrangle with a message for one of the doctors, she paused to watch the building work on the corner tower, reflecting that there wasn't much to sing about these days. How carefree she had been just a few short months ago, her only worry that her secret would be discovered and that she would be prevented from doing what she loved most. In the face of the misery all around her it hardly seemed to matter now.

When she got back to the office Miss Nightingale was waiting for her. She handed her a sheet of paper. Another list, Arabella thought with an inward sigh. But she was wrong.

"Your instructions, Miss Raynsford. The boat will be leaving soon and I do not have time to explain everything in detail. But it is all written there," she said, smiling. "I have just received permission to inspect the other hospitals. I am to take ten of my nurses to Balaclava."

124

"I have heard things are even worse there. You will have much to do." Arabella held her breath, hoping that she would be allowed to go too.

"I will go with an easy mind knowing you are here. You know my methods and will keep things running smoothly until I return."

"You mean I am to be in charge?" Arabella asked.

"You will answer to the Chief Medical Officer and the other doctors, but, yes, you will be responsible for the requisitions and seeing that everyone carries out their duties," the older woman replied.

When she had gone, Arabella looked around the empty office, scarcely able to believe what had happened. Here she was, after only a few weeks, in a position of responsibility such as she had never dreamed of. She was determined to make a success of it and to justify Miss Nightingale's faith in her.

She went in search of Maisie, eager to tell her what had happened. Since coming to Turkey, the two girls had become close friends, although Arabella had still not managed to persuade her former maid to stop addressing her as "Miss".

She found Maisie in the kitchen with three of the nurses. They did not notice her as she paused in the doorway and listened to their chatter.

"I came for the money," one of the girls said. "It's hard work but good pay. I can send money home to my family."

"My pa would go mad if he knew what I was doing," said another. "He thinks nursing is only one step up from selling your body."

"That's not fair," Maisie said. "If he could see how hard you work, he'd be proud of you."

"Well, nursing has always been done by very lower-class girls — the dregs my pa called them when I told him what I wanted to do." The girl laughed. "He thinks I've gone into service and travelled abroad with a posh family."

"I think Miss Nightingale is trying to change all that. She wants us to train properly, to be respected for what we do," said Maisie.

Arabella stepped forward. "I think she is beginning to succeed. And when the men go home, they will surely spread the word about how they were looked after. It will take time, but attitudes will change."

"Hope so, Miss," said another nurse, turning from the stove where she had been stirring a pot of soup.

Arabella told them that Miss Nightingale had left for Balaclava and read from the instructions she had left. They all admired Miss Nightingale and she only hoped that she would inspire the same sort of respect.

It was hard. Arabella had no trouble with the nurses, although she knew some of them resented the responsibility she had been given. But the nuns took no notice of her at all, continuing to do things in their own way. As for the doctors, although they had come to admire and respect Florence Nightingale, they were not so sure about Arabella.

She found it very difficult to lower her gaze and bite her tongue when they criticized her work or tried to give her orders. But she was determined to keep things running smoothly until her mentor's return from the battlefront.

Despite Miss Nightingale's injunction to have nothing to do with their patients, Arabella found that was the one rule she could not obey. Each evening, when the men had been settled down to sleep, she would go round the wards and see that all was in order. She told herself she was only doing what Florence herself did. She knew that the men must miss her nightly rounds when she would stop at each bed and murmur a few words of comfort, tuck in a blanket here and there, raise a soldier's head so that he could drink a little.

Arabella was determined to follow in Miss Nightingale's footsteps and came to look forward to these quiet moments late at night — not that it was always quiet, of course. Even in the middle of the night a ward crowded with sick and injured men was filled with coughs, groans, snores, sometimes wild shouting from one reliving the nightmare experiences up on the slopes above Balaclava.

The paid nurses thought their work done when they had washed, fed and settled the men for the night. The nuns were more compassionate, but their idea of comfort was to murmur prayers and make the sign of the cross.

One night the men were particularly restless, a new intake of soldiers suffering, not from wounds received in battle, but from some unexplained fever. Many of them threw off their covers in delirium, moaning and crying out.

Arabella moved from bed to bed, the flickering light from her lamp throwing shadows on the walls. She paused by the side of a young man, a boy really, who looked too young to have left his mother, let alone to end up in a foreign country fighting a bloody war. She sat on the edge of the bed and bathed his face, smoothing his hair back from his damp forehead.

She murmured soothing words, then began to hum a tune under her breath. As he gradually quietened she carried on humming, and almost without realizing it, began to sing one of the songs from her music hall days. The words of "Home, Sweet Home" caught in her throat but she carried on, her voice gaining in strength.

The young soldier's eyes opened and he smiled, then his eyes closed again and he fell into a more normal sleep. Around her, the noisy ward stilled, and she turned to find some of the men leaning up on their elbows, staring at her. She stopped and stood up abruptly. "I'm sorry. I'm disturbing you. Besides, you should all be asleep by now." She tried to sound stern and authoritative, smoothing her skirt and hurrying towards the door.

A burly sergeant spoke up, his voice gruff. "Don't stop, Miss. We was just startin' to enjoy it. Please, carry on."

Arabella shook her head, her voice tight with unshed tears. "I can't. I shouldn't have started." She hurried away, hoping no one would report her lapse to Miss Nightingale. She'd be sent home for fraternizing with the soldiers, no matter how innocent her intentions.

Discipline was all important even when the men were away from the battlefield.

When she got back to the cubbyhole which she called her room, Maisie was already there. "I heard, Miss," she said, smiling. "It was lovely — just like old times."

"Not quite, Maisie." She sat down on the edge of the bed. "I shouldn't have done it. Someone will report it to Miss Nightingale when she returns. I won't be allowed to stay. But I couldn't help myself. And once I started it was as if I were in a different place. All the dirt and disease, the smells, the horror — all disappeared. I was in another world."

"You'll go back to that world one day," Maisie assured her.

The next day when Arabella did her morning round she saw to her delight that the young soldier, Private Williams, was almost recovered from his fever. He was well enough to be moved to the convalescent ward where the soldiers were able to prepare their own meals and clean their own kit while waiting for a ship to take them home — or back to the battlefront, depending on how badly they'd been wounded.

"It seems your singing's a miracle cure," Maisie laughed.

"Don't be silly," said Arabella, flushing. But she was pleased. And as word of the girl with the voice of an angel spread around the hospital she found it harder to resist the sick men's pleas to sing to them as they settled down for the night. The nurses looked on in disapproval and Arabella knew she'd be in trouble when Miss Nightingale returned from her inspection of the other hospitals.

There had already been jealous murmuring when she had been given so much responsibility — "and her not a proper nurse", as she'd heard one of the women saying.

"Maybe. But she works as hard as any of you — even as hard as Miss Nightingale herself," Maisie said, trying to stand up for her mistress.

But the other woman scoffed. "She's just a society miss, one of those bleeding do-gooders. Who's she think she is, anyway?"

Arabella couldn't help overhearing and she stopped in the doorway, trying to tell herself she really didn't care.

But Maisie knew how much it hurt. "Take no notice, Miss," she said. "They're just jealous."

"I'm only trying to help. And if my singing can make those poor men forget their suffering in these awful surroundings for just a few minutes, I feel I'm doing some good."

"Miss N won't like it though. And word will get to her. One of those cats will run tittle-tattling, you can be sure."

"Well, I'll just have to make the most of it while I can." Arabella attempted a lightness of tone she did not really feel. Miss Nightingale would send her back to the Mastersons's and once they heard what she'd been up to, she'd be on the next boat back to England.

She'd have to keep her word — marry and settle down to a boring predictable life. As she tried to get comfortable in the hard bunk bed she thought that maybe it wouldn't be so bad — if only the man her parents had picked out for her were not the loathsome Oswald Delaney.

The image of Nat Sloane's face danced before her closed eyes and she couldn't help smiling. She'd managed to get her own way so often in the past — surely there must be something she could do. But the smile faded at the thought of Delaney's cruel smile and threatening posture the last time she'd seen him. Despite her rebellious nature, Arabella loved her parents and would do anything to protect them. Although she didn't want to believe her father would knowingly become involved in anything underhanded, he had, after all, done business with Oswald. And even if he were innocent of any illegal dealings, Oswald could make things difficult for him if she did not do as he asked.

As she settled into uneasy sleep, she wondered why the Irishman seemed so keen on the match. Her modest dowry could mean nothing to a man who already possessed so much.

CHAPTER
ELEVEN

Arabella didn't have time to dwell on her own concerns. Sometimes she didn't even stop to eat as, now that the fighting had started again, more sick and wounded men began to pour into the hospital each day. She was kept busy trying to find beds for them, as well as making sure that Miss Nightingale's strict standards were kept up and that the "comforts for the soldiers" sent from England were fairly distributed.

It was taxing work and she was worn out. "You must rest," Maisie urged. "You'll be no use to anyone if you fall ill."

But at the end of each long day she still insisted on doing the rounds of the wards and, at their request, she would often sing to the soldiers. "It makes them feel better — and it makes me feel good too," she said.

"Let's hope Miss N doesn't get to hear about it. I'm sure she won't approve," Maisie said.

"I'll worry about that when she returns," said Arabella, secretly hoping that it would not be too soon.

So she was smitten with guilt when a ship arrived, bringing not just another consignment of patients, but the news that Miss Nightingale had been taken ill at the

Castle Hospital in Balaclava and that there were fears for her life.

There were tears in her eyes as she relayed the news to the nurses. "She has gone down with a fever and will have to remain at Balaclava. There is no possibility of moving her at present. Let us hope that the skills she has taught the nurses there will be sufficient to help her pull through." She paused and looked at them sternly, knowing she must appeal to their goodwill to accept her authority for a little longer. "I know how much you admire Miss Nightingale — as do I," she said. "I am relying on you to act as if she were here in person — to keep up the standards of cleanliness and decency that she has taught you so that when she returns she will be proud of you all."

Those who had rebelled against Arabella's supervision had the grace to look a little ashamed and there were murmurs of agreement. She felt no sense of triumph at their capitulation. She was just pleased that she would not have a battle of wills every time she asked someone to do something.

She left them to their duties and made her way to the room in one of the towers that had been set aside as a convalescent ward for those waiting for a ship home. It had been Miss Nightingale's decision to separate those on the road to recovery from those who were gravely ill. Arabella had to agree that they seemed to make more rapid progress in the more relaxed atmosphere away from the sick and dying.

Maisie had made it her responsibility to care for the convalescents. They did not need nursing as such but there were many ways in which she could make herself useful. As Arabella approached along the corridor she heard the sounds of argument above a wailing sound that was only just recognizable as music.

She threw open the door to find herself face to face with a burly Cameron highlander, his bagpipes tucked under his arm, his face red with the effort of playing as loudly as possible. Behind him, several soldiers from the regiment of engineers protested vigorously, while Maisie stood with her hand clapped to her mouth to stifle her laughter.

Suppressing the urge to laugh too, Arabella put on her sternest expression. "What on earth is going on here? You are disrupting the whole hospital."

"Tell him to stop, Miss," one of the soldiers begged. "It's giving me an 'eadache."

The Scotsman lowered his instrument and the sound died away with a final squeal of escaping air. "I was only practising, Miss," he said. "Sarge says I'm fit enough to go back to the regiment and I'll have to be able to play when the fighting starts again." He grinned. "The pipes puts the fear o' God into them Russkies, so it does."

"That's as may be," Arabella said. "But I can't have you upsetting the other patients."

He had the grace to look shamefaced. "I were only joshing, Miss. He said he couldnae abide the pipes — like a cat squealing, he said. So I had to show him, didn't I?"

"We'd rather listen to you singing, Miss," said one of the others.

134

"I haven't got time now. Maybe later," she promised. But she wished she'd never started it. She was busier than ever now and she was beginning to realize how Miss Nightingale would react when she heard what had been going on — as she surely must before long.

As spring gave way to summer the heat became almost unbearable. To add to the soldiers' discomfort, a plague of flies descended on the hospital. Arabella found that she had to be stricter than ever to keep up Miss Nightingale's standards. Scrupulous cleanliness was the only way to keep the insects and consequent risk of infection at bay.

The nurses, particularly the older and more experienced among them, although they had seemed to accept her at last, began to rebel, resenting what they saw as her interference.

"But what can I do?" she asked Maisie, almost in tears after yet another altercation. "Miss Nightingale put me in charge but they take no notice. Can't they see I am only passing on her instructions?" She sank down on the edge of her bed and covered her face with her hands. "Oh, I wish I had never come to this dreadful place."

Maisie patted her back awkwardly. "You don't really mean it, do you, Miss?"

Arabella gave a short laugh. "Not really. Imagine what my life would be if I had stayed at home."

Maisie was saved from answering when a knock came at the door to their tiny room and a nurse poked her head round it. "Can you come, Miss Raynsford? A

135

new contingent of men has arrived and there is nowhere to put them."

While she was busy sorting out accommodation for the new arrivals, another messenger arrived carrying a note from Lady Masterson. She thrust the paper into her pocket and carried on with her work. When everyone was settled and the evening meal was being distributed, Arabella at last had a few moments to herself. She sank into a chair in Miss Nightingale's office, smiling gratefully as Maisie appeared in the doorway with a cup of tea.

"What did her ladyship want?" Maisie asked.

Arabella had completely forgotten the note that had been delivered earlier. She felt in her pocket and drew out the crumpled envelope. As she read, the colour drained from her face and she gasped. "Oh, no."

"What is it?" Maisie put her hand to her lips. "Not Master Harry?"

Arabella hastened to reassure her. "It's not bad news, Maisie — at least not that sort of bad news. I'm sorry if I frightened you. It's Mr Delaney. He is here — in Turkey. The letter is an invitation from Lady Masterson to join them for supper this evening. Oh dear, how impolite she will think me — I didn't even send a reply saying I could not come."

"But surely her ladyship realizes your work here is more important than a supper engagement?" Maisie shifted her feet impatiently. "But what of Mr Delaney? Why is he here? And why didn't he tell you he was coming?"

"I don't know, Maisie." Arabella almost snapped at her friend. What *was* he doing here — and did it have anything to do with the strange man she had met in the souk? She only knew she didn't want to see him and she had the perfect excuse. Miss Nightingale had left her in charge and she had no time for social engagements. "I must write a note to her ladyship," she said.

She scribbled a note of apology saying she had not got the invitation in time as she had been busy with her duties. Hoping she would be forgiven the white lie, she also said that she regretted that her work at the hospital meant she would not be able to see Oswald during his stay in Constantinople.

"Aren't you going to write to Mr Delaney too?" Maisie asked when Arabella handed her the sealed note with instructions to make sure it went across on the next ferry boat.

"I have nothing to say to him. Besides, if he was so eager to see me, he should have let me know he was coming and given me time to make arrangements."

She was still angry with him for getting her involved in what she thought of as his nefarious dealings. She knew she should confront him about it but she was strangely reluctant to do so. She should have been pleased at having an excuse to refuse his marriage proposal but, until she was sure her father was not involved, she could say nothing. Then there was Nat. What part did he play in all this?

Maisie hurried off with the note, leaving Arabella feeling sick, her heart racing, as she tried to sort out her confused feelings. With a sigh she drained her cup and resolutely put those feelings aside. Her work here was far too important to her now and she must devote all her energies to it for the time being. When Miss Nightingale returned — if she recovered from her illness — that would be time enough for Arabella to start worrying about her own personal life.

She did her usual round of the wards and, when one of the soldiers begged her to sing, she could not refuse, although tonight her heart wasn't in it. He asked for "Home, Sweet Home" and she tried to persuade him that another song would be more suitable. She feared she would break down and cry if she sang it.

"What about 'Sweet Polly Oliver'," she asked.

There was chorus of approval and she smiled and launched into the ballad of the girl who dressed as a soldier to follow her love.

As she reached the last verse, there was a commotion at the other end of the ward. "Sir, you cannot go in there without permission," Maisie declared loudly.

Arabella stood up and peered through the dim lamplight, recoiling as she recognized the voice of Oswald Delaney. "Since when do I need permission to speak to my fiancée?"

He pushed Maisie aside and strode up the ward. "So there you are, Arabella. Why did you choose to ignore Lady Masterson's invitation?" he demanded.

Arabella took a deep breath. "Good evening, Mr Delaney. What a surprise. Would you care to come to my office where we can talk in private?" She bent to the

138

soldier whose covers she had been straightening. "There now, Private Evans. You must try to sleep now."

She swept out of the ward, leaving Oswald to follow. She entered the office and hurriedly put Miss Nightingale's desk between them, gesturing him to take the chair opposite.

"Now, Oswald," she said, smiling sweetly. "I know you must be eager to see me after so long apart but I hardly think it appropriate for you to come bursting in here and disturbing me at my work."

"Your work?" He gave a most ungentlemanly snort. "Singing to the common soldiery like a —"

She continued to smile, determined not to let him ruffle her temper. "I admit that is not part of my duties but it calms the men, helps them to settle down for the night."

"And that takes precedence over spending an evening with your fiancé and your hostess?"

"Lady Masterson appreciates that my work keeps me at the hospital these days so that I have no time for social engagements. If I had received her letter earlier I would have sent my apologies. However, I know she understands. As for you, Mr Delaney, we are not yet formally engaged so you have no right to make demands on me."

"You don't understand." He stood up and made to come round the desk towards her. "Arabella — I had to see you."

There was desperation in his voice and, if Arabella had believed his emotion was in any way connected with his feelings for her, she might have been moved.

139

But she recalled only too clearly his menacing tone when he had threatened her in the drawing room at Essex House.

Despite the uneven thumping of her heart, she spoke coolly. "Oh, and why is that, Mr Delaney?"

"You know why, Arabella. After all, haven't I asked for your hand in marriage? It has been several months —"

He hesitated and Arabella interrupted. "Could your eagerness to renew our acquaintance have anything to do with the delivery of a certain letter?" she asked.

The mask of pretence slipped, revealing Oswald's true nature. His eyes gleamed and he leaned over and grasped her wrist. "Why did you not deliver it? I know the man contacted you. But I have not received a reply."

Arabella snatched her hand away and rubbed her wrist. "I gave the letter to that man — as you instructed. He approached me again a few days later with his reply which was included in a letter I wrote to you immediately afterwards."

"I have received no letter from you."

"It must have gone astray. I assure you I did write —"

"Well, what did it say?"

"I can't remember exactly. So much has happened since then. I believe the man said that you had not supplied enough of the goods you had promised and he needed more before he would pay you. I assume it had something to do with supplies for the army." Arabella

140

had seen how fragile Oswald's temper was and now she was afraid to reveal her suspicions.

"Why would you assume that?" he asked, a glint in his eyes.

"You do business with my father and I know he supplies copperas for your gunpowder mills."

Oswald snorted again. "Your father's copperas beds are worked out. He has let me down badly."

"So if you no longer do business with him, why —?"

"He owes me money." Oswald dismissed her gasp of horror with a wave of his hand. "That doesn't matter. My business here is far more important. You must see this man again and give him a message from me."

"I cannot leave the hospital while Miss Nightingale is away. Why can't you deal with him yourself now you are here?"

"It would not be wise for me to be seen with him," Oswald murmured.

"So, I was right to think you were up to no good. What is it — are you a spy as I suspected back in England?"

Oswald laughed. "You are quite wrong, my dear." He reached out a hand as if to placate her. "I merely wish to avoid recriminations from those in society who see wrong in anyone profiting from the war — especially an Irishman."

Arabella wasn't sure she believed him but she smiled too. "If that is all it is, I cannot blame you. After all, my father's living comes from the same source." As she spoke she remembered Oswald's devastating statement about the copperas beds at Whitstable. But that wasn't the only source of the family's wealth. How could her father owe money to Oswald? She felt again the familiar impatience that convention kept her ignorant of matters to do with business. Women were not supposed to be worried by such things yet she was sure her brother Harry, although completely disinterested in the business, was fully informed of what was going on.

"So, will you meet my contact again and deliver another message?" Oswald asked interrupting her thoughts.

"I've already told you, I cannot leave the hospital."

"You must. It is of great importance — not just to me. If this deal is completed, I will be able to keep my promise to relieve your father of his debt."

"Why would you do that?"

Oswald smiled, his teeth gleaming in his dark face. "It is a condition of his giving consent to our marriage."

Arabella gasped. She could not believe her father would make such a bargain, however bad his financial problems were. "I don't believe you," she said.

"It's true enough, me darlin'."

"But why? I mean, why make a bargain that has no profit in it for you?"

"Ah well, I could be telling ye that I fell for your charms the moment I saw you — which would be true enough, I suppose. You're a fine looking girl and you have a bit of spirit, which I like in a woman." He grinned as Arabella began to blush. "However, I have bought a house in London and I wish to be accepted in polite society. For that I need a wife — from a good,

142

respectable family like the Raynsfords." He paused and again that mocking glint appeared in his eye. "Respectable," he repeated.

"Mr Delaney, I think you've said enough. I would like you to leave now," Arabella said, hoping her voice sounded firm and dignified. She came round the desk and edged past him, opening the door. To her relief there were people passing in the corridor. She hoped no one would realize how long she had been alone with Oswald.

"Ah, but I cannot leave until you have agreed to do that little errand for me," he said.

"And I have told you I cannot."

His affable manner changed. "You will do as I say, miss. How would your new friend Miss Nightingale take it if she were to learn that, far from being a respectable *lady*, you are nothing but a common music hall performer?"

So he did know. It wasn't just hints and suspicions now. But she mustn't let him see how his accusation had affected her. She drew herself up and looked him in the eye. "She would not believe you. Besides, Mr Delaney, you have no proof. And if you try to spread this story around, I will sue you for slander."

His response was a bellow of laughter. "We shall see, Miss," he said, striding off down the corridor.

Arabella was still shaking when Maisie came in with her supper.

"Lady Masterson sent some eggs," she said, setting down the tray.

"Why, Miss, you look quite pale. Are you sick?"

"No, I am quite all right."

"Sit down, let me pour you some tea." Maisie pushed Arabella gently into a chair, patting her shoulder. "Are you sure you're not sick?"

"Yes, I am — sick of that man thinking he has some hold over me and can force me to do his bidding." Her anger exploded and she continued to rail against Oswald Delaney while Maisie tried to calm her.

When she ran out of words, Maisie handed her a handkerchief, biting her lip before speaking. "Miss, when you say he tried to force you — did you mean —?"

"Oh, no, not that." Arabella hastened to reassure her friend. A gleam of humour appeared in her eye. "He wouldn't dare." She shook her head. "He wants me to carry another message for him — he wouldn't tell me what it's all about and I think that, far-fetched as it may seem, he really is a spy."

Maisie gasped. "You refused, of course. What did he say?"

"He threatened me. How dare he?"

"You must tell someone. If he is a spy, he should be stopped."

"Who can I confide in without implicating myself? The doctors and officials here resent my very presence since Miss Nightingale has given me so much responsibility. As for the Ambassador, he thinks me an empty-headed society girl. No one would believe me. And Mr Delaney can play the part of a gentleman very convincingly."

"Well, Miss, as you say, you cannot leave the hospital at present and he will hardly want to draw attention to himself if he is up to no good. So, stay here and get on with your work. Wait and see what happens," Maisie advised.

"I don't think I can do that, Maisie," Arabella said, shaking her head. "You see, he knows — about the Half Moon."

CHAPTER
TWELVE

The knowledge that Oswald knew about her double life did not dismay Arabella as much as she had once thought it would. The thought of having her secret exposed to London society had faded into insignificance compared with what she had witnessed over the past few months — the agony of torn limbs and shattered bodies, the sickening smells and muffled groans.

Since coming to the barrack hospital she had begun to realize how very trivial her concerns were. Besides, being top of the bill at the Half Moon Theatre now seemed like a half-remembered dream.

Once she had thought that maybe, when the war was over, she could go back to that life. She was stronger now and would be able to stand up to her parents, insist that her life was her own to do with as she chose. She would refuse to marry Oswald and make her own way as a singer — and if her family disowned her, so be it.

Now, as she did her late night round of the dimly lit wards, stooping to murmur a word of comfort here, straighten a blanket there, she realized that it had been only a foolish daydream.

Whatever her father had done, she loved him and would not see him ruined through any action of hers. She had no idea how the situation had come about — even if Henry was no longer able to make money from the copperas works, he had his fleet of colliers and a stake in the harbour at Whitstable as well as shares in the burgeoning railway industry.

"It can't be true," she muttered, giving one last glance at the sleeping men before leaving the ward. As she made her way down the dim corridor by the flickering light of her lamp, a horrifying thought popped into her head. Had her father been gambling? She could think of no other reason why he would owe money to someone like Oswald Delaney.

Back in her cubbyhole of a room, Maisie was already in bed and appeared to be asleep. But she had turned the bed down and placed a cup of hot milk ready for Arabella on the nightstand.

As she undressed, Arabella glanced fondly at her loyal friend, who, although she worked as hard as any of the nurses, always had time to care for her, just as though she were still her maid back in London.

"Thank you, Maisie," she whispered.

Maisie yawned and sat up. "I wasn't asleep, Miss. Is everything all right?"

"Not really. I keep thinking about Mr Delaney — what am I going to do?" She sank down on the hard bunk and put her head in her hands. "I keep going over it in my head and there's only one thing for it. I must do as he says."

"No, Miss. You mustn't. Suppose he is a spy — you know what they do to spies, don't you? And if you're caught they'll think you're one too."

"I don't see any way out of it. If I don't, he'll tell my parents about the Half Moon — and the scandal would kill my mother."

Maisie gave a half laugh. "He won't tell, Miss. Just think — he wants to marry you. Any scandal would reflect on him too. It's just a threat, don't you see?"

Arabella nodded thoughtfully. Maisie was right. Oswald had confessed that he wanted to marry well so that he would be accepted in polite society. He couldn't have it both ways. She sat up straight. "I'll call his bluff. He can do his own dirty work. But to keep him sweet I'll agree to marry him when I get back to England."

Maisie shuddered. "Will you really go through with it?"

"If I have to." Arabella said, getting into bed and turning out the lamp.

"But what about Mr Sloane?"

Arabella pulled the blanket over her ears and pretended she hadn't heard. She didn't want to think about Nat. But in the darkness the image of his dear, honest face would not go away and tears squeezed between her eyelids.

The next morning Arabella had intended to delegate her duties to one of the older nurses and take the ferry across to Constantinople. She would call on the Mastersons and hope that they could tell her where

Oswald was staying. The sooner she got this hateful errand over the better.

But before she had finished breakfast a nurse appeared, panting with the news that a ship had arrived in the night carrying soldiers wounded in an assault on the besieged fortress at Sebastopol.

"There's hundreds of them, Miss. The stretcher bearers are bringing them up to the hospital now," she said, her eyes wide. Despite her experiences over the past few months, the girl still hadn't got used to the devastating injuries which seemed worse with every new influx of patients.

Pushing her plate aside, Arabella leapt up and followed the girl down the corridor, steeling herself against new and unimaginable horrors. Directing the stretcher bearers to the few empty beds in the ward, she had no time to dwell on the sights and smells that assailed her. She gave orders that some of the men, although they were still far from well, should be moved to the convalescent ward to make way for the new casualties.

The more seriously wounded were lined up in the corridor outside the operating theatres awaiting their turn under the surgeon's knife. Despite their horrific injuries they were uncomplaining, muffling their groans and even in some cases managing a feeble joke. The nurses could only try to comfort them and calm them before their ordeal.

Arabella had gone to the kitchen to fetch another jug of water and on her return one of the nurses plucked at her sleeve. "Please, Miss Raynsford, one of the officers was asking for you."

"I haven't got time to stop. I'll speak to him later," she said, impatient at the interruption.

"You don't understand — it's one of the wounded officers. He's at the end of the corridor. He asked if you were here."

Arabella felt a churning in her stomach. She knew that her brother had recovered from his wounds and had returned to duty a few weeks ago. Surely poor Harry hadn't been wounded again.

She thrust the jug of water at the nurse and followed the pointing finger to where a Captain in the Royal Engineers lay on a stretcher. It wasn't until she bent down and wiped the blood from his face that she realized it was her brother's friend James Wilson.

He looked up at her through pain-shadowed eyes. "Is it really you, Arabella?" he croaked.

She knelt beside him and took his hand. "It's really me, James. Don't worry, you'll be all right now."

His grip was feeble but he managed to raise her hand to his lips and kiss it. "Tell Charlotte that Harry's all right, will you? He's the one that got me to the ship," he said. "Good old Harry, wouldn't have made it without him."

Arabella's eyes filled with tears. "Oh, James," she whispered. The orderlies appeared and picked up the stretcher. She gazed after him as he disappeared into the operating theatre, the tears flowing more freely now. She knew how many men failed to come out of there alive. She would have to write to Charlotte. But

150

how could she tell her friend how seriously her brother was wounded, not to mention that the man she loved was still in the thick of the battle?

She drew a deep breath and stood up. She couldn't sit here and cry over one man when so many were in need of her care. As she turned away, wiping her eyes on her apron, she bumped into someone. Murmuring an apology, she would have passed by but the man took her arm.

"Miss Raynsford — Arabella — are you all right?"

With a gasp she recognized Nat Sloane. "What are you doing here?" she asked.

"I got caught up in the bombardment."

"What happened? Are you hurt?"

"I'm all right. I came to help carry the stretchers." He hesitated. "I should get back — there is much to do."

"Is the siege over?"

"Not by a long way. It had been quiet for a while and the officers decided to make an assault. It was no use." Nat grimaced and wiped a hand across his forehead. "I think the Russians have had time to strengthen their defences — we should have been able to take both the Malakoff Tower and the Redan. But our men were beaten back." He sighed. "As you can see, there were heavy losses."

"But what were you doing there?" Despite her feelings for him, she felt all her old suspicions flooding back. Nat wasn't a soldier. Why was he anywhere near the battle area?

"Don't you remember? I came out to advise the army on building the road between Balaclava and Sebastopol."

Arabella still wasn't convinced. "My brother is a Royal Engineer — I am sure there are men in his regiment with the knowledge to build a road. Besides, I thought the road was finished months ago."

Nat winced at the sarcasm in her voice. "You're right, of course. But the winter rains washed much of it away. It needs strengthening. It was your brother who recommended me. I have been in this part of the world before and know the terrain well."

Arabella immediately felt ashamed of her doubts. Harry obviously trusted him and she knew her brother was a good judge of character. "I'm sorry." What more could she say?

She made to turn away but he put his hand on her arm. "You have no right to be suspicious of me. In fact, it should be the other way round. Didn't I see you speaking to a very undesirable character in the market place? And haven't you had dealings with Mr Delaney in recent weeks?"

"My relationship with Mr Delaney is none of your business," said Arabella, her face flushed with indignation.

"Oh, yes. You are to marry him, I hear." His voice was bitter.

"No, that's not true. I mean — we are not officially engaged." Arabella found herself stammering, remembering her conversation with Maisie. She had meant it at the time. She would marry Oswald if it would help her

152

family. But, face to face with Nat, and despite her reluctant suspicions, she could not deny what her heart had been telling her ever since she first met him — he was the man she loved. Surely it would be better to remain an old maid than to spend the rest of her life with the wrong man.

"The man himself seems pretty sure of it," Nat said, interrupting her thoughts.

"Well, *I'm* not sure. He is not the man I love," she said, colouring at the admission.

"Ah, I see." Nat's voice wavered and he pushed his matted hair off his forehead.

His hand came away bloody and Arabella gasped. "You are hurt. Sit down."

"It's nothing," Nat said faintly. But he allowed her to help him down on to the floor where he leaned his back against the wall of the corridor.

When Nat came to he found himself lying on a bunk in a small room that was little more than a cupboard. Another bunk occupied the opposite wall and between them was a nightstand with a carafe and water glass on it. There was no window but a lamp burned on a small table just inside the door.

As memory returned he groaned and raised his hand to his head, feeling the rough bandage which covered the wound. He had thought it merely a scratch and had managed to ignore the throbbing in his head during the voyage to the hospital. He must have been bleeding all that time until finally loss of blood had caused him to faint — right in front of Arabella.

He smiled at the memory. He was angry with her — both for her suspicions and for her involvement with the Irishman. But she had fought back, showing the spirit he so admired in her. His smile faded. He believed her when she said she had no intention of marrying Delaney. But she had hinted that she was in love in with someone else.

As he wondered who the lucky man could be, a mental picture came to him — Arabella bending over a wounded soldier, taking his hand, speaking tenderly — her brother's friend, Captain Wilson. He must be the one . . .

It made sense. They had known each other since childhood, their families were connected. But Nat knew Mrs Raynsford would never allow a match with an impoverished army captain. James stood as much chance of marriage with the beautiful Arabella as he did himself.

In spite of this, Nat felt a surge of jealousy and his head began to throb. He groaned again and tried to sit up. As he turned towards the door it opened and a young woman entered.

"How are you, Mr Sloane? Feeling better? Miss Arabella asked me to check on you. Do you need anything?"

Nat smiled as he recognized Arabella's maid. "I would like a drink please, Maisie. My throat is parched."

"You know me, sir?" Maisie poured water from the carafe at the bedside.

"Of course. We have met several times, both here and back in London," Nat said, struggling to sit up and take a sip from the glass. He put it back on the nightstand and swung his legs over the side of the bunk.

"Don't try to get up, sir. You lost a lot of blood. Miss Arabella insists you stay here until you are recovered."

"If it is that serious why am I not in the hospital?"

"It isn't serious. You will be well enough to leave after a rest. Besides, the hospital wards are full — we have no more beds."

Nat looked across at the empty bunk a question in his eyes.

"That is my bed, sir," Maisie said with a grin.

"And whose is this?" Comprehension dawned as Maisie continued to smile.

"Yes, sir. Miss Arabella gave you her own bed."

He could not stop the thought entering his head that this was the closest he was likely to come to sharing her bed. He gave a harsh laugh and tried to stand. He had to get out of here before he said something he regretted. But the room began to move as if he were still on board ship and he was forced to sit down again.

"I told you not to get up," Maisie said. She made him take another drink and pushed him gently back on the pillow, covering him with a blanket. "Rest is what you need. I'll get Miss Arabella to look in on you when she is less busy."

Nat felt too weak to protest. Still, he resolved to slip away from the hospital before he had to confront Arabella again. But weariness swept over him and he could not stop himself from dozing off. As his eyes closed he remembered he had not asked Maisie about Captain Wilson. Jealousy burned once more as he remembered the gentle look in Arabella's eyes when she had taken the young captain's hand, the tears as he was carried away to the operating theatre. Nevertheless, he hoped James would be all right. He could not bear to think of Arabella's grief if he were to die.

When he woke, the lamp had gone out and the room was lit only by a sliver of light from the partially opened door. The air was heavy in the windowless cubbyhole and Nat's body was drenched in sweat. He shifted restlessly as voices came to him from the corridor. "Go away, let me sleep," he muttered.

He turned over in the narrow bunk, stiffening as he recognized the voice beyond the doorway. There was no mistaking that Irish accent.

"Well, me darlin'. You've decided to do what I want, have you. Sensible girl. Your mama and papa will be pleased you've come to your senses at last. And if you behave, there'll be no need for them ever to find out about the other business." Oswald gave a low chuckle and Nat's hands curled into fists. He should go out there now, challenge the man, knock his grinning teeth down his throat.

But even as he pushed the covers back and struggled up from the bed, he knew it was useless. For one thing, he was too weak to fight, and for another he might make things worse for the girl he loved. For, although at first he'd been sure Delaney was referring to their engagement, Nat had heard the unmistakable threat behind the other man's words. He wasn't sure what the

156

"other business" was but it seemed that Arabella had got herself into deep water and punching Oswald Delaney on the nose wasn't the way to help her.

As the footsteps receded along the corridor, Nat lay back and closed his eyes. He heard the squeak of the door hinges and someone approached the bed. "How are you feeling now, Nat?" Arabella asked softly.

He kept his eyes closed, breathing deeply and evenly as though he were still sleeping. Her hand reached out and touched his cheek and he heard her sigh. "Thank god you didn't hear all that," she murmured.

He wanted to speak then. But something made him keep quiet.

She sighed again. "Oh, Nat, what am I going to do?" Her voice choked on a sob but before he could react, he heard the swish of her skirt, and the closing of the door.

CHAPTER
THIRTEEN

As she sat making out a list of requisitions to pass on to the Supply Officer, Arabella's concentration wavered. She could not stop her thoughts returning to Nat Sloane. When she had entered the room, determined to confide in him and ask his advice, he had been sleeping and she had been reluctant to disturb him. She had to admit now that her earlier suspicion of him was unfounded. She had merely been trying to find reasons why she should not admit to being in love with him.

But would he accept her apology? And, more importantly, would he believe that Oswald Delaney was the villain here? Whether he was a traitor or not, the Irishman was surely involved in something shady. He pretended to be in love with her, but only to further his own interests and to get her to do what he wanted. But how could she explain all this to Nat without revealing her own involvement? Reluctantly, she had decided to say nothing and had crept out of the room, leaving him to sleep.

She shook her head and screwed up the sheet of paper she had been working on. She couldn't concentrate on lists with so much else on her mind.

Dismissing her own concerns, her thoughts turned to James. She was sure the surgeons would have had to amputate his arm and she prayed he would survive — so many didn't.

Feeling guilty for worrying about her own problems when so many others were suffering, she pushed her papers aside and stood up. It was almost time for rounds anyway. She'd go and see James and then she would have to write to Charlotte. She couldn't let her friend wait until she received the official, impersonal, notification that her brother had been wounded.

James had been moved to the ward and even before she reached his bed Arabella could see the bandaged stump. Inured as she had become to such sights, she still blanched with horror at the thought of her old friend's suffering. Despite the heavy dose of laudanum, he moved restlessly, throwing off the blanket and muttering in his sleep. His face was sheened with sweat and Arabella wiped it away with her own handkerchief.

"You'll be all right, James," she murmured. "I'll take care of you."

From the doorway Nat watched as Arabella bathed the young captain's forehead, saw her eyes fill with tears. He had intended to speak to her before returning to Balaclava. But he couldn't bring himself to intrude on the tender scene. He stumbled away on unsteady legs, his heart heavy. He had no doubt of his ability to win her away from the obnoxious Oswald Delaney. But how could he compete with her feelings for her childhood sweetheart?

159

As he made his way down to the harbour he determined that, even if Arabella never returned his love, he would watch over her. He would make his own inquiries and once he had discovered what Delaney was up to he would have no hesitation in exposing him.

But he would only do so if he could be sure that Arabella was not implicated. The girl he had fallen in love with might be rebellious and high-spirited but he knew she would never knowingly do anything wrong.

He couldn't help smiling as he remembered the moment he had realized just how far her rebelliousness had taken her. He'd been a guest at Essex House and Arabella was seated at the piano in the drawing room. She played the first few bars of "On Wings of Song" and, as she began to sing, her clear voice soaring up to the high ceiling, she glanced at him. His stomach lurched and he had the feeling she was singing just for him. She wasn't, of course. But it was exactly the feeling the well-known singer, Bella Forde, engendered in the patrons of the Half Moon. And that voice — there was no mistaking it even as he realized that she was trying to modulate it, to hold something back. The similarity of the names was the final proof. How many others had guessed her secret? Several in the room were patrons of the Half Moon but Nat hoped none of them was astute enough to make the connection.

So far she seemed to have got away with it. Nat sighed. Whatever happened, he wouldn't be the one to betray her. He hadn't back then and he certainly wouldn't now.

When he reached the harbour he saw that the ship in which he had accompanied the wounded to Scutari had loaded up with supplies and was almost ready to leave. He looked about for a boat to take him out to her, anxious to get back to Balaclava as soon as possible. He couldn't stand by and watch Arabella give her heart to another man.

"Hey, boatman," he yelled as a small craft edged its way up to the harbour wall.

The man looked up and nodded. But as Nat was about to jump down, he spotted two men in deep conversation. One was the rough-looking man who had accosted Arabella in the souk, the other was Delaney.

He shook his head at the boatman. "Later," he said.

The man shrugged and pulled at his oars.

Nat pushed his way through the crowds thronging the harbour and stepped behind a pile of bales, hoping he hadn't been spotted. Peering out cautiously he strained to hear what was being said.

The men weren't speaking English and he bit his knuckle in frustration, wishing he had taken the trouble to learn at least a few words of Turkish. He began to edge closer but had to dodge back when Delaney glanced round.

The Irishman was clearly nervous, pulling at the other man's sleeve and drawing him into the shadow of a nearby warehouse. It gave Nat the opportunity to draw nearer.

The man was gabbling something which he could not understand until one word came clearly — "*Nyet*".

Nat gasped. It was one of the few Russian words he knew. Was Delaney really doing business with the enemy? Nat didn't want to believe it. He had long suspected the Irishman of shady dealings but he had thought that the man was only profiteering from the war — not a crime in itself even if morally wrong. But this was treason.

Nat's outrage was tinged with relief. Arabella couldn't possibly be involved in this — at least not knowingly. She would never conspire with those against whom her brother and sweetheart were fighting.

He thought back to that day months ago when he had come upon the man harassing Arabella and her maid in the souk. His suspicions had been aroused when he had seen her slip something to him. He had tried to dismiss it from his mind, telling himself the man must be a beggar and that she had been giving him money.

Now he wondered if Delaney had prevailed on her to pass a message and, if so, how he had managed to persuade her. Knowing Arabella, she had probably agreed merely for the sense of adventure. But even if she'd refused, Nat wouldn't put it past Delaney to exert pressure on her.

The two men were still arguing and Nat heard the Irishman say, "Speak English, dammit."

"You understand me well enough, Mr Delaney. Rest assured, I will have the goods I was promised or I will make trouble for you."

Nat tensed as Delaney laughed. "Trouble? I think not, my friend. You are the one on enemy territory. I could have you arrested and shot as a spy."

"You forget. I have a — how do you say — a trump card. I am sure you would not wish any harm to come to the beautiful young lady I met in the market place last winter."

"She has nothing to do with this — she was merely a messenger."

A gabble of Russian followed and Nat moved away. The temptation to confront the pair had been almost overwhelming but he had quickly realized that it would do no good to show his hand. Delaney was a friend of the Mastersons and a welcome guest at the Embassy here. They would believe his word over that of a humble engineer. He had to wait until he had proof.

The ship he had hoped to board had departed and Nat decided to cross over to Constantinople and seek a bed for the night. Despite his impatience to return to his work at Balaclava, he felt he'd be better employed keeping an eye on Delaney. As he waited for the ferry, he wondered if he ought to return to the hospital and warn Arabella of what he had discovered. But he wasn't sure if she'd believe him. After all, she'd been suspicious of him until recently. And, despite her recent protests, the last time he'd spoken to Harry, he had seemed certain that his sister and Delaney would be married on her return from the Crimea. Her family were all in favour of the match.

Crossing the choppy waters of the Bosporus, Nat felt a wave of despair. His head ached from his tortured thoughts as much as from the bandaged wound. Whichever way his thoughts turned, he could not see a happy ending for himself. He might be able to stop Arabella from marrying Delaney by exposing him as a traitor — but there was still Captain Wilson, young, good-looking and a friend of the family.

Arabella was finding it hard to write to Charlotte. By the time her letter arrived James's family would probably have been informed that he'd been wounded. But they would not be given any details. Should she mention his arm? She sighed and crumpled the paper, reaching for a fresh sheet. Was it kinder to say nothing or would the shock be even greater when he arrived home with an empty sleeve? If he arrived home at all.

She looked up at Maisie who was sitting on her bunk mending a stocking by the inadequate light of the one lamp. "How was James?" she asked.

Maisie had helped to dish out the suppers that evening. She shook her head. "The lad is very poorly. One of the nurses gave him a drink but he didn't swallow much."

"I'm writing to his sister." Arabella put her head in her hands. "Oh, Maisie, I don't know what to say to her." Her voice choked on a sob.

"Just say what you usually do when you write to the men's relatives — that he's being looked after and that he sends his love. No need to go into details. After all, we don't know yet —" Maisie's voice trailed away.

Arabella nodded. She knew what Maisie had been trying to say. James might die in spite of their efforts.

So few of the wounded recovered from surgery, especially after the amputation of a limb. Why distress her friend unnecessarily?

"It seems wrong to give her false hope," she said.

"There's always hope," Maisie said.

Arabella nodded and dipped her pen in the inkwell. Her letter was as cheerful as she could make it in the circumstances. She spoke of the improvements that had been made to the hospital since she'd arrived, not forgetting to mention Harry's bravery in getting James to the ship. "*And, of course, he has the devoted care of myself and Maisie to help him on the road to recovery*," she ended.

She blotted and sealed the letter with a fervent prayer that her optimism was well founded. It was time for her rounds. James wasn't the only one in need of her care.

While she had been writing, she had not once thought of Nat Sloane. When she had returned from her earlier rounds, Maisie had told her he had left the hospital and returned to Balaclava. His wound wasn't serious and there was no reason to detain him.

Arabella was disappointed that he hadn't bothered to say goodbye. But she had been busy and no doubt he was anxious to return to his work too.

Now, as she quietly made her rounds of the wards, she blushed at the thought of their encounter in the corridor, how she had almost blurted out her feelings for him. Thank goodness she had been distracted by his wound and thank God it had turned out to be only a superficial cut, despite the huge loss of blood.

She smiled at the memory of him asleep on her bunk. He'd looked so tired and vulnerable. How she had longed to confide in him, to tell him of the threats Oswald had made and how she was tempted to give in to him. If she thought Nat returned her feelings and would not be shocked by the revelation of her double life back in London, she would have called Delaney's bluff. Would he understand?

Deep in thought, she scarcely noticed as a hand clutched at her skirt.

"Miss, aren't you going to sing to us tonight?" the man asked.

Singing was the last thing on her mind. If she tried she felt she would choke. She was feeling far too emotional at the moment. What would the men think if she broke down in tears? She quickly thought of an excuse. "I'm afraid I have a sore throat, Corporal. Maybe tomorrow?" She patted his arm and moved on.

When she reached the ward where James was she went quickly to his bedside. He seemed to be sleeping peacefully but his face was flushed, his forehead damp. As before, she bathed his face, tucked the blanket around him and moved to the next bed. She could not spend too much time with him at the expense of the other patients.

Back in her office there were more letters to write as well as her daily report for Miss Nightingale, who, although on the road to recovery, was still not fit enough to travel. Arabella had received a note from her saying that she was anxious to return to Scutari as soon as possible.

166

"I'm pleased she's better. I had begun to think she wouldn't recover," she told Maisie. "But what will I do when she returns?"

"What do you mean?" Maisie asked.

"I'll have to give up all this." Arabella waved a hand round the cluttered little room. "Miss Nightingale will want her office back. And she won't need me any more."

"Will you really mind, Miss? After all, it's a big responsibility. And you're always tired. You could go back to Lady Masterson's, have a bit of a rest."

"I don't need a rest," Arabella snapped. In truth, she was tired and often frustrated with the demands of the job, but she had begun to enjoy it. There was a sense of satisfaction in seeing how the improvements Miss Nightingale had instigated were beginning to bear fruit.

"Well, I'm sure Miss Nightingale will find something for you to do. After all, she's been ill and may not be well enough to work as hard as she did before." Maisie gave a short laugh. "Mind, I wouldn't be too sure about that — you're a pair, you are. Neither of you knows when to slow down."

Arabella smiled. "You're right, of course. But it's not just that. I'm afraid she'll be angry with me."

"Angry? She should be pleased. Everyone knows what a good job you've done." Maisie was indignant.

"But someone will tell her about the singing — and I know she won't approve."

"Why ever not? As far as I can tell, it does no harm — might even do some good. Besides, even those

167

nurses who tried to make trouble at first have come round to you, Miss. They won't say anything, I'm sure."

Arabella sighed. "Let's hope none of the men lets it slip." She could never understand why it was acceptable for a young society lady to sing to friends in the privacy of her own home, but not in public. What was so shameful about bringing pleasure to so many?

But now she wished she hadn't given in to that first impulse a few weeks ago. Since then, it had become a regular thing after the lamps were turned low and the men were settled for the night. She only chose soothing, gentle songs — it was almost like singing lullabies for a fractious child.

Well, it would have to stop, Arabella decided, as she finished writing her report and told Maisie it was time to get ready for bed.

A few days later another boatload of wounded arrived and Arabella had no time for singing or anything else beyond organizing beds and fresh linen. The corridors were once more lined with broken, bleeding bodies awaiting their turn under the surgeon's knife.

Each night she fell exhausted into her bed. By now, she was so accustomed to the hard bunk that she scarcely noticed the discomfort and, on the rare occasions she thought back to her former life, it was as if her bright clean room in Essex House was part of an almost forgotten dream.

Neither Oswald nor Nat Sloane returned to the hospital during those hectic days and, even if they had,

Arabella would probably not have noticed. Her personal life was non-existent.

One morning she woke from a vivid dream. She and Harry were children once more. They had been playing in the garden at Mill House with Charlotte and James. As she sat up, their shouts of glee still ringing in her ears, her heart began to thump. Had something happened to Harry?

When Maisie brought her morning tea, she thrust the mug aside and dressed hurriedly. "Have any new wounded been brought in during the night?" she asked.

Maisie shook her head.

James — it must be James, she thought. "Have you seen Captain Wilson lately? How is he?"

"Still poorly, Miss — but making progress I think."

There was a knock on the door and a nurse asked if Arabella could come to look at a patient. There was no time to go and see James. Besides, she told herself, it was only a dream.

The rest of the day passed in a blur of exhaustion and it was evening before Arabella could give a thought to her friend. Poor James, he would think she didn't care. And she did — even if not quite in the way he hoped.

Ignoring Maisie's pleas that she should eat something and take a short rest, she hurried towards the ward where she had last seen James only to find that his bed was occupied by another man, a lieutenant.

She felt herself begin to sway. No. He couldn't have died without her knowing. A nurse came and took her arm. "Were you looking for Captain Wilson, Miss?"

Arabella nodded.

"The stump has become infected. The doctor said the rest of the arm must come off if we are to save him. The orderlies took him away to await surgery."

"When?"

"A few moments ago."

Without waiting to hear more, Arabella rushed out of the ward. The surgeons performed their operations in the far block of the hospital and patients waited their turn in the corridor. Never before had the passages seemed so endless to Arabella as she stumbled between the makeshift beds, searching each face for that of her childhood friend. If only she had gone to him this morning, she thought. Maybe she'd have seen the signs in time to do something about it. No one survived a second amputation — usually the infection had progressed beyond the point where it would do any good or the patient was already so weak that the shock killed him.

In the dimly lit corridor she almost passed by him. He was almost unrecognizable, his normally ruddy face now tinged a greenish grey, his eyes sunken. The bandage covering the stump at his elbow gave off a sickly smell, blood and pus seeping through it.

Arabella knelt beside him and gently wiped his face with the corner of her apron. "James, it's me — Arabella. Let's see if we can make you more comfortable."

His eyes opened but he did not seem to recognize her.

She began to unravel the bandage, clamping her mouth shut and breathing shallowly against the smell — a smell she had never become accustomed to in all her months at the hospital. Angry blackish-red streaks marched up the remaining stump of arm reaching beyond the shoulder.

Arabella's breath hissed through her teeth. When blood poisoning had reached this stage it was too late for surgery. Why hadn't someone noticed? Why hadn't *she* noticed? She was consumed with guilt, even as the logical part of her brain insisted that it was impossible to save everyone. There were just too many patients and too few resources.

Forgetting all the rules about not becoming personally involved, Arabella gathered James in her arms, rocking him gently and murmuring words of comfort. She wasn't sure if he could hear her but she told him about her dream of the children they had once been. As she recalled those happy times, tears rolled down her cheeks.

Gradually she became aware of a feeble hand touching hers, a whisper, the merest breath. "Sing for me, Arabella."

At first she couldn't think of a song. Then she remembered Brahms's cradle song and she hummed the first few bars. The words came back to her and, as she began to sing *"Lullaby and good night —"*, she brushed the hair away from James's face.

He smiled and his eyes closed.

As she reached the last line — *"angels guard thee from harm, thou art safe in my arms"* — she looked

171

down and realized that he was no longer breathing. She began to sob, rocking him in her arms. She was scarcely aware of the hand that fell on her shoulder, the angry voice.

"What is this meaning of this unseemly display? Get up at once."

Arabella's hold on James's lifeless body tightened, her tears falling faster.

"Miss Raynsford, I command you to go to my office — now."

Arabella looked up and her blurred vision took in the stern face of Florence Nightingale. Pulling herself together, she gently laid James's head back on the pillow and stood up slowly, smoothing her crumpled apron.

Ignoring her mentor's wrathful glare, she said in an amazingly steady voice, "Welcome back, Miss Nightingale. I hope you are fully recovered."

"It seems I have returned not a moment too soon. Go to my office, Miss."

The doctors and nurses had paused in their work and they stared openly as Arabella fumbled her way along the narrow passage between the beds until she reached Miss Nightingale's office.

She ignored them, closing the door behind her and sinking into a chair, only to stand again as Miss Nightingale entered. She stood with her hands clasped in front of her, head bowed as the older woman paced the small room.

Finally she stopped and faced Arabella. The anger had gone, replaced by a look almost of perplexity.

"How could I have been so mistaken?" she said. "I thought I could trust you. I gave you a position of great responsibility, relied on you to maintain the standards I set and you —"

She paused and Arabella looked up, tried to speak. But Miss Nightingale cut her off with a wave of her hand. "I do not want to hear excuses. Your behaviour speaks for itself. I had heard rumours of your association with the men, but I refused to believe it. I put it down to jealousy of the favour I have shown you. But I cannot deny the evidence of my own eyes. Embracing the patients is *not* part of your duties —"

"But Miss Nightingale, he was —"

"He was dying and you were offering some sort of comfort, no doubt. But that is no excuse." She sighed and went to sit behind her desk. "Miss Raynsford, if you knew how I had struggled — to get the people back home to accept that nursing is a respectable career, to get the doctors to let us do our job, to —" She ran out of words and shrugged helplessly.

"I'm sorry, Miss Nightingale. If you would just let me —" Arabella was sure she would be forgiven her lapse in judgement once she explained about her relationship with James, her childhood friend.

But she was not allowed to speak. "I could overlook one incident. However, there is the matter of entertaining the men — singing, and encouraging them to sing too."

So she had heard then, thought Arabella. One of the doctors had probably informed her. She almost smiled at Miss Nightingale's next words. "I will not have my hospital turned into a common music hall."

But she quickly sobered when the other woman continued. "I have no recourse but to send you home." Her voice softened. "You must see that I cannot allow you to stay. But rest assured, your family will not get to hear of this — not through me, at any rate. I will spare them your shame. We will say you have been ill." She waved a hand. "You are dismissed, Miss Raynsford. You may as well go to your room and start packing now. You can take the early morning ferry to Constantinople. I will send a message to Lady Masterson to expect you. She will arrange your passage home."

Tears welled up in Arabella's eyes and her throat closed. Even if Miss Nightingale had allowed her to speak she would not have been able to. She turned away, groping for the door handle.

CHAPTER
FOURTEEN

When she reached her room she tore off the sash with its embroidered "Scutari Hospital" — the sash she had worn with such pride — and threw it across the room. Her starched white cap followed it. Anger at the injustice of Florence Nightingale's rebuke was followed by grief as the reality of James's death hit her. A sudden picture of his pain-ravaged face rose in her mind and she lay down on her bed and gave way to hysterical sobs.

She didn't hear Maisie come in and she flinched as a hand touched her shoulder.

"Are you all right, Miss? What's happened?" asked the maid.

"James is dead," sobbed Arabella.

"Oh, Miss, I'm so sorry. Such a nice lad, always so considerate. But we knew it was touch and go, didn't we?" She stroked Arabella's hair. "Come on now. It's not like you to give way. Sit up and bathe your face and I'll fetch you some tea."

"I don't want any."

"Well, you can't lie there feeling sorry for yourself. Besides, you'll have to write to Miss Charlotte again, won't you?"

"I'll be able to tell her myself," Arabella said, sitting up and dashing a hand across her eyes.

"What do you mean?"

"I'm being sent home." Arabella burst into tears again. She hardly noticed as Maisie picked up the scattered clothing and began to tidy the room. But when the other girl touched her shoulder, offering the steaming cup, she sat up and dried her eyes. Between hiccoughs and shuddering sighs she told Maisie what had happened.

"But I didn't do anything wrong," she wailed as she finished the story. "How could she imply that I had done something shameful? And now she's sending me home in disgrace."

"Maybe it's time you went anyway, Miss," Maisie said. "You're exhausted and you won't rest. It's only a matter of time before you really fall ill. And now Miss Nightingale's back —"

"She won't need me, you mean." Arabella sighed. "I can't go home, Maisie, I just can't."

"I understand. But surely Miss Nightingale will want to keep it quiet — the reason, I mean. She won't want a scandal to ruin the work she's done here."

Arabella nodded. "She did say she would tell everyone I was ill, a believable excuse for my return — but only to spare my parents."

"Well then." Maisie folded her arms over her bosom. "You'd best get some sleep if you're to get the early morning ferry. I'll finish your packing." She held up the embroidered sash. "Do you want to keep this?"

176

"I don't really care." Arabella turned away as Maisie carefully folded the sash and placed it in the trunk.

When Maisie shook Arabella awake the next morning it took a few moments before she remembered the events of the previous evening. And, as she did so, another thought struck her.

"I can't go home, Maisie, I just can't," she repeated.

"Where else would you go? Besides, the arrangements are made. An orderly brought a message from Miss Nightingale. You are to stay at Lady Masterson's until a passage is available to Marseilles."

"But you don't understand." Arabella grasped the maid's arm. "I promised Mr Delaney that I'd marry him when I get home. And I must keep my word or he will make my family suffer."

"Well, you certainly can't marry him — not after what you told me. Why don't you tell your father what he's really like?" Maisie asked, laying the last of Arabella's things in the trunk and closing the lid.

"I don't know if he'd believe me, Maisie. Anyway, suppose he's involved in whatever Oswald's up to as well?" Her eyes filled with tears. "What am I to do?"

"I don't believe Mr Raynsford would do such a thing," Maisie said. She pulled an old carpet bag from under her bunk and began to stuff things in it.

"What are you doing?" Arabella asked.

"Packing, of course."

"But you haven't been dismissed. I don't expect you to leave because of me."

"I can't let you travel alone, Miss." Maisie said.

"But you love your work here. I'm sure Miss Nightingale would want you to stay."

"I go where you go. No argument." The maid's voice held a note of finality and Arabella smiled.

"I must admit I'd miss you. Are you sure?" She touched the other girl's arm. "There is one more thing you can do for me."

"Anything, Miss."

Arabella laughed. "That's it — you must stop calling me 'Miss'. I know we've had this conversation before but I must insist. From now on I am 'Bella' — after all you have proved yourself a good friend and friends call each other by their Christian names."

"Very well, M — Bella." Maisie grinned and fastened the buckles on the bag. She went to the door and peered out into the corridor, grabbed the arm of a passing orderly. "Can you take Miss Raynsford's luggage down to the ferry, or if you haven't time, find someone to do it?"

She turned back into the room, laughing. "Come along then, *Bella*, if you want to get the early boat. Have you thought what you're going to say to Her Ladyship and Miss Lavinia?"

When Lady Masterson greeted them, she was still holding Miss Nightingale's note. "I'm sorry to hear you have been ill, Miss Raynsford," she said. "But then, much as I admire my friend's work, I never really felt that the barrack hospital was a suitable place for a lady. I am not surprised you succumbed to a fever."

178

So Miss Nightingale had kept her word. She had not revealed the true reason for dismissing her. Arabella felt only mild relief. She didn't really care about anything at the moment.

Lady Masterson took her arm and led her into the drawing room, dismissing Maisie with a wave of her hand. "You know where Miss Arabella's room is, don't you? Get her things unpacked and then go down to the kitchen."

When Arabella was seated she glanced around the room, with its cream-coloured drapes and a pale patterned carpet, as if she had never seen it before. It was so light and airy. After so many months incarcerated in the gloom of the barrack hospital, which despite their efforts never seemed really clean, Arabella had forgotten how pleasant such surroundings could be. Even so, she wished things could have turned out differently, that she was still on the other side of the Bosporus, doing the work that had come to mean so much to her.

Lady Masterson's concerned voice interrupted her thoughts. "Would you like some refreshment? You do look a little pale, my dear. Still, a few days' rest will do wonders. You must stay here until you are strong enough to travel."

Arabella felt a twinge of guilt at the other woman's concern. She couldn't keep up this pretence for long. She put a hand to her forehead and said in a faint voice, "I'd like to go to my room, if you don't mind, Your Ladyship."

"Of course. Maybe you'll feel well enough to come down for dinner."

To her surprise, Arabella managed to sleep for several hours. She must have been more exhausted than she'd realized. When she woke feeling refreshed, she stretched and sat up, suddenly realizing where she was. The memory of Florence Nightingale's stern face, her angry words, made her flinch. Had her behaviour really been that reprehensible? She didn't think so. But others didn't agree. She had known in her heart that once the news of her singing reached Miss Nightingale, it would be the end of her work at the hospital. The older woman's strict moral code would not allow her to be lenient with Arabella when she was so rigorous with the others in her charge.

Understanding did not make her feel any better though. But it was no use looking back. She had to accept that that part of her life was over and she must decide what to do next. Going home to return to resume the narrow life of a society lady or, worse still becoming the wife of a man she despised, was out of the question.

When Maisie came into the room carrying a can of hot water, a towel over her arm, she smiled and said, "Well, what shall we do for our next adventure?"

"I should think you've had enough of adventures. Besides, your family will be pleased to have you home. And Miss Charlotte will be delighted to see you again."

Poor Charlotte, Arabella thought. Thank goodness she would never know the reality of how her brother had died. But surely it would be a comfort to know her friend had been with him at the end and that he had died in her arms.

As Arabella washed and dressed, revelling in the luxury of plenty of hot water and soft towels, she said, "I must write to Charlotte. I don't think I could speak about James without breaking down and that would upset her too. A letter will be easier for both of us."

"You'll have to face her some time," Maisie said.

"Yes, but not too soon. Besides, I've decided — I'm not going home just yet."

"You don't mean to stay here, surely?"

"Oh no. I'll leave as soon as a ship is available. But I don't want to go back to England." She smoothed her gown and smiled. "I might stay in France."

Maisie didn't reply and Arabella left the room. As she descended the wide staircase and approached the dining room she heard voices, the rumble of male laughter. She hadn't realized Lady Masterson had guests. She couldn't face anyone at the moment and she was about to turn away and return to her room when the door opened.

Seeing her, the footman held it wider and motioned her into the room, announcing her name to those already seated at table.

It was too late to flee and Arabella summoned a smile as Lady Masterson said, "I'm so pleased you feel well enough to join us, my dear."

As the footman pulled out a chair for her, Arabella realized who the guests were.

"A nice surprise for you, Arabella," said Her Ladyship. "I quite forgot to mention earlier that your fiancé was dining with us tonight. And, of course, you know Mr Sloane?"

"Yes. How is your head, Mr Sloane?"

He smiled and touched the bandage. "It is much better, thanks to your ministrations," he said.

"It was nothing." Arabella sat down next to Oswald, her heart thumping. How would she get through the next few hours? She looked across the table at Nat, who was now speaking to Lavinia Masterson. She was smiling adoringly at him and he seemed to be enjoying the conversation. Not for the first time, she wondered if she had been mistaken in hoping that Nat might feel the same way about her as, she now acknowledged, she felt about him.

If only there was some way she could let him know that, in spite of everyone's assumption that Oswald and she were betrothed, she had no intention of marrying him. Her earlier decision to do so in order to spare her family from shame and scandal had quickly been reversed at the sight of him.

How could these people be taken in by him, she wondered, as Oswald took her hand and said, with his usual sardonic smile, "I am so sorry to hear you have been ill, my dear. Perhaps now you will take my advice and return home. I am sure your parents will be glad to welcome you."

"I am quite well, Mr Delaney. I had a touch of the fever and just need a few days' rest, that's all."

Nat leaned towards her. "Does that mean you will be returning to Scutari?"

"No, Mr Sloane. I have decided to return to England. But first, I will stay for a few days in France. I have friends in Paris. I do not feel up to making such a long journey, so a short break will do me good."

"What are your plans when you return to England?" Nat asked. "Will you continue nursing?"

Before she could reply, Oswald broke in. "Certainly not. We will be getting married as soon as my business here is finished." He still had hold of Arabella's hand and he squeezed her fingers on the word "business".

She forced a smile and pulled her hand away as the footman placed a dish in front of her. The smell of the rich food made her feel dizzy. She had been used to plainer fare at the hospital, when she remembered to eat at all. She managed a few mouthfuls and put her knife and fork down.

"Are you still unwell, Miss Raynsford?" Nat asked.

"Just tired," she answered.

"It must be hard for you watching so many young men die — especially hard when it is someone you have known for so long. I was so sorry to hear about Captain Wilson. If only we could have got him to the hospital sooner."

"You did your best. We all did."

Lavinia pouted and interrupted. "I wish we could talk about something else. This is hardly a fitting subject for the dinner table."

Arabella swallowed her tears and her anger. "I'm sure you are right," she said. She turned to Nat. "I'm surprised you're still here. I thought you had returned to Balaclava. You seemed in such a hurry to leave."

"I missed the boat," he said.

"And we persuaded him to stay," Lavinia said, touching his arm and smiling.

"But not for long. I must get back to my work," Nat said. "I shall probably not see you again until I am back in England."

"You must come to our wedding," Oswald said, wiping his mouth with his napkin, and turning to Arabella. "You must make sure Mr Sloane's name is on the guest list, my dear."

"Of course." She picked up her fork again in order to avoid looking at him. Surely he must notice how her hand was shaking though? She put it down again. "I'm sorry, I feel a little faint." She stood up and turned to Lady Masterson. "If you will forgive me, Your Ladyship."

She scarcely noticed as the men stood up and she stumbled from the room. At the foot of the stairs, she grasped the newel post, willing her legs to stop shaking. Maisie appeared as if she had been waiting for her and helped her up the stairs.

In her room she gave way to tears. "I can't do it, Maisie. I can't keep up this pretence. They all think I'm going to marry Mr Delaney. There's no way out of it."

"You can't, Miss. He's a devil, that one. You must tell someone what you suspect. And if he carries out his threats, well at least you'll know you've done the right thing."

"I'm not concerned about myself, you know," Arabella said, sitting at her dressing table and wiping

184

her eyes. "You know what my mother's like — any scandal would kill her. And if my father is involved with this gunrunning or whatever it is, he would be ruined. Finding out that I've been singing in a music hall would be the least of their worries then."

Maisie took the pins out of Arabella's hair and began to brush it with long soothing strokes. "You need to confide in someone. Why don't you tell Mr Sloane? He doesn't seem the sort of man who'd be shocked by your singing and he's in the right place to find out just what Mr Delaney is up to."

"But he knows about the man we met in the market. And he thinks I was a willing messenger for Oswald. Will he believe I was under pressure?"

"I'm sure he will. Why don't you write him a note?"

Arabella brightened immediately. "Why didn't I think of that?" She jumped up and went to the little desk under the window.

It took a long time to write it all down, with much crossing out and sighing and screwing up of sheets of writing paper. But at last it was done. As she blotted the letter and sealed it, a thought struck her. "Maisie, I don't know where he's staying. And he might be gone by the time we find out."

Maisie reassured her. "I'll go down to the harbour first thing in the morning. Someone will know if a boat has left and, if he was on it, I'll get someone to take it to him by the next one."

Arabella had to be content with that. At least she had done something. Now, all she had to do was get away from here, before Oswald tried to involve her further in his so-called business. Already, a plan was forming in her mind but she wasn't ready to confide in Maisie just yet.

The next few days passed slowly for Arabella. Now that she had decided what to do, she couldn't wait to get away from Constantinople. At least the delay meant that there was more chance of hearing from Nat before she left.

But no word came and she wondered if he had even received her letter. When Maisie had gone down to the harbour she had learned that he'd already left. She had spoken to a sergeant from James's regiment who was returning to duty on the next ship. He knew Nat and promised faithfully that he would deliver the letter as soon as he landed at Balaclava.

"Did you have to pay him?" Arabella asked.

"I did — with a kiss." Maisie had smiled mischievously.

Arabella had laughed properly for the first time in weeks.

"You're looking better, my dear," Lady Masterson said when she came down for luncheon.

And she had to agree she was feeling more herself. The grief for James and the other young men under her care had not lessened but she was now more able to accept that she had done everything she could for them.

She had begun to realize too that, although her illness had been manufactured as an excuse for her leaving Scutari, she really had been exhausted by the work of the past few months. And as her health improved she found it hard to play the convalescent.

As she gazed out of the window at the harbour with the towers of the barrack hospital looming in the distance, she felt the old boredom returning. If only she had something to do.

Lavinia, busy at her embroidery, glanced at her. "Wishing you were back there?" she asked.

"Not really," Arabella replied, realizing that she spoke the truth. At first she had missed the routine of the hospital as well as the feeling that she was doing something worthwhile. But that part of her life was over. Besides, Miss Nightingale would never allow her to return.

Lavinia looked at her closely. "You don't look ill. Maybe you just needed a short rest. Why don't you ask to go back? I know you don't really want to marry Mr Delaney and it would at least give you an excuse to delay the wedding."

"How did you know I didn't want to get married?"

"I'm not sure. It's just the way you look at him. It's not the look of a woman in love," Lavinia said.

"Marriage isn't always about love," Arabella said. "It is a good match and my parents approve."

Lavinia returned her attention to her embroidery and said no more until they were interrupted by a maid bringing tea. Arabella wished she could confide in the other girl. But she had never really taken to her, and knowing that Lavinia seemed to be falling in love with Nat made it impossible to reveal her own feelings.

As the days passed it became harder for Arabella to contain her restlessness and, as it became obvious that Nat had either not received her letter or wasn't going to reply, she longed to be gone. At last word came that a ship had arrived in the harbour and would be leaving for Marseilles early the next day.

It was with relief that she said her final goodbyes to the Mastersons and she and Maisie boarded the ship. They stood at the rail watching the final loading of convalescent soldiers who had been discharged from the hospital and Arabella swallowed a lump in her throat.

When she had seen the stretchers being brought aboard she had stepped forward to offer assistance. The nursing sister in charge had laid a hand on her arm. "Miss Nightingale has told me that you are not to be allowed any contact with the patients," she said gently. "I'm sorry."

Now, she could only watch.

There was a rattle of anchor chains and the ship began to move away from the harbour wall. The early morning mist had dispersed and Arabella turned for a last look at the sun-gilded towers of the hospital. Despite the traumas of her months in Turkey it had been an experience she would not have missed for anything.

Her only regret was that she had ever allowed herself to become embroiled in Oswald's activities. Was it too late to put things right? And, if Nat had received her letter, would he help her?

CHAPTER
FIFTEEN

Dawn was breaking as the stage coach entered Paris and Arabella lifted her head from Maisie's shoulder and sat up. The other occupants were waking too, anxious to reach the coaching inn and stretch their legs after the long and arduous journey along muddy, potholed roads.

As the coach crossed one of the many old bridges spanning the River Seine, Arabella caught a glimpse of the spire of Notre Dame Cathedral towering over the other buildings. She leaned forward, eager to take in the sights of this vibrant city. On the journey out to Turkey, she had hardly noticed a thing in her impatience to reach their destination. Now, the familiar excitement which new places and new experiences always produced in her rose up and she couldn't wait for the coach to stop.

As the wheels ceased turning, she jumped down, hardly waiting for the coachman to lower the steps for her. Maisie followed more slowly, looking around and wincing at the babble of foreign words, the noise of wheels rumbling over the cobbled streets.

When their luggage was unloaded and piled on the ground at their feet, she asked anxiously, "Where are we going to stay, Bella? Do you know how to find these friends you told Her Ladyship about? Do they know we are coming?"

Arabella laughed. "I do have friends — but not in Paris. We are going on to London in the morning." Ignoring Maisie's shocked expression, she took her arm and followed the porter, who was carrying their bags into the inn.

The maid looked confused. "Why did you say we were staying here then?"

"We are only spending one day in Paris. Then we get the coach to Calais."

Inside the inn she asked for a room for herself and her maid and ordered breakfast to be brought to them. When they were seated at a table by a window, looking out onto the cobbled square, she told Maisie what she had planned.

"I wanted Mr Delaney to think I was spending time here before returning to England," she said. "I know he's still out there, conducting his 'business' as he calls it, but he'll rush back the minute he knows I'm home."

"But won't your mother or father let him know?" Maisie frowned. "You know your mother can't wait to start planning your wedding. She'll have the invitations sent out as soon as we get back to Essex House."

"We're not going to Essex House."

"Where then?"

"The Half Moon." Arabella laughed as Maisie's mouth dropped open. "Don't you see — it's perfect. I can rent a room from your sister and I can start singing again."

Maisie looked doubtful. "But Mr Delaney knows —"

"Yes, but he won't hear that I'm back there. Who's going to tell him?"

"He'll find out somehow."

"By the time he does it will be too late. I don't care about scandal and gossip — not if it means he gets caught. If I don't hear from Nat soon I've made up my mind to speak to my father. I need to find out how much he knows about Mr Delaney's goings-on. I'm quite sure that if he is involved it is quite innocent on his part. And if I can make him see that Oswald is a traitor, he will know how to deal with it." Arabella took a final mouthful of coffee and smiled. "My mother will soon change her mind about his suitability as a husband." She stood up. "Anyway, I'm not going to worry about it today. Finish your breakfast — we're going to see the sights."

Arabella's high spirits didn't last long. She and Maisie spent an enjoyable day strolling through the Tuileries Gardens and along the Champs-Élysées to the splendid Arc de Triomphe. But back at the inn reality seeped in and she felt a churning in her stomach at the thought of what the next few days might bring. Sam Fenton had probably found a new singer to take her place and wouldn't want her back. Vi might not have a room to let. That wasn't the worst of her worries though — she had money of her own and knew she could manage for a while.

The thought that plagued her was that Nat, even if he'd received her letter, might not believe her — worse, he might not want to help. She had told him to send a reply to the Half Moon knowing that, even if she wasn't able to stay there, the Fentons would pass it on.

Then there was the fear that somehow Oswald would discover that she had returned to London and was about to betray him. Who knew what he might do? She had learned enough about him by now to realize that he was entirely ruthless.

During the rough crossing from Calais to Dover her thoughts chased each other round in circles. The final part of the long journey seemed interminable until, exhausted by her worries, she fell into an uneasy doze. At last Maisie shook her awake and she realized the coach was entering the outskirts of south London.

"We're home," Maisie said and the joy in her voice brought home to Arabella how homesick her friend had probably been and how much she had sacrificed to follow her to Turkey. She did not deserve such loyalty and devotion and she resolved to be kinder to the maid in future and not to take her so much for granted.

As the coach rumbled over London Bridge, she looked out of the window at the familiar scene and realized that she too had missed the bustle of her native city. But in her heart she knew it wouldn't be long before the routine of everyday life would start to pall and she would be seeking new adventures.

As she had hoped, Vi Fenton welcomed them both with equal pleasure, ushering them into the cosy kitchen at the back of the theatre. Sam, summoned from backstage where he had been supervising rehearsals for the coming night's entertainment, appeared in the doorway, rubbing his hands and beaming.

"Well, bless my soul — you're back." He hugged Maisie and kissed her, and then, before she could protest, he had grabbed Arabella round the waist and planted his whiskery lips on her cheek too.

At Vi's horrified gasp, he quickly released her.

"I'm sorry, Miss, I couldn't help meself. I'm that glad to see you," he said, his face red.

Arabella laughed. "I'm glad to see you too, Sam. And it's good to know I'm welcome."

"Of course you are, me dear," Sam said.

"Stay as long as you like," Vi confirmed.

Before long they were seated at the table, the inevitable cups of tea in front of them. With many interruptions and exclamations, Maisie and Arabella told their story. They didn't dwell on the horrors they had witnessed at Scutari but Arabella was loud in her praise of the work Florence Nightingale had done. "Things are a lot better now than when we arrived," she said.

Sam looked at her shrewdly. "But that's not the whole story is it?" he asked. "I thought you were to stay for the duration of the war — and it's not over yet. So why have you come back?"

"You're not ill, either of you?" Vi interrupted with an anxious frown.

Arabella laid a hand on her arm. "Don't worry, we're both perfectly well." She paused and decided to be blunt. "I was dismissed for misconduct."

Vi gasped and Sam's eyes widened. "I don't believe it," he said.

"It wasn't Bella's fault. She didn't do anything wrong," Maisie said.

"A misunderstanding, was it?" Vi asked.

Arabella looked at their honest faces and decided to tell them everything. "And Maisie insisted on leaving with me — she has proved a true friend," she finished. She turned to the other girl and smiled. "I don't know how I'd have managed without her."

"She's a good girl, our Maisie," Vi agreed, pouring another cup of tea.

Sam turned to Arabella. "This trouble you had — is that why you don't want to go home?"

She nodded. "I can't face them yet. Are you sure it's all right for me to stay here?"

"Of course. In fact, I'm delighted — you'll have no excuse for not gracing the stage." He laughed. "Give me a few days to swap the acts round a bit. You'll need a bit of rehearsal too. I don't suppose you've learned any new songs where you've been."

"I'm looking forward to singing again, Sam."

Vi gave a little cough. "I don't know if that's a good idea, Sam," she said.

"Why ever not?"

"Look what happened last time. Just when we were playing to full houses, she ups and goes off to Russia or wherever." She turned to Arabella. "I don't mind renting you a room, love. But we can't be let down again — and besides, you're supposed to be getting married soon."

194

Arabella swallowed. "I won't be getting married. My engagement to Mr Delaney was never official. And now that I know a bit more about him, I know I could never marry him."

She took a sip of tea to moisten her throat and, knowing that she owed it to these kind people to be honest with them, she once more launched into explanations, revealing her suspicions and uncertainties.

When she'd finished, Sam cleared his throat. "If what you say is true, you must have proof. Can't accuse the man on suspicion alone." He snapped his fingers. "I know, why don't I have a word with Sergeant Keen?"

"A soldier?" Arabella asked. "What can he do?"

"A policeman," Maisie said. "You remember. He took care of that ruffian who was annoying you the last time you sang here."

Arabella had a vague recollection of the man, a memory which became clearer as she saw the flush on Maisie's face. He had often been at the theatre, hanging about after the performance and she had teased the other girl about her devoted admirer. "Will he really be able to help?" she asked.

"We can only ask — that's if you don't mind me telling him. We shouldn't hold anything back — even Delaney's threats to you. And he's bound to ask what hold he has over you."

"I don't care for myself and if it means exposing him and stopping him from hurting my father —"

"Will Bella have to go to the police station?" Maisie asked.

"I'll have a word in private. The sergeant often comes in for a quick pint when he comes off duty. And he keeps an eye on the place for me, makes sure there's no rough stuff or hanky-panky."

"That's settled then," said Vi, beginning to clear the tea things away. "Now let's sort out rooms for you girls."

Arabella had been at the Half Moon for a week and she was getting restless. Sam wanted her to sing but felt she needed new songs and time to rehearse before taking to the stage again.

To fill the time between rehearsals, she tried to help Vi around the house, but she wouldn't hear of it. "It's not right," she said firmly. She still thought of Arabella as a "lady", despite Sam and Maisie's acceptance of her as "one of them". She had seemed quite shocked when Maisie called her former mistress Bella.

It was hard for Vi to do the same even when Arabella tried to put her at her ease, saying, "I'm just Bella to my friends."

Vi reluctantly agreed to the informality but still tried to wait on her, jumping up and taking her plate away whenever Arabella tried to do it herself.

One morning, Vi and Maisie had gone to the market, leaving Arabella to wander about the house sighing in frustration. They had pressed her to go with them but she was worried about being seen by someone who knew her. Besides, she still hoped for a letter from Nat and she had to be here when it arrived.

196

After tidying her room she went through the connecting door to the theatre which was now entirely separate from the house. She had been amazed at the changes in the months since she'd been away. The old pub had been gutted, making room for more seats and there was now just a bar which was only manned during the interval and for a short time before performances started.

"We're getting a better class of audience now," Sam had told her proudly.

There were new plush seats in the main auditorium and a gallery above where those who could not afford a proper seat could watch the show. Instead of the smoky old lamps, gas lighting had been installed.

She wandered between the rows of seats, imagining herself up there on the stage once more, thinking of the songs she used to sing back in the barrack hospital. She had tried them out here with Sam playing the piano for her but he'd shaken his head. "No, that won't do. People want something cheerful. They don't want songs about dying soldiers and lost lovers."

As she turned to go back to the house she heard voices from backstage.

"Sam, is that you?" she called.

He parted the curtains and peered through the gloom. "Bella, me dear. I was just coming to fetch you. There's someone wants a word with you."

It's Nat, he's back, she thought, running down the aisle between the rows of seats, her heart thumping, a joyous smile lighting up her face. But the man who accompanied Sam was tall and broad, with a red face and a bushy moustache. She recognized the high hat, dark blue coat with gleaming brass buttons and buckled belt even before Sam had introduced him.

"This here's Sergeant Davie Keen."

"You were a constable last time we met," Arabella reminded him.

"Got me stripes a couple of months ago," he said with a proud smile.

"Congratulations."

He gave an embarrassed cough. "Sam says you have something to tell me. It sounds like a very serious matter, Miss Raynsford. I'd like to hear the story in your own words, if you don't mind."

"Perhaps we could go into my office," Sam suggested, leading the way to the little room at the back of the theatre. There were only two chairs and Sam offered to go and fetch some refreshment. "I expect the missus is back by now. I'll get her or Maisie to bring it."

"So your sister-in-law's back with you, is she?" Sergeant Keen said and Arabella smiled as his ruddy face grew even redder.

Sam nodded and left and the policeman turned to Arabella. "Sam's told me what you suspect about this Delaney feller, but I need more details."

Arabella sighed. "I don't know where to begin."

"Take your time, Miss," said the sergeant.

Once she started, it all poured out — the letter she'd been asked to deliver, the rough man who'd accosted her and later turned up dressed as an Arab, Oswald's threat to implicate her father if she told anyone of her suspicions.

198

Finally she drew a deep breath and said, "The worst thing was when he blackmailed me."

Sergeant Keen pursed his lips. "Blackmail's a very serious crime — and very hard to prosecute. Usually, the person being threatened would rather pay up than have their secrets exposed." He looked at Arabella shrewdly. "I can't imagine that a respectable young lady such as yourself would have anything to hide, although there must be some reason why you're lodging with the Fentons rather than going home to your family."

Arabella blushed. "I thought Sam would have told you — or that you might have recognized me." She hesitated. "I'm Bella Forde — the singer."

The sergeant smiled. "I must admit I'd noticed the resemblance, Miss, but I thought it a coincidence. Now you mention it though —"

It hadn't been so hard to own up, Arabella thought, relieved that her secret was out. At any rate, the policeman didn't seem too shocked.

He echoed her thoughts. "I can see how your friends and family might react if they found that out," he said. "But I've met some very respectable people in the theatre business — the Fentons, for example. And what about Miss Jenny Lind, the Swedish nightingale as they call her? She's accepted in the highest circles."

Arabella had had the same thought but she knew there was little chance of her mother agreeing. A suitable marriage to someone with money and property was the only "career" she deemed acceptable for her daughter.

Sergeant Keen was still speaking. "Now, as to this Mr Delaney, it seems clear he's up to no good. Supplying arms and explosives to the enemy is treason. Of course, he's Irish, albeit he has a home and business here. So maybe just sending him back to Ireland is the answer. I'd like to see him thrown in jail but I'm not sure we have enough to go on." He paused and pulled at his lip. "I'll have to speak to my superiors and see what they recommend. It certainly needs investigating."

"But what about my father?" Arabella's eyes filled with tears. "I know he wouldn't do anything to help the Russians — my brother was wounded and now he's out there fighting again. But Father's been doing business with Oswald for more than a year now and he might be implicated through no fault of his own."

"Don't worry, Miss. If he's innocent we'll make sure he isn't involved, but you must realize, we have to investigate."

"Of course." She wiped her eyes and tried a smile. "Thank you for listening and believing me. I feel better knowing something will be done."

"Will you be here if I need to speak to you again?"

"Yes, I feel safer here. I don't think Oswald will think of looking for me here — he thinks I'm staying with friends in Paris."

There was a tap on the door and Maisie came in carrying a tray which she set down on the corner of Sam's desk. She glanced from one to the other and then concentrated on pouring tea. "Is everything all right?" she asked.

"I've told Sergeant Keen everything and he is going to get his superiors to investigate."

"I knew he'd help," Maisie said with a broad smile. She paused. "When you say you've told him everything, do you mean —?"

"Yes, he knows about Bella Forde."

Maisie giggled. "I bet he didn't guess."

"Your mistress had everybody fooled — but I did have my suspicions."

"Oh, you policemen are suspicious of everyone," Maisie said.

"I wouldn't mind taking you into custody, young lady," he said with a grin.

Maisie gave him a playful push and Arabella, sensing that there was more to their banter, slipped quietly out of the room.

She made her way to the stage where Sam was tinkering with the piano. He stood up when he saw her and beckoned her towards him. "I think I've got just the song for you, Bella love," he said. "Come and give it a tryout."

She plucked the song sheet from its stand and read the title. "'The Soldier's Tear'? I thought you wanted something cheerful," she said.

"I changed my mind when I came across this one — it suits your voice, Bella love. I can get Nancy to do the bawdy stuff in the first half — the patrons love it — but they lap up these sentimental songs too. This is just the thing to send them home with."

Sam played the introduction and she began to sing, hesitantly at first, then as she got the feel for the words and the music, her voice grew stronger and the notes soared up to the high ceiling — "*A soldier stood on the battlefield, His weary watch to keep.*"

Despite the pathos of the words, she felt lighter of heart now she had unburdened herself to someone in authority. It was easy to give herself up to the one thing that had always brought her solace when she was troubled — her singing. As she sang, she was unaware of the shadowy figure who had let himself into the theatre and now sat in the farthest row.

CHAPTER
SIXTEEN

Arabella's pure voice filled the theatre with its sweet sound. Sitting in the shadows at the back of the auditorium, Nat couldn't take his eyes off her. As he took in the words of the song, tears filled his eyes. She was so obviously singing from the heart and he wondered if she was thinking of the young Captain Wilson who had died in her arms.

Had he done the right thing in seeking her out? When the soldier had approached him at Balaclava bringing Arabella's letter he'd still been trying to decide what to do about Delaney. Their encounter at the Mastersons's had left him in no doubt that the man was determined to marry Arabella. And she had not contradicted him. She had told him she wouldn't marry the Irishman, but something must have happened to make her change her mind.

Nat didn't care. He still loved her. And, desperate as he was to try and stop Delaney from aiding the enemy, he wouldn't do anything to hurt her. He had left for the battlefront still undecided what to do. Then he received Arabella's letter and he realized that she was just as anxious to expose the Irishman as he was. Maybe her seeming acquiescence to Delaney had been a pose.

Buoyed up by this thought, he had made discreet enquiries about the Irishman's accomplice and learned that he was a dealer in guns and explosives who had no compunction about selling to either side in any conflict. Now, although he had no hard evidence, Nat felt sure he could convince the authorities that they had a traitor in their midst.

Leaving his work in the Crimea in the hands of his colleagues, he had hastened back to London. It had been tempting to stay in Paris in hopes of seeing Arabella but without knowing the names of her friends there, it would have been impossible to locate her. So here he was, back at the Half Moon where he had caught his first glimpse of Bella Forde over a year ago.

Like every other man in the audience that day, he had fallen in love with the beautiful singer, telling himself that she was singing just for him — but like them he had known it wasn't real love. And then he had been introduced to the lovely Arabella Raynsford — dark, not fair, with sparkling grey eyes and a warm smile. It had been love at first sight.

As he listened to her singing now, he remembered the first time he'd heard her in the drawing room at Essex House, the lurch of his heart as he recognized that voice. Surely everyone else must recognize it too, he thought. He had glanced around the room, noting the smiles of the ladies as they nodded or flicked their fans in time to the music, the men gazing at Arabella with unfeigned admiration. Apart from the group of Harry Raynsford's fellow officers, Nat realized, the assembled guests were not the sort of people to frequent the music halls. And then he'd caught sight of the smirk on Delaney's face. So he knew too. He could hardly believe it when he heard that Arabella was to become engaged to the Irishman, wondering how he felt about his fiancée's secret career.

But despite knowing she was promised to another man, Nat had not been able to get her out of his thoughts — or his heart.

He had come to the Half Moon hoping for news of her, unable to believe his good fortune when he saw her come on to the stage with the proprietor of the theatre. He listened, entranced, and when the song came to an end he stayed in his seat, unsure how to approach her. Maybe he should just slip quietly away.

As she finished singing, Arabella heard a movement from the back of the theatre. It could have been Maisie or Vi but her heart thudded. Suppose Oswald had tracked her down? Scotland Yard might be on to him, but she knew he was still dangerous. She would not feel safe until he was in custody. She came to the edge of the stage, peering into the half-darkness. "Is there someone there?" she called.

Sam grabbed her arm. "Wait a minute," he said. "It could be anybody." He raised his voice. "Who's there? Don't you know we're closed?"

The man stood up and Arabella sighed with relief. "Nat, what are you doing here?" she called and, turning to Sam, "It's all right, it's Mr Sloane."

"I thought you were in Paris," said Nat, coming down the aisle to the foot of the stage.

"That's what I wanted everyone to think," she replied with a smile.

"Haven't you even let your family know you're back in London?"

"I can't. If I go home, my mother will inform Mr Delaney — and I don't want him to find me." She could see the questions hovering on Nat's lips and she turned to Sam. "Should we go into the house? I have so much to tell Mr Sloane."

"Good idea, love," said Sam. "Follow me, young feller. We've got a couple of hours before we open up for business. And I'm sure Vi will ask you to stay for a bite to eat."

If Nat was surprised at the other man's easy familiarity he did not show it and followed the two of them through the connecting door and along a narrow passage to the Fentons private quarters.

"Take him into the parlour, Bella me dear, and I'll let the girls know who's arrived," said Sam.

Arabella sat in an armchair to the side of the fireplace and gestured to Nat to take the other. He refused to sit but stood just inside the door taking in the cosy room, so different from the setting in which he had been used to seeing her.

"It's a bit different from the hospital isn't it, Nat?" she said, knowing that he had not been thinking of those grim surroundings but of the graceful drawing room at Essex House or the home of the Mastersons where they had last met.

"Do you really belong here, Arabella?" he asked.

"Yes, I do." She leaned forward, her voice gentler. "I feel far more at home here than I ever did back there — and I'm not talking about the hospital." She shook her head. "I suppose you got my letter."

"Yes, that's why I'm here. I need to know —"

"I told you everything; why I was dismissed; why I felt I had to bow to Oswald's wishes."

Her voice broke and he pulled the other chair closer, sat down and took her hands in his.

"I understand that you felt you had no choice. I wish you had confided in me earlier."

"I wish I had too. But at the time I wasn't sure if you were involved as well. You kept appearing unexpectedly with no convincing explanation for your presence."

"I was keeping an eye on Delaney — and on you," Nat said. He squeezed her hands in his. "Now we have to decide what we are going to do about him."

"I have spoken to a policeman. He is looking into it."

"Do you think that was wise? He may think you are involved, especially since your father has similar business interests to Delaney's."

"He has promised to keep me and my family out of it."

"Are you sure you can trust him?"

Arabella snatched her hands away. "Of course I trust him. He's a friend of Sam's. Besides, I had to confide in someone. I wasn't sure if you had received my letter — or even if you would act on it."

"You misjudge me. Of course I acted on it. I would do anything to stop you marrying that man."

Arabella's heart skipped a beat. So he did care. She smiled and touched his arm, asking tentatively, "Why do you not want me to marry Oswald?"

"He is not worthy of you. Any man who would threaten a young lady's reputation is a villain in my book." His voice faltered and his face reddened. "Besides, your father is a good man. He does not deserve to be ruined by such a man. He must rue the day he ever invited him to his home and introduced him to his daughter."

It was not the answer Arabella had hoped for but she sensed that, although Nat hadn't revealed his feelings, he did love her. Was he afraid her family would not accept him, or was it the fact that he now knew she'd been flaunting herself on the music hall stage?

The old rebelliousness resurfaced. As if she cared what he thought. He was not the man she thought him if he was so easily swayed by convention. But still, he had promised to try and help her, and for that she was grateful.

She was trying to think of a suitable reply when the door opened and Maisie announced that the meal was served. "We eat early so as to be ready for opening," she explained, directing them to the dining room.

Vi had surpassed herself with a table laden with cold meats, pies and puddings. Arabella was sure she would not be able to eat but, to her surprise, she managed to do justice to her hostess's cooking and she was pleased to see that Nat tucked in with vigour.

"A far cry from the fare we had to endure in the Crimea, Mrs Fenton," Nat said, licking his lips enthusiastically.

"So I heard from Maisie and Bella. Half-starved they looked when they got home. Filling out nicely now," said Vi, squeezing Maisie's arm.

"You always were a good cook, Sis," said Maisie.

Nat smiled, appreciating the friendly atmosphere round the table and thinking how well Arabella seemed to fit into this world, as naturally as she did in the society she had been brought up in. Maybe it was her tendency towards the theatrical that made her so adaptable, he thought. And, as she offered him another piece of pie, accompanied by that devastating smile, another thought struck him. Had she been merely playing a part — that of the helpless female in need of male protection? Once more, the doubts crept in as he remembered her agreeable demeanour at the Mastersons's when Delaney had forcefully declared that she would not carry on nursing when she returned to London.

The conversation swirled around him and once more he found himself torn between his love for Arabella and his unwillingness to be taken in by a pair of sparkling eyes and a beautiful smile.

He was brought back to the present when Sam spoke to him. "We've left everything in the hands of Sergeant Keen," he said. "If you have any further evidence you should speak to him too."

"I can't add anything to what you already know. Delaney's a wily creature and seems to have covered his tracks." Nat put down his napkin and sighed. "I think I should visit Mr Raynsford — we need to know his part in all this."

Arabella stood up, pushing her chair back abruptly. "No. You can't think he is involved. I won't allow you to speak to him."

"I'm not accusing him," Nat said, his anger rising at her assumption. "But he needs to know what's going on. I'm surprised you haven't spoken to him already. But I suppose you were too concerned with making sure they don't discover your secret life — *Miss Bella Forde.*"

He too pushed his chair back and stormed from the room, leaving a stunned silence behind him.

Nat regretted his hasty action the moment he had left the Half Moon Theatre but it was too late to go back. He had been unpardonably rude in the face of the Fentons's hospitality, not to mention that he had probably forfeited his chances with Arabella.

As he strode along, oblivious to the passers by, the cries of the street sellers and the rattle of cab wheels on the cobbles, he asked himself why he let these doubts creep in. Why was he so unsure of himself? He had enjoyed liaisons in the past — none of them serious — and he had always been confident with the opposite sex. But then, none of his former relationships had been so important to him. Until he met Arabella he had never really believed in love, the kind that lasted forever, that dominated one's every waking thought and, most importantly, put the loved one's well-being before all else.

But she had been in love with James Wilson. And because he could not believe that she would ever feel the same way about him, he sought for reasons why he should not love her. It was no use though. Even the fact that she sang in public didn't matter to him. He didn't care what polite society thought. Besides, why shouldn't she share her God-given talent with a wider audience? What was so wrong about bringing pleasure into people's often drab lives? If anything, he admired her for her courage in flouting convention.

He sighed, knowing that even if he never got the chance to tell her so, she would always remain in his heart.

Exhausted by his emotions, he reached the street corner and hailed a cab, asking the cabbie to take him to the lodging house he always used when he was in London. He settled back in his seat, trying to still his racing thoughts. Was there anything else he could do? Despite Arabella's protests, he still felt that her father should know what was going on — if he didn't already.

He reached up to knock on the roof of the cab. "I've changed my mind — take me to Essex Square."

At the Raynsfords's house he hesitated on the steps leading up to the porticoed front door, his hand hovering over the bell pull. It was rather late to be calling unannounced but he knew that if he did not do it now, he might never summon the courage to do so.

The door opened to reveal a liveried footman who looked down his nose at Nat's dishevelled appearance.

It was too late for Nat to change his mind though. "May I speak to Mr Raynsford? It is an urgent business matter. My name is Sloane — Mr Nathaniel Sloane."

The footman, still looking supercilious, opened the door wider and gestured him to enter. "Wait here, sir. I will enquire whether Mr Raynsford is at home."

It seemed an age before a door opened and, instead of the expected footman, Henry Raynsford hurried toward him wiping his chin on a linen napkin.

"I am sorry to intrude, Sir. I did not realize you would be at dinner," Nat said.

"No matter, you are here now. And besides, we had just finished. It is only Mrs Raynsford and myself — we have no guests tonight." Henry gave a little chuckle. "We'd better go into the library. You know how my dear wife dislikes any discussion of business in the home."

He ushered Nat into the snug room and offered him a chair, picking up a decanter and gesturing. Nat nodded. Maybe a snifter of brandy would help to calm him after his emotional journey here.

He wasn't sure how to begin and for a few moments the two men silently sipped at their drinks.

At last Henry looked up. "Now, then, young man. What's the trouble?"

As Nat shook his head in denial, Henry chuckled again. "Look here, I know you wouldn't visit unannounced unless there was something on your mind." He paused and his face creased in concern. "Oh, Lord. It's not Harry is it? We've not had a word since he returned to the front."

"No, not Harry." Nat hastened to reassure him.

"Thank God. We heard about young Wilson, of course." Henry shook his head. "Sad business, that." He looked up. "Well, out with it, man."

212

Nat decided to take the plunge. No use beating about the bush. "How well do you know Oswald Delaney?" he asked.

"Good businessman, made a lot of money in gunpowder, owns land in Ireland." Henry looked sharply at Nat. "Why do you ask. What's your business with him?"

Nat closed his eyes briefly, fervently hoping he had not misread the other man's character. But he refused to believe Arabella's father would be involved in anything underhanded. He leaned forward, clasping his hand between his knees. "It is a rather delicate matter, Sir. I have reason to believe that Delaney's business dealings are not entirely honest. I thought I should warn you, knowing that you have done business with the man — not to mention him being engaged to your daughter."

Henry began to bluster. "Don't bring my daughter into this. Besides, this engagement is my wife's doing — she wants a good match for the girl."

"Are you sure it is such a good match though, Sir?"

The older man sighed and the colour left his face. "I must confess, Sloane, I have been having doubts on that score. But tell me what you know. If it is merely suspicion —"

Nat decided to tell the whole story, leaving out Arabella's part in it. "As you know, I have been in the Crimea advising the army on various engineering works out there. I came across Mr Delaney on several occasions." He hesitated and Henry motioned impatiently for him to carry on.

"I believe he is there to further his own interests. My suspicions were aroused by his furtive behaviour and I have seen him consorting with some decidedly unsavoury characters."

"Well, naturally, he would have to deal with the locals, given the nature of his business." Henry began to bluster again.

Once more Nat was forced to question how much the other man knew about what Delaney had been up to and he spoke abruptly. "The man I saw him with was a Russian."

Henry's face went even paler. "You mean he was consorting with the enemy?" He leaned forward and put a hand on Nat's knee. "Are you sure there is not a reasonable explanation?" he pleaded.

"I'm sorry, Sir. It was quite obvious that their meeting was not innocent. I overheard them talking and it was clear to me. Delaney is supplying arms and ammunition to the enemy."

"And I have been supplying him with copperas for his gunpowder mills." Henry sighed. "Does that make me guilty too?" He stood up and began to pace the room. "I assure you, Mr Sloane, I had no inkling of this — none at all."

Nat believed him wholeheartedly and he sighed with relief. Should he mention Arabella's involvement now? Surely, if he told Henry how the Irishman had duped her into carrying messages for him, he would realize that the engagement must be broken off.

But there was no need for him to say anything. Henry threw himself back in his chair and grabbed his

214

brandy glass, gulping the liquid down and rubbing his hand across his mouth. "How could I have been taken in like that? Granted, the man has charm and my wife took to him. I thought that doing business with him would help my family." He paused, looking keenly at Nat. "I am speaking in confidence, young man. My wife knows nothing of this and I want to keep it that way. I hope you can be trusted."

"Of course, Sir." Nat hastened to reassure him.

"I am in financial straits. My copperas beds down in Whitstable are almost worked out. I have invested heavily in the railway but have yet to see a return on my money and, foolishly, I allowed Delaney to help me out. He loaned me money with the proviso that he would not want to be repaid if he and Arabella married. I insisted that it must be a businesslike arrangement and made over two of my ships to him as collateral." He sunk his head in his hands and groaned. "How could I have been so taken in?"

Nat nodded sympathetically. Knowing Caroline Raynsford's ambitions for her daughter, it was easy for him to see how the situation had come about. Blinded by Oswald Delaney's charm, his riches and his estates in Ireland, she had persuaded Henry of the advantages of a match. Never mind what Arabella wanted.

His thoughts were interrupted as Henry raised his head. "Well, young man, what do you think I should do about it?"

Nat was tempted to tell him that it was all in hand, that Sam Fenton's policeman friend was dealing with it. But that would mean explaining how he came to know the theatre manager. He had promised Arabella that he would not reveal her secret and he would keep his word.

He compromised. "It is a difficult decision, Sir. If you denounce him, he is sure to try to implicate you."

"That is what worries me. It would kill my poor wife if the family were involved in a scandal. She values our good name above everything."

Nat couldn't help thinking that Caroline Raynsford valued riches far more or she would not have tried to force her daughter into marrying someone she did not even like — let alone love. And if she had guessed at Henry's financial difficulties, it would explain why she had been even more eager to foster a match between Delaney and Arabella.

Henry refilled his brandy glass and took another gulp before offering the decanter to Nat. "One thing is sure, I cannot let my daughter marry that man. Thank the Lord the engagement is not yet official. We had planned to announce it when Arabella returned from the Crimea."

"Is she not home yet, Sir?" Nat asked innocently. "I heard from the Mastersons that she left Constantinople some days before me."

"She wrote that she was spending some time in Paris." Henry shook his head. "I do not know these friends she mentioned. She must have met them while she was abroad."

Nat smiled inwardly. So Arabella had managed to dupe her parents. They clearly had no inkling she was already in London. Maybe he could convince her to

216

return home now that there was no possibility of her being forced into marriage with Delaney. Much as he liked and respected the Fentons, he didn't feel that the theatre lodgings were really a suitable place for her.

As Henry went to refill his glass, Nat shook his head. "I wonder if I might make a suggestion," he said. "I could approach the authorities without involving you. After all, I was the one who witnessed him collaborating with the enemy. Once the seed is sown, he will be closely watched. It is only a matter of time until he is caught."

"Excellent idea, Mr Sloane. I can't thank you enough for bringing this to my attention." Henry stood up and shook Nat's hand.

"Thank you for believing me, Sir. I must confess I was a little nervous of approaching you. After all, I have no real proof of what Delaney is up to. And, having done business with the man, you may well have taken his word over mine."

Henry shook his head. "I have had my doubts about his honesty for some time. But my wife assured me that he was quite smitten with Arabella — and she with him — and I was reluctant to do anything which would interfere with her happiness. And, I have to admit, at first he did seem most genuine."

"It's a good thing that we discovered his true nature in time," Nat said. "Besides, I wouldn't worry about your daughter. I do not think she is as enamoured of Delaney as your wife thinks."

"Really? What makes you say so?"

Nat couldn't reveal that Arabella herself had told him. He thought quickly. "She was distraught at the death of Captain Wilson," he said.

"They had known each other since childhood. But I'm sure she thought of him as a brother. She would have told me if there had been anything more to it — and I would not have allowed her to become engaged to Delaney if I had thought she was in love with someone else — no matter what my wife may have wanted." Henry rang for the footman to see Nat out, shaking his hand and thanking him again.

As Nat made his way to his lodgings he was pleased with how well the meeting had gone. Now, he could leave the police to deal with Delaney. But what was he going to do about Arabella? Would he get the chance to apologize?

CHAPTER
SEVENTEEN

Arabella was still smarting from the argument with Nat — if you could call it that. He had stormed out without giving her a chance to explain her concerns. Besides, how dare he imply her father had something to do with Oswald's crimes.

She finished her rehearsal for that evening's performance and Sam left her to check the beer barrels in the cellar. She remained on the stage, seated at the piano and running her fingers over the keys.

Bored, she wondered what to do with herself until it was time to get changed. She would have helped Violet in the kitchen but she knew her offers of help would be rejected. The older woman still tended to treat her as an honoured guest and found it hard to adopt the easy familiarity that Maisie and Sam had achieved.

Maisie had gone out with Sergeant Keen. It was his day off and they had gone to listen to the band in the park. When they got back she must ask him if there was any news of the investigation.

She sighed impatiently. What could a sergeant in the Metropolitan Police Force do when the criminal wasn't even in the country?

Sam came up from the cellar and looked surprised to see her still on the stage. "You look fed up, me dear," he said. "Thinking about that young man of yours?"

"He's not my young man," she snapped and then smiled apologetically. "I was just wondering where this will all end. In a way, I hope Oswald stays in Russia, or goes back to Ireland. That way, he can't hurt me or my family."

"But he should be punished, Bella love. You saw all those poor young men in the hospital, the injuries and suffering. The stuff he supplied to the enemy could have been responsible."

"Maybe — but they'll get their guns and ammunition somewhere, somehow. What does it matter? There'll always be wars — and young men like my brother and James will suffer." Her voice was bitter.

Sam shrugged. "You're right, me dear, of course. But I still say he should be thrown in jail."

"Don't take any notice of me, Sam." Arabella stood up and shuffled her sheets of music into a tidy pile. "I wonder if Nat went to see my father, after all," she said.

"If he did, I'm sure it wasn't to accuse him. That young man has your interests at heart. He wouldn't do anything to hurt you or your family," Sam said.

Arabella thought he was only trying to make her feel better. His mention of her family being hurt made her feel guilty. She should have gone to see her parents before now. They must be wondering why they had received no word from her.

She made up her mind. She'd go tomorrow. Perhaps Nat had already convinced her father of Oswald's treachery, but if not she herself would tell him everything that had happened. Surely then her mother must see that a marriage was out of the question. If her parents withdrew their consent to the match, there would be no advantage to him in revealing her secret singing career — at least that's what she tried to tell herself.

Sam patted her arm. "Stop worrying. Come and have some tea and a bit of a rest before we open up. Maisie and the sergeant will be back soon."

The young couple were already in the parlour and Violet was bringing in the laden tray. Arabella was pleased to see Maisie looking flushed and happy. Would her own story have such a happy ending too, she wondered.

"I suppose it's no good asking if there's any news," she said as she took a chair next to Sergeant Keen.

"Not as such. As you know, I passed on your suspicions to my superiors and they said they'd look into it. But they don't confide in me. I'm just a lowly sergeant." He took a bite of the cake that Violet had handed to him, balancing the plate and the cup and saucer on his knee.

Arabella looked disappointed and Maisie chimed in. "Tell her what you told me, Davie," she said.

He swallowed his cake and took a gulp of tea before answering. "It seems the powers that be are forming a new division to deal with this sort of thing — spies, anarchists, not your usual thieves and ruffians," he said. "Special Operations I think they're going to call it."

"Tell them the rest," Maisie urged.

The sergeant's face grew redder. "Well, I'm not sure, mind, but I think I might be picked for this new branch of the force. It'll mean a rise in pay too — that's if I get it." He looked at Maisie and smiled. "We'll be able to get married then."

Maisie had gone a bit pink too. "Davie asked me this afternoon. We're going to get a ring on his next day off."

Amid the laughter and congratulations, Arabella felt a lump in her throat, once more wondering if she'd ever be lucky enough to become engaged to the man she really loved. For, despite her earlier annoyance with Nat, she had already forgiven him his sarcastic remark.

The next morning Arabella set off for Essex House, her stomach churning at the thought of the coming confrontation. What would she say if her mother still insisted that she was to marry Oswald? She would refuse, that's what, she thought, taking a deep breath as the cab drew up outside the house. She would just have to be firm. They couldn't force her into marriage. And if all else failed she would tell her parents how he had managed to coerce her into carrying messages for him.

Maisie had offered to accompany her but she wasn't sure how her former maid would be received at her parents' house. She had felt it would be easier to face the ordeal alone. But now, as she mounted the steps, she wished her friend were with her.

The footman welcomed her, looking behind to see where her luggage was. "My bags are following later," she said, following him into the wide, panelled hall. "Are my parents at home?" she asked.

"Mr Raynsford is in the library and the mistress is in the morning room," he said. "Shall I announce you?"

"Don't bother. I'll go straight in. Could you tell my father I'm here and ask him to join us?"

Caroline Raynsford was seated at her writing table under the window, her back to the door. She didn't look up when it opened but tutted impatiently. "I said I wasn't to be disturbed," she said.

"Not even to welcome me home, Mama?"

Caroline stood up, almost knocking her chair over. "Arabella. Why didn't you let us know you were coming? And why haven't you written? We were getting quite worried about you." She put her hands on her daughter's shoulders, kissed her on each cheek, then held her away, looking her up and down. "You're so thin. Are you quite recovered from the fever?"

"Yes, Mother. I still get a little tired but in time I will be my old self again."

"I knew I should not have allowed you to go," said Caroline. "Still, you're home now." She glanced over Arabella's shoulder. "Are you alone?"

"Of course. Who were you expecting?"

"I thought Mr Delaney —" She picked up a letter from her desk and waved it. "He wrote that he was joining you in France and hoped to travel home with you."

Arabella's heart sank. So he was still playing the part of the loving fiancé. And her parents had fallen for it. It seemed that Nat had not been here after all and they were still in ignorance of what Oswald had been up to.

Well, she would have to tell them herself. "I haven't seen him since I left Turkey," she said, thankful that in this at least she was speaking the truth. Now she would have to start lying about where she'd been since then.

She was saved from having to say any more as her father entered the room, enfolding her in a welcoming embrace and kissing her cheek. "My dear, we are so pleased to have you home with us at last. The house has seemed quite empty with both you and your brother away."

"Is Harry all right? I haven't heard anything for ages."

"He's well. We had a letter yesterday," Henry said, shaking his head. "We heard about poor James — sad business. You were with him at the end I hear."

Arabella nodded.

"That was a great comfort to his mother and to Charlotte," said Henry.

The memory of those dreadful moments in the dank corridor of the Scutari Hospital had faded a little since Arabella's return to London. But now it all flooded back in a tide of sadness — not just for James but for all the young men who had been in her care. "It was dreadful," she said, her voice choking a little. "I can't begin to tell you what it was like."

Caroline hastened to interrupt her. "There's no need. I'm sure you want to put it all from your mind now you are home." Her voice sharpened. "You knew before you left that it would not be a pleasant

224

experience. Well, you got your own way and I hope you have learned your lesson."

"I certainly learned something," Arabella snapped.

Henry intervened. "Now, my dear. Let's not have any tantrums. You're home now and, as your mother says, you can put all that unpleasantness behind you."

Deflated, Arabella sank into a chair. It was no use, they'd never understand. Her mother sat beside her and rang the bell for a maid. "I'm sure you need some refreshment after travelling such a long way," she said.

Arabella almost laughed, thinking of the ten-minute cab ride from the Half Moon Theatre. But she could see that her mother was anxious to resume an appearance of normality and she managed a smile. "I wasn't sure if you were even in London," she said. "Have you been down to Kent this summer?"

"We stayed for a couple of weeks only this time. Your father had to be in London and without you and the other young people, it was so dull."

Arabella carried on trying to make polite, meaningless conversation until the tray had been brought and the maid had gone. She knew that once they were alone, the questions would start.

Caroline turned to her daughter. "I cannot understand why you came home alone. Why did you not wait for Mr Delaney?"

"I didn't know he was going to Paris. As I told you, I have not heard from him. The last time we met was at the Mastersons' just before I left. Besides, his whereabouts mean nothing to me." There, it was out.

Arabella waited for the outburst she was sure would follow.

"But you are to be married. I assumed you would be eager to begin the arrangements for your wedding —"

"Then you assumed wrongly, Mama." Arabella put her cup down and stood up, striding over to the window.

Before Caroline could answer, Henry interrupted. "My dear, I'm sure Arabella has her reasons."

"I don't understand. Have you quarrelled?"

"I discovered what kind of a man he really is, Mama." She came over to where her mother sat and knelt in front of her, taking her hands. "If you knew —" Her voice broke.

Caroline looked bewildered, shaking her head.

Henry put a hand on her shoulder. "Arabella is right. He is not the man we thought he was. I'm sorry, my dear. I didn't tell you because I didn't want to distress you. Besides, I felt I couldn't say anything to you until I was sure." He glanced at his daughter. "You know, don't you?"

She nodded.

"Know what?" Caroline asked, looking from one to the other.

"Delaney is a charlatan, a fraud, a criminal —" Henry began to bluster.

"He is a traitor," Arabella said quietly.

"It's true then? I did hope young Sloane was mistaken," said Henry, glancing at Arabella. "How did you find out?"

226

In a quiet voice she told them how Oswald had asked her to deliver a letter when she reached Constantinople. "That was when I first became suspicious. But I told myself it was nothing. When his messenger accosted me in the market, I knew something wasn't quite right."

She went on to tell them about her meeting with Nat Sloane, his own suspicions and her dawning realization of what Oswald was up to. "I didn't know what to do, who to turn to," she said.

"Is that why you stayed in France?" Henry asked.

"I needed time to think. I couldn't come home," she said with a catch in her voice. "I was afraid. He said that if I accused him he would involve me, especially as I'd carried the messages for him."

"That swine should be horsewhipped," Henry said.

Caroline held a handkerchief up to her eyes. "I can hardly believe it. Such a charming young man —"

"We were all taken in, my dear. Men like him rely on their charm and plausibility. He certainly took me for a fool." Henry's voice was bitter.

"What are we going to do?" Caroline asked. "He can't get away with this."

"Don't worry, my dear. The man is already under investigation. I feel sure he will be caught and punished."

Arabella and her mother began to question him at the same time and Henry held up a hand. "When Mr Sloane came to see me, he told much the same story. He knew I'd done business with the man and wanted to warn me —"

"Henry, don't tell me you —" Caroline whispered.

"Of course not. My dealings with him were entirely innocent, although I may have trouble proving that."

Arabella sighed with relief. She told herself she'd always believed in her father but now she had to acknowledge that there had been one or two moments when she had doubted him.

As Henry tried to explain why his business had gone wrong and that he had only been trying to salvage something from the wreckage, she began to understand the strain he had been under too. "We would have been ruined, my dear," he concluded.

"Are we not ruined already because of that man? Who will do business with you in the future once it becomes known that you have been consorting with a criminal?" Caroline spoke bitterly, seeing her plans for their advancement in society tumbling about her ears.

"Sergeant Keen said he would try to keep the Raynsford name out of it," Arabella said.

Her mother turned on her. "And how do you know of this police person?" she snapped.

Arabella wished she hadn't spoken. "He and Maisie are to be married," she said.

"Are you speaking of your former maid — the girl I dismissed for insolence?"

"Yes, Mother. I did not tell you in my letters as I knew you would disapprove." She took a deep breath. "Maisie came out to the Crimea with me. She worked alongside me at the hospital and has proved herself a true and loyal friend."

Caroline gasped and would have spoken but Arabella went on. "It is thanks to her and her fiancé that we have a chance of catching Oswald out and seeing that he is punished for his treachery. I would not have thought of seeking help from the police by myself."

"I do not see how this man can help us. I was under the impression that the new police force was formed to patrol the streets and keep us safe from thieves and vagabonds."

"That is only part of their work, Mama. Davie — Sergeant Keen — told me that he is to be part of a new section formed especially to deal with spies and traitors."

Caroline dabbed at her eyes with her handkerchief. "I cannot believe that you — my daughter — have been consorting with these people." A frown creased her forehead. "And how did you meet this man? Did you not say that you had just returned from France? I thought you had come straight from Dover."

Arabella thought quickly. How could she confess that she had been back for several weeks? "Maisie and I arrived in London very late and I did not want to disturb you. We stayed overnight with Maisie's sister and it was there that I met Sergeant Keen. He told me that Oswald was being investigated." That last part was the truth, at least.

"Well, you're home now. There's no need for you to have anything more to do with these people." Caroline picked up the bell on her writing table and summoned the maid. When the girl came to take the tray away she gave instructions for Arabella's room to be prepared and asked her to dispatch someone to fetch her things.

Arabella jumped up and said she would write the directions. As she quickly scribbled a note to Maisie, she realized she should not have come home yet. Now she would be expected to put the experiences of the past year behind her and settle down to the boring life of an obedient and dutiful daughter. Worse still, once her mother had recovered from the shock of discovering how mistaken she'd been in her choice of suitor for Arabella, she would be on the lookout for another eligible young man.

But what choice did she have now? Whatever happened, though, she was determined to carry on singing as long as possible. Surely there must be a way. She added a sentence to the note asking Maisie to meet her in the park the following day.

The sun was shining and Arabella breathed deeply of the scent of new-mown grass, relishing the freedom after the stifling hours spent answering her mother's interminable questions. The previous evening they had gone over everything a dozen times, only to start up again at breakfast.

Arabella couldn't wait to get away and, pleading fatigue, had gone to her room. From there she had crept down the back stairs and managed to slip out unnoticed.

She took her friend's arm and opened her parasol. "I had hoped that Mama would allow you to return to work for us. I miss you already and Burton is such a dour old stick," she said.

"You should have stayed with us," Maisie said.

"I wanted to, but we knew it wasn't going to be for ever. I had to go home some time." Arabella sighed.

"You will still be singing though? Sam was very upset when you left so suddenly. He's just had some new posters printed."

"Don't worry, I won't give it up. It's the only thing worth living for now. All we have to do is work out how I'm going to do it."

"That's easy. You'll just have to say you're sick. Pretend that the fever you had in Turkey has come back."

"But I didn't have a fever."

"I know that, silly. But Lady Masterson thought you'd been ill and we kept up the pretence so that no one would know why you really left the hospital." Maisie giggled. "I'll have to get busy with the make-up though. You look far too healthy at the moment."

Arabella nodded. Although she had assured her mother that she was now quite well, Caroline had made quite a fuss of her and accepted that she needed to rest. It might work.

When her father had mentioned Nat's visit, she had held her breath, but of course, if he had mentioned her singing at the Half Moon, her father would have tackled her about it. Could she trust him to keep her secret a little longer? And was it worth the risk of being found out?

Arabella decided that it was. She couldn't contemplate giving up now that she had experienced once more the thrill of being on the stage.

As they strolled in the park, heads bent together, occasionally breaking out into giggles, the girls planned how "Bella Forde" could carry on singing without being exposed.

The weight of responsibility that Arabella had carried at the Scutari Hospital began to fall away from her. Her months there had been a satisfying experience but, she now realized, not one that she wanted to last for ever. She was no Florence Nightingale. But the thought that in some small way she had helped young soldiers like her brother and her childhood friend ensured that she would never regret going.

As the girls parted at the park gate, Arabella sighed. "I'm sure to get caught eventually. But we'll make the most of it while we can."

Maisie grinned. "Don't forget to put the pillows in the bed. And leave the lamp on low — and the bottle of laudanum on the bedside table. If anyone looks in on you, they'll see the medicine and think you're sleeping."

"Do you think it will work?"

"It did before," Maisie said, giggling.

CHAPTER
EIGHTEEN

It was not hard for Arabella to persuade her mother that she was still suffering from the effects of her months at the barrack hospital. Maisie passed on her skill with theatrical make-up and Arabella soon learned how to fake a convincing pallor together with dark blue and purple shadows under her eyes.

Sometimes she didn't even have to act. The late nights at the theatre left her exhausted, emotionally and physically. And throughout those last few weeks of the summer and into autumn, she spent many afternoons lying under the trees in the garden, a blanket over her legs.

At least the news from the Crimea was encouraging. There had been a big battle in August when the Russians had attempted to relieve the siege at Sebastopol. They were defeated by French and Sardinian troops and then, in September, after a heavy bombardment, the Russians evacuated the city. From then on everyone knew that the war could not last much longer.

Despite her parents' attempts to keep the news of the fighting from her, Arabella managed to read the papers occasionally. She still felt involved in the events in that far-off country and felt an urgent need to know what was happening. Sometimes, when she slipped into a doze, she would dream that she was back at the hospital and would wake, sobbing and shuddering. The experience had taken more out of her than she had realized.

She knew that her parents were worried about her, but when Caroline suggested they should go down to their country house for a few weeks, she made excuses. She had to stay in London. Since there had been no word from Nat, she told herself that she was resigned to a loveless future. Her singing meant everything to her now. It was all she had.

"I don't feel well enough to travel," she told her mother, when the suggestion was made yet again.

Caroline patted her arm and said soothingly, "I thought the country air would do you good. But never mind, perhaps all you need is rest."

Arabella stifled the guilt she felt, knowing that in a few hours she would be plumping up the pillows under her eiderdown in the semblance of a sleeping body, and slipping quietly down the back stairs.

Maisie was always waiting for her at the corner with the cab she had hired and, once on the stage, she forgot everything as the music embraced her.

Gradually, as autumn turned to winter, she began to regain her zest for life. On the evenings that she was billed to sing at the Half Moon, the theatre was packed. Word of the return to the London stage of the popular Miss Bella Forde had quickly spread and her admirers crowded round the stage door hoping for a glimpse of the reclusive singer.

So far, Sam had managed to fend them off with stories that she was still recovering from the illness that had kept her off the stage the previous year. The patrons, all of whom fancied themselves in love with "Beautiful Bella", respected her wish for privacy — most of the time.

One night, however, when Sam was sure that they had all gone, he opened the door to Arabella's dressing room and beckoned her out into the passage. "It's all clear, me dear. Cab's waiting."

She hurriedly said goodnight to Maisie and Sam and walked out into the street. Thick fog curled up from the river and she pulled the hood of her cloak closer around her.

As she stepped across the pavement towards the cab, a hand reached out and clutched her arm. She shied away, stifling a scream.

The young man in soldier's uniform let go immediately. "I'm sorry, Miss Bella. Didn't mean to startle you. I just wanted to give you these — a token of my appreciation, like."

He thrust a posy of violets into her hand and Arabella stammered her thanks.

The cabbie leaned down from his perch. "Everything all right, Miss?"

Before she could reply a voice called out from the enveloping mist. "What are you up to, man? Leave the lady alone."

"Sorry, sir. It's just — I had to thank her. You see, I recognized her, sir, from the war. She looked after me when I was wounded. She used to sing to us in the hospital."

Arabella climbed into the cab, her knees shaking. She looked out of the window, only then noticing the wooden peg leg which echoed hollowly on the pavement as the man disappeared into the fog. She leaned back against the seat and ordered the driver to take her to Essex Square.

As her breathing gradually steadied, she realized she was still clutching the wilting posy. But her thoughts were not on the soldier who had given them to her. She was wondering what would happen when she reached Essex House. For she was almost sure that the voice admonishing the soldier who'd accosted her was that of her brother Harry.

The following morning Arabella remained in her room as long as possible, anxious to avoid speaking to her brother. Had he been at last night's performance? Had he too recognized her? And could she rely on him to keep her secret?

She had stayed awake until the early hours, listening for his return home. But when she finally dozed off just before dawn she still had not heard him come in. Perhaps he had spent the night at his club or at the regimental barracks. But he was sure to visit his family as soon as his duties permitted. What was he doing in London, she wondered, and why hadn't he let his family know he was home?

236

As she allowed Burton, her mother's maid, to help her dress and arrange her hair, she vaguely remembered Charlotte reading from a letter a few days before. They had been taking tea together and Arabella, who had returned late from the theatre the previous evening, was feeling the strain of responding to her friend's chatter. She had closed her eyes and let her voice fade away.

Had Charlotte said something about Harry coming home on leave? All she could remember was her friend excitedly declaring that she would have a spring wedding.

When she entered the dining room her mother was still at the table reading a letter. She looked up as Arabella came in and smiled.

"It's from Harry. He's in London already. But he says he has duties to perform before he can come home."

"What a pity," Arabella said, her heart fluttering with relief. She helped herself to food from the sideboard and sat down, toying with her fork. "Does he say why he has returned? I thought he would have to stay until the war ended."

"He says it is all but over. He has been sent home to see to the training of new recruits. Apparently there are young men still clamouring to join up and fight."

Arabella didn't reply. She didn't want to get into another argument with her mother who, despite the death of James and her own son's injuries, couldn't seem to grasp that war was not the heroic project she imagined. Whenever she tried to tell Caroline what it had really been like, she was reminded that the subject was not fit for ladies' ears.

That afternoon when Charlotte came to call, her face was aglow with the news that Harry was back.

"He called yesterday but was only able to stay a few moments before returning to the regiment. Did you see him?" she asked.

Arabella hesitated, wondering whether to mention that he had been outside the theatre. But that would unleash a barrage of questions and Charlotte would be hurt that she had not confided in her before. Besides, she might be risking their friendship by confessing to what Charlotte would think of as unseemly behaviour. Maybe she wouldn't be shocked by the singing, but she'd be horrified at the thought of deceiving her parents. Maybe it would be best to keep her secret a bit longer.

"Mother had a letter this morning so I knew Harry was back in England," she said at last.

"We must talk about the wedding — yours too," Charlotte said eagerly.

"I'm not getting married," Arabella said, smiling at the confusion on her friend's face.

"But you are engaged to Mr Delaney. I had hoped we could have a double wedding."

"I hate Mr Delaney — and I am happy to inform you that my parents no longer think he is a suitable match."

"But why? I thought —"

Arabella couldn't tell her the real reason without revealing all that had happened while she was in

Turkey. "I believe he and my father had a disagreement — a matter of business," she said.

Charlotte smiled. "I know you weren't happy about marrying him so I'm pleased for you." Her face fell. "But you must marry some time. You don't want to be an old maid."

To Charlotte such a fate was unthinkable but Arabella knew there were worse things. "I don't want to get married," she said. How could she explain how she felt to her conventional friend?

Charlotte leaned over and put a hand on her arm. "I'm sorry, Arabella. I should think before I speak. You're still grieving for James, aren't you?" She blinked away a tear. "I miss him too."

"I was very fond of James, but I didn't love him — not in the way you mean. Of course, I'm sad that he died but —" Her voice trailed away.

Charlotte smiled. "There must be someone else then. I know —"

But before she could speak, the footman announced that more visitors had arrived. Arabella was relieved. She did not want to talk about Nat. He still had not been in touch and she was beginning to think he would never forgive her for her masquerade as Bella Forde. Her hopes that he might understand and forgive her deception seemed to be in vain.

Tea was served and her mother joined them to greet the new guests. To Arabella's relief the rest of the afternoon was taken up with talk of Charlotte's wedding and she was able to close her eyes in pretended exhaustion.

★ ★ ★

When Harry sent word that he was joining them for dinner and would be bringing a friend, Charlotte was invited to stay too. Several other guests had been invited and Arabella knew she would have to face her brother. She had dozed most of the afternoon and her mother would not accept fatigue as an excuse for continuing to avoid their guests.

Caroline came into Arabella's room to find her lying on the bed making no effort to dress for dinner.

"This won't do, my girl," she said. "You have been home for several months now and your health is greatly improved." She sighed. "I know you hate these social occasions but it is expected of us. I will not allow you to fall into your old habits of pleading headaches whenever we have guests."

"I'm sorry, Mama. I'll do my best to be polite," she said.

"Why should it be such an effort? These people are our friends. Besides, you must mix in society. How will you ever find a husband otherwise?" She jabbed a finger at her daughter. "And don't say you wish to remain single. I will not hear of it. Perhaps you will change your mind when you meet Harry's friend, Major Broomfield. Now get up and make yourself ready. I will expect you downstairs in ten minutes."

She swept out of the room and Arabella, with a deep sigh, stood up and rang the bell for Burton.

The meal seemed to last forever and Arabella found it hard to indulge in small talk while her mind was occupied with worrying about whether Harry had guessed her secret. Beyond greeting her with a brotherly kiss, he had hardly spoken to her. All his attention was directed to Charlotte, who had made no secret of her joy at his safe return.

Arabella tried to tell herself it was a guilty conscience which had caused her apprehension and she turned to her neighbour at the table. With an effort she responded to Major Broomfield's pleasantries and was relieved that he seemed to expect little from her beyond a smile or nod of agreement. To her surprise he proved to be an entertaining companion, although she couldn't help comparing him with Nat.

At last Caroline Raynsford gave the signal for the ladies to leave the room and Charlotte took Arabella's arm as they went into the drawing room. "Doesn't Harry look handsome in his uniform," she said.

"You always say that," Arabella laughed.

"And what about Major Broomfield? You seemed to be getting on very well."

"I was merely being polite," Arabella said.

In the drawing room, she soon became bored with the ladies' conversation and she went and sat at the piano, running her fingers over the keys. She didn't really want to sing tonight, preferring to save her voice for the theatre the following evening, but the guests seemed to expect it. When the men rejoined them, Harry came across to the piano with his friend and picked up some sheets of music that were lying on top of it.

"What are you going to sing for us tonight?" he asked. He turned to the major. "Do you have any preferences, Robert?"

"I heard a song at the theatre the other evening," the major replied. "It's called 'A soldier stood on the battlefield'." He turned to Arabella. "Do you know it, Miss Raynsford?"

"Oh, no, not that one," Arabella said quickly. "It's far too sad. Let's have something more cheerful." She snatched the pages from her brother and started to rifle through them.

Harry began to laugh and she almost dropped the music as she listened to his anecdote. "Did I tell you what happened the other evening as I was returning to barracks? I'd just passed the Half Moon Theatre when I saw a soldier from our regiment accosting a lady. He was being most persistent and I remonstrated with him. As she got into the cab, I realized it was that singer, the one everyone's talking about." Harry laughed again. "The fellow seemed to think he knew her — said it was a girl who'd nursed him out in the Crimea."

Major Broomfield joined in the laughter. "Poor fellow must have been injured in the head. Can you imagine the celebrated Miss Forde nursing in the Crimea?"

Arabella deliberately let the sheet music slide to the floor and stooped to gather it up. So it had been Harry outside the theatre. But had he recognized her? Surely he would have confronted her by now if he had.

When her hands had stopped shaking and her breathing had returned to normal she resumed her seat at the piano.

"I'm going to sing 'My Mother Bids me Bind my Hair'," she announced and began to play. At first her voice wavered and she heard her mother say to her neighbour, "I'm afraid Arabella is out of practice. She has not been well since her return home."

But as usual, once she began to lose herself in the music, her voice gained in strength and she forgot everything around her.

As the last notes died away there was a smattering of polite applause from her mother's guests.

Major Broomfield, who had remained standing beside the piano, bowed over Arabella's hand. "May I say, Miss Raynsford, that your singing surpasses even that of the so-called 'Beautiful Bella'? Dare I hope that you will sing for us again?"

"I'm sorry, sir. I must decline. I am still far from well." She beckoned to Charlotte. "It's your turn now." She gave up her place and went to sit with the guests, avoiding the admiring gaze of Major Broomfield and the quizzical looks from her brother.

Throughout the rest of that interminable evening, as Charlotte clung to Harry's arm and hung on his every word, Arabella managed to avoid talking to him. She couldn't escape the knowing looks he threw in her direction though. It could have been because of the attention Major Broomfield was paying her, but she couldn't help the sinking feeling that he had begun to suspect her secret.

She wasn't left in doubt for long. As she joined her parents in saying goodnight to their guests while they waited for the footman to collect their coats, Harry drew her to one side, gripping her arm and keeping his voice low. "So, did you think I hadn't recognized my little sister?"

It was no use denying it. "Are you going to tell anyone?" she asked, shaking him off and tossing her head as if she did not care.

"I haven't decided yet. Does Charlotte know?"

"Of course not."

"How could you risk your good name like this?" he asked.

"It is safe enough. No one else has guessed." Arabella crossed her fingers at the lie. She suspected that Harry was more worried about advancing his army career than her good name. But she couldn't blame him. He had fought as hard as she had to escape the life mapped out for him by their parents.

She took his hand. "Please, don't say anything," she pleaded.

"You must give up this nonsense," he said.

"I can't."

Charlotte called across the hall. "Harry, we're ready to leave now."

He smiled and nodded. "I'll be with you in a second." He turned back to his sister. "We can't discuss it now. I'll call tomorrow if I can get away."

"We're supposed to be taking tea with Charlotte and her mother."

"Send a message that you are unwell. I'll tell them I am on duty so that we can talk alone."

Once more, Arabella was left to spend a sleepless night, wondering if she was to be exposed. She thought back to their childhood when she and Harry had been so close. When they were in the country they had spent hours together, roaming the woods and hills, watching their father's ships in the harbour, collecting shells on the shore. He had taught her to ride, to sail and shoot with a bow and arrow. They had always been up to some mischief or other to the despair of their mother who deplored her unladylike ways.

Arabella knew that Harry's army career meant a lot to him but she wondered when he had become so stuffy and conventional. Didn't he realize that her singing meant just as much to her? She had to try and make him understand.

CHAPTER
NINETEEN

To his credit, Harry did try to be sympathetic. He turned up in the late afternoon while their father was still at his office and their mother was out visiting.

Arabella rang for tea, making light conversation until the maid had left. But when she was sure they would not be disturbed again she burst into passionate pleading.

"Harry, you mustn't tell. I beg you. Mama will send me to the country, she will make me marry some stuffy gentleman —"

To her surprise, her brother leaned back in his chair, trying to hide his grin. "Don't get yourself in such a lather, little sister. I have no intention of telling."

Before he could say any more, she leaned forward and grasped his hand. "Oh, thank you. I hoped you'd understand. I couldn't bear it if I had to give it all up now."

His face became serious. "You don't mean to carry on, surely? That's not what I meant. Rather, my not telling is on condition that you stop this nonsense."

"Nonsense, is it? How could you say that? I thought you realized how much it means to me. You know how I have always loved to sing."

"Yes, but — in public? In a music hall?" Harry's mouth twisted in repugnance.

"It's a theatre, actually. A most respectable place — as you must know if you've been there." She stood up and began pacing the floor. "I don't understand why it is so bad. The Queen herself attends the theatre. And what about Miss Jenny Lind? She is fêted everywhere she goes and is accepted in the highest circles."

"That's true," Harry said, nodding thoughtfully. "I confess I do not see the difference. But it is not what I think that matters." He put his cup down and stood too, taking her arm. "Please, come and sit down. Try not to get so agitated."

She shook him off but after a moment resumed her seat. "I can't help getting agitated, Harry. It's all very well for you going off with the regiment to far-flung places, free to follow your career. Why should it be different for me just because I'm a girl?"

"It just is," Harry said, sitting opposite her. "I know you think I am only worried about the family name, but I really do understand how you feel." He took her hand. "Surely you must see that you can't carry on like this. For one thing —" He paused and sighed. "You may not like it, but what you do reflects on the rest of us — on me. If you are discovered, it could affect my career. I am due for promotion, and then there's my marriage to Charlotte."

"Oh, it's not fair." Tears welled up and Arabella dabbed at her eyes with her napkin. "I'm sorry, Harry. You know I wouldn't do anything to hurt you or Charlotte."

"Are you sure she doesn't know what you've been up to?"

"Of course."

"How did you get involved in all this?"

Arabella told him about her first visit to the Half Moon Theatre with Maisie. "I only did it for a bit of fun," she said. "I never dreamed I'd be able to carry on."

"This happened before you went out to Scutari?"

Arabella nodded. "I vowed I wouldn't take the risk again. But when we got back, Sam was so pleased. He said everyone had been talking about me. When he asked me to sing again, I couldn't say no."

"Well, you must say no now," Harry insisted. "If not for the family, then for your own good name. You will be found out sooner or later. You have sung for our guests and I know that some of them visit the music halls. The similarity of your voice — not to mention the name. Someone will work it out before long."

He was right, Arabella knew. Perhaps it was time to bring her singing career to an end, hard as it would be. She was about to say so when Harry said. "You do realize that your fiancé is a frequent patron of the halls," he said.

It was a moment before she fully took in his words. In a burst of anger she said, "If you mean Oswald Delaney, I suppose you are not aware that he is no longer my fiancé. Our engagement was never formalised — for which I'm very thankful. If I were to marry him it would cause even more of a scandal than news of my singing on the stage."

Harry's cup jerked in his hand, splashing his uniform breeches. "What do you mean? I have heard nothing to his detriment."

"I thought Papa might have said something."

Harry shook his head. "Tell me."

His eyes widened as Arabella related once more how Oswald had managed to ensnare her in his nefarious schemes. His anger was even greater than their father's had been. "What is being done about him? The man's a traitor."

"He will be arrested as soon as he returns to this country," Arabella assured him. "Sam's policeman friend has alerted the authorities and Mr Sloane is helping."

"I don't understand why Delaney involved you," Harry said.

"He needed a messenger and he knew I would do anything to protect Papa."

"What has Father to do with it?"

Arabella explained and, although Harry found it hard to take it in, he could see how it had happened. "I realized Father's business was in trouble. We knew the copperas seams would be worked out soon and there would be little for me to take over. That's why he gave in and allowed me to join the army instead of following him into the business." He shook his head. "I didn't realize he had mortgaged two of his ships to Delaney though."

"That's the hold Oswald had over him. If I agreed to marry him, he was prepared to let him off the loan and return the ships to Papa. I only discovered this a few days ago." She gave a small laugh. "Perhaps you're wondering why he was so keen on marrying me?"

Harry laughed too. "I know brothers are supposed to say such things, but anyone can see you're quite a catch. You must know that all the chaps in the regiment are in love with you. Why should Delaney be any different?"

Arabella was grateful to him for injecting a lighter note into the conversation but she frowned. "He wasn't in love with me — not really. He was just seeking an advantageous marriage. He felt that linking his name to the Raynsfords would advance him in society."

Harry laughed again. "I almost feel sorry for him — he certainly didn't know what he was letting himself in for."

"He deserves everything he gets," Arabella said.

Her brother nodded and put his cup and saucer down. "Poor Father. He must have been under a great strain trying to keep his troubles from us and carry on as usual. Does Mama know about all this?"

"Yes. She was most upset, of course." Arabella couldn't help a little smile. "I think she was more annoyed about misreading Oswald's character. She had been at such pains to convince me he was a suitable match."

"And now she will have to start all over again husband-hunting for you," Harry teased.

"Oh, no. I have made it quite plain that I must be allowed to choose my own husband or not marry at all."

Harry laughed. "I can imagine dear Mama's reaction to that." He stood up and his face became serious. "I must report for duty now, but I'll find time to talk to Father about this dreadful business. I may be able to help in some way. And you, my dear impulsive little sister — please tell me you will give up this performing nonsense."

"I don't know if I can, Harry," she said sadly.

"At least, try not to take any risks — and not just for my sake." He kissed her cheek and was gone.

In an effort to take her mind off things, Arabella went into her father's study and picked up *The Times* newspaper. Lately, she had been too taken up with her own problems to think about the war and what might be happening out in the Crimea. Harry had told her that since the siege was raised, the two armies were at an impasse. Like last year, the coming of winter also meant an end to any real fighting until the spring. How much longer would it go on?

Her heart sank when she read of the cholera epidemic which had broken out in Scutari. She turned the page and her spirits rose when her eye was caught by the mention of Miss Nightingale. Despite the way she had been dismissed, her admiration for the older woman had not diminished, especially since she'd returned to England and begun to realize how the people at home viewed her. For, despite the continued antipathy of the medical and military establishments, to the mothers and sisters of the soldiers she nursed, Florence Nightingale was a heroine. Arabella couldn't help wishing that things had turned out differently. In a way, she felt she should still be out there, helping to overcome those problems which Miss Nightingale was still encountering.

As she noted the headline in the newspaper she smiled and eagerly read on. A meeting of Miss Nightingale's supporters had decided that she should be recognized for the work she had done. They had agreed that a fund should be set up to establish an institute for the proper training of nurses which would be named in her honour.

"How wonderful," Arabella murmured. "A real victory for her and something to look forward to when she comes home." She jumped up and pulled the bell for the maid. She had to tell Maisie about it. She'd have time to pay her a visit before her parents returned home.

Before she had time to ring, the door opened and the maid appeared holding a silver tray with a card. "Mr Delaney is here, Miss."

Arabella gasped. She couldn't face him yet. "Tell him I'm not at home," she instructed.

But the door was flung back and Oswald strode into the room. "But you *are* at home, aren't you."

"How dare you burst in here?" Arabella's chin went up and she clenched her fists at her side. She turned to the maid. "Fetch Jennings quickly," she said.

The maid nodded and scurried out. As the door closed behind her, Oswald grasped her arms, gripping them painfully. "I warned you, Miss. Now, you must accept the consequences."

"I don't know what you mean." Arabella was shaking. She had been so sure he would be arrested as soon as he reached England. Yet here he was threatening her once more.

"You've been telling tales about me," Oswald said, giving her a shake.

Arabella glared at him defiantly. "I only told the truth. You are a liar and a traitor. I'm surprised you haven't already been arrested."

"So you *are* the one who betrayed me." His hands tightened on her arms. "One of my associates warned me I was in danger of being caught. How did you find out?"

"It wasn't so hard to work out that your business wasn't legitimate. If the letter I carried for you was so innocent why did you need to threaten me? I had my suspicions right from the start."

He gave her another shake and then let his hands drop to his sides. Muttering something about "interfering women", he began to pace the room.

Arabella watched him warily but when he turned back to her he seemed calmer. "Well, my dear, there must be a way out of this dilemma. If you have only suspicions and no proof, you must convince everyone that you made up this story. Perhaps you saw it as a way to break our engagement." He nodded and smoothed his moustache. "Yes, I'm sure you can do it — after all, you are quite the performer, as we know."

As she opened her mouth to make an angry retort the door opened and Jennings came in. "Is everything all right, Miss?" he asked.

Oswald laughed. "Just a lovers' tiff, Jennings," he said.

The butler looked at Arabella. "Are you sure, Miss?"

"Yes. You may leave us."

The butler bowed and retreated to the door. Before he closed it, Arabella called. "The minute my father gets home, could you tell him Mr Delaney is here."

She turned back to Oswald. "Shall we sit down and discuss this calmly?" she said.

"Very sensible, my dear."

They sat facing each other, neither speaking for a few minutes. Arabella's thoughts raced. Sergeant Keen had assured her that Delaney would be arrested as soon as he returned to England. How had he managed to evade the authorities? She daren't ask without revealing how much she really knew about his activities.

"I heard you were in Paris," she said striving to keep her voice even.

"I was only there for a few days. Lady Masterson said you were there, visiting friends. When I couldn't discover where you were staying I returned to Ireland. I had some business to attend to."

"I see." So that was how he had evaded arrest. The police had been looking out for him at Dover. Arabella stifled a gasp as something else occurred to her. She knew there had been some trouble in Ireland and remembered reading in the newspaper about a group called the Fenians. Was Oswald connected with them, supplying them with gunpowder too? It would explain why he felt no compunction in betraying the English and Scottish troops fighting out in the Crimea.

"I took the ferry from Dublin and came down on the railway train. It got me here much faster than the coach. I couldn't wait to see you again, my dear."

254

He smiled but there was a cruel twist to his lips and Arabella wondered how she could ever have thought him charming. He was trying to exert that charm now, leaning forward and earnestly mouthing compliments. But Arabella hardly listened. If he hated the English so, why was he determined to marry into an English family? It wasn't for money, since he knew her father was almost ruined. But it would be the perfect cover — a respectable family with a son in the army.

Rage almost boiled over and she longed to lunge at him, to rake her fingernails down that sneering face. But she maintained her outward calm, hoping that he would think she was swayed by his words. Anything to keep him here until her father got home.

He took one of her hands and she tried not to flinch. "So, you see, my dear, there is no need for us to quarrel. I will keep your little secret if you will keep mine. It is not such a bad bargain, after all."

Nat left the Half Moon boiling with frustration. He'd hoped to see Arabella as well as to find out if there was any news of Delaney's whereabouts. But he'd been disappointed on both counts.

He hadn't seen Arabella since their disagreement and he still wasn't sure how she'd react when they next met. But he desperately wanted to apologize and reassure her that he wasn't shocked at all by her singing. To his disappointment, he'd learned from Sam that Arabella had returned to her parents' home a few weeks previously. It seemed that her family still hadn't found out what she'd been up to and so far she had managed to leave the house on the nights she was scheduled to perform at the Half Moon without any problems.

"She's on again tomorrow night," Sam said and Nat resolved to attend the performance and speak to her in the interval.

As for Delaney, Sam said there was still no news although it was believed that he was no longer in Paris. Sergeant Keen had reported that a watch was being kept at Dover, the most likely place he would enter the country.

Where was the man, and what was he up to? Nat ground his teeth. He had a new project that he should be starting work on soon. But first he must make sure that Arabella and the Raynsfords were safe from the Irishman's machinations.

He turned his coat collar up against the cold and jammed his hat further onto his head. He'd try to see Arabella's father and find out if he had any news. He would probably be at his club, Nat thought, turning his steps in that direction. It would have been quicker to take a cab but he needed the time to gather his thoughts.

As he strode along, thoughts of Arabella invaded his mind and his heart beat a little faster. He didn't care about her singing, about her involvement with Delaney or the fact that her parents would probably oppose their match. He had to see her and declare his love for her.

If she rejected him, he would return to the Crimea and throw himself into his work, heedless of any

256

danger. But first he would make sure that Delaney got his just deserts.

Henry Raynsford had just left his club and was about to step into a cab when Nat got there. He hurried forward and, taking off his hat, shook the older man's hand. "Any news, sir?" he asked.

Henry shook his head. "I was hoping you'd have heard something."

"I've just come from the Fentons's," Nat said. "Sergeant Keen was there but he couldn't tell me anything."

"The man seems to have disappeared completely. But I'm sure he will try to contact me if he manages to slip into the country unobserved. He'll want to make sure my debt to him is repaid." He smiled bitterly, gesturing at the cab. "Why don't you come home with me? I'm sure Arabella will be pleased to see you."

Nat felt himself colouring. So Henry had guessed that he was in love with her. He hardly dared hope that the older man's words meant that Arabella felt the same way.

During the short cab ride Henry made small talk but Nat hardly listened. His heart was beating faster at the thought of seeing Arabella, wondering how he would greet her and if she had forgiven him for his outburst the last time they met.

Jennings met them at the front door, saying in a low voice, "Mr Delaney is here, sir."

"Where is he, the scoundrel?" Nat would have pushed past him but Henry grabbed his arm.

"Don't be so hasty, Sloane," he said, turning to the butler. "Where is he now?"

"In the drawing room with Miss Arabella. I tried to stop him entering, sir, but he pushed past me. I was reluctant to leave them alone but Miss Arabella said she was all right. I told the boot boy to stand outside the door and if he heard anything untoward to fetch me immediately. I hope I did the right thing, sir," Jennings said anxiously.

"Yes, of course. Thank you, Jennings." Henry turned to Nat. "Fetch Sergeant Keen. I'll try to keep him here, lull his suspicions. Go on, man, hurry."

Nat didn't want to go. How could he leave, knowing that Arabella was alone with Delaney? But Henry was right. The policeman would know the best course of action.

He hurried down the steps, praying that he'd quickly find a cab to take him back to the Half Moon where Davie Keen was spending his day off in company with Maisie and the Fentons.

Arabella's eyes constantly flicked towards the door. She hoped Jennings would obey her instruction to let her father know that Oswald was here. Surely he'd send for Davie Keen and her nightmare would be over. Why wasn't he home yet? And where was her mother?

Oswald noticed her agitation and laughed. "Your parents won't be any help to you. If you so much as open your mouth to say anything other than a polite greeting your secret will be out. I mean what I say. You

258

will be ruined, my dear. No respectable man will want you once it becomes known what you've been up to."

Arabella tossed her head in pretended indifference. But she did not reply. She wanted to tell him that his threats meant nothing, that she didn't care so long as he was punished for the misery he had inflicted on her family. She was sure her father would have weathered his financial difficulties if Oswald had not interfered. But she knew that once she unleashed an angry outburst she might not be able to stop herself from saying too much. Better to let him think she was still intimidated by him.

The door opened and she looked up, expecting to see one of the servants but to her relief her father entered the room.

Before she could speak, he strode across to Oswald, hand outstretched. "Ah, Delaney, you're back then. I trust you had a pleasant journey." He gave a little chuckle. "I see my wife has not returned home yet. So — you young people have been alone." He stroked his moustache and chuckled again. "Still, as you are to be wed —"

"Papa —" Arabella threw him an imploring glance and he came towards her, taking her hands and kissing her cheek.

"Arabella, my dear, you have not offered Mr Delaney any refreshment. Why don't you ring for the maid?"

When she opened her mouth to protest he kept hold of her hands and tightened his hold. "I know we are expecting guests for dinner but I'm sure we can find room for one more." He turned to Oswald. "You will stay, won't you, sir?"

Arabella knew that the family were to dine alone that evening and she smiled at her father, giving a small nod to show that she had interpreted his message. She had guessed that the guests he referred to were Sergeant Keen and his colleagues. "Yes, please stay, Oswald. We have much to talk about," she said with a smile as she rang the bell for the maid.

She gave the order for refreshments, asking the maid to inform cook that that there would be one more for dinner. She sat down between her father and the man she had come to hate, marvelling at Henry's calm exterior as he asked polite questions about Oswald's journey and their mutual business dealings.

As time passed, the conversation flagged and Arabella noticed her father glancing more frequently at the clock on the mantel. He was clearly expecting someone to arrive. Had he sent Jennings or one of the footmen to fetch Sergeant Keen? Her impatience and excitement grew. At last, Oswald was going to pay for his crimes. She only hoped that his arrest would be swift and he wouldn't be given the chance to blurt out any counter-accusations.

If Oswald noticed her agitation he gave no sign, maintaining his air of urbane charm as he recounted an anecdote concerning one if his Irish tenants.

When the door opened at last Arabella jumped up. But it was Jennings announcing the arrival of Mr Sloane.

"Nat," she whispered. What was he doing here? And where were the police?

"Good evening, Sloane," said Henry. "You are the first to arrive."

"The others will be here soon, sir," Nat said. He bowed formally, acknowledging Arabella and Delaney.

"Business acquaintances," Henry explained. He turned to Jennings. "Is my wife home yet?" he asked.

"The mistress went straight up to change for dinner, sir," said the butler, bowing and leaving the room.

Arabella noticed that he had left the door ajar but her father, who was closest made no attempt to close it. When he spoke his voice sounded louder and more hearty than usual.

"Well, Sloane, what news?"

"It seems you were right, sir," said Nat. "The *Lady Caroline* was intercepted in the Thames, laden with ammunition and, as we suspected, it was not bound for our troops in the Crimea. The captain confessed — his destination was Odessa and that port is still in Russian hands."

Arabella gasped. "But the *Lady Caroline* is one of your ships, father," she said.

"Not any longer, my dear. That fine vessel now belongs to Mr Delaney." He turned to Oswald. "That's so, isn't it? Can you deny that you are supplying munitions to England's enemy?"

Oswald stood up and began to bluster. "I had no knowledge of this — I assure you. It must be a mistake."

As he continued to protest his innocence, his eyes flicked towards the drawing room door. At the same time, he was gradually edging in the direction of the French windows.

Arabella glimpsed a movement in the hall outside and hoped that it was Davie Keen. What was he waiting for? Oswald was nearer the window now. She couldn't let him escape.

Was Davie hoping to hear a confession? She decided to try and goad Oswald into speaking. "What about the messages I carried for you — and that man I met in the market in Constantinople?" she asked.

He smirked. "I thought I explained to you, my dear. He is a business colleague."

"A *Russian* business colleague, Delaney?" Nat spoke up. "Don't try to deny it — I saw you with the man myself."

"Spying on me, eh? I knew I couldn't trust you." He turned to Arabella, venom in his eyes. "As for you, Miss. I warned you what would happen if you spoke out."

"I don't care," Arabella spat, her eyes sparking defiance.

Nat laid a hand on her arm. "Leave Arabella out of this," he said.

"Arabella is it?" Oswald's lips curled in a sneer. "Don't you mean Bella Forde — the celebrated music hall performer?"

CHAPTER
TWENTY

Arabella was locked in her room, forbidden to talk to anyone, her dinner brought to her in silence on a tray by the maid, Burton.

She had wept herself dry, her eyes red-rimmed and sore, her face blotchy, hair awry where she had torn at it in frustration. Broken ornaments and jars littered the room, thrown in a temper when no one answered her outraged screams.

Her only consolation was that seconds after Oswald's drastic revelation, Sergeant Keen and his men had burst into the room and overpowered the traitor. If only her mother had not chosen to enter the room at the moment of Oswald's revelation, she might have managed to talk her way out of things.

At first Caroline Raynsford had refused to believe her daughter capable of such deceit but Oswald would not be silenced. Struggling against the restraint of two burly policemen, he insisted on revealing the details of Arabella's double life.

"Oh, yes," he said. "She may have tried to disguise herself but I recognized her straight away. You would not believe the salacious remarks I heard outside the theatre while I waited for her. The stage door johnnies were out in force, all wanting the favours of the Beautiful Bella." Oswald's lips twisted in a sneer and he would have said more.

Henry interrupted his tirade. "If you had discovered what my daughter was doing, why did you not inform me? As her fiancé, did you not feel you had a duty to stop her from ruining her life?"

"He's not my fiancé — I've already said I won't marry him. And, Papa, how can you think of such a thing now that you know he is a traitor?"

Caroline's face blanched and she clutched her husband's arm for support. She gave a weak moan. "No one will marry her if word of this gets out." She seemed more concerned with her daughter's reputation than the fact that her husband had been doing business with a criminal. "How will we ever live this down?"

Oswald spoke confidently. "No one need ever know. Withdraw the charges against me, make these peelers let me go — tell them you were mistaken."

Davie Keen stepped forward. "Enough of that sort of talk. We have enough on you to make a charge." He nodded to the policemen. "Take him away."

"I'll see that the name of Raynsford is ruined," Oswald screamed as, still struggling and mouthing obscenities, he was marched outside, down the steps and into the closed carriage that would take him to police headquarters.

In the silence that followed, Arabella moved towards her mother. "I'm so sorry, Mama —"

Caroline pushed her away. "You wicked girl. I always knew you were wilful and disobedient but I never dreamed you would risk your reputation — let alone that of your family. How could you?"

"I just wanted to sing," Arabella said, a catch in her voice.

"Well, you will sing no more — certainly not in this house or anywhere else. Go to your room at once."

"Please, let me explain."

When she refused to move, Caroline grabbed her arm and hustled her out of the room. Her fingers pinched Arabella's arm as she almost dragged her up the stairs, pushing her into her room and slamming the door.

Now Arabella sat on the edge of her bed surveying the damage she'd wrought and trying to sort out her muddled feelings. Was the anger she'd felt because she'd been found out? Or was it the fact that Nat had been a witness to her humiliation?

She sighed and began to gather up the broken pieces of china. It was her own fault. Hadn't she always known she'd be found out one day? She should have come straight home from Scutari and never gone near the Half Moon theatre again. But she'd known from the first moment she stepped on to the stage that first night that it was what she wanted. She'd always loved singing, but pretty drawing room songs sung to an indifferent piano accompaniment, while a would-be suitor turned the pages of the music, could not compare with the euphoria she experienced when she went on stage. The hush that descended over the auditorium as she began to sing, the glorious sounds floating up to the gods, the tumultuous applause as the notes died away — this was what she lived for.

Would she ever know that feeling again? She must. Even while she'd been working at the hospital she had dreamed of returning to her true career, as she thought of it. She couldn't bear the thought of giving it all up.

Why didn't anyone understand? Even Nat . . .

She sat back on her heels, clutching a broken china figurine and tears welled up again. She had hoped that Nat, at least, would understand. He had seemed less bound by convention than most of the young men she knew. But she couldn't forget the way he had almost spat her assumed name at her as he'd left the theatre the last time she had seen him. And he had hardly spoken to her at all during the recent confrontation with Oswald.

She went over to the window and looked out across the square. It had begun to rain and a misty halo surrounded the globe of the gas lamp on the corner of the street. There were few people about and Arabella had the wild thought that if she climbed out of the window and ran away no one would see her — or care.

A half laugh, half sob escaped her. Where would she go? She'd be welcome at the Half Moon but that was the first place anyone would look for her. Looking down at the steep drop on to the spiked railings below, she knew it had indeed been a wild thought.

She threw herself on the bed again. Well, they couldn't keep her locked up forever. When they'd decided what to do with her, they would let her out. They were sure to try and marry her off — probably to a stuffy old widower in the country where she'd be hidden away until the scandal died down.

But she couldn't wait for that to happen. She went to the door and once more began pounding on it, screaming at the top of her voice, "Let me out, let me out."

In the shocked silence that followed Arabella's ejection from the room, Nat gave an embarrassed cough. He wished he had not been here to witness Arabella's humiliation or her parents' discomfiture at Oswald Delaney's revelation.

He hoped they would not disown their daughter completely. Naturally they were scandalized, but in Nat's opinion it was the deceit that was more shocking than the action. He stood up and prepared to leave.

"Don't go, Sloane," Henry said, going to the sideboard and lifting a decanter. "Have a drink. Dinner will be served when my wife comes downstairs."

"I think I should go, sir. You and Mrs Raynsford will surely wish to be alone."

Henry waved a hand, motioning Nat to remain seated, and handed him a glass. "Well, what do you think of this business, eh?" he asked.

Nat wasn't sure if he was referring to Delaney's arrest or his daughter's theatrical career. He took a sip of the whisky and said diplomatically, "It's a good thing he's been caught."

"Yes, yes, of course. I'm as relieved as you are. But I'm talking about Arabella. Did you know what she was up to?"

Nat wanted to protect her and settled on a half truth. "I guessed. The voices are similar. And I'd seen her at the Fenton's — the people who own the music hall. Arabella's former maid is related to them. I thought she was just visiting. Even now, I'm not really sure —"

"She did not deny it. And Delaney seemed very confident." But Henry's voice wavered as if he was reluctant to believe his darling daughter had deceived them all.

"Delaney could have been trying to deflect attention from himself," Nat said.

"Maybe, and yet —" Henry gave a short laugh. "I always knew she had spirit. Clever too. It must have taken some ingenuity to trick us all."

There was a tinge of pride in his voice and Nat smiled. He'd always admired Arabella's spirit too.

Henry sighed. "Her mother will never forgive her though. She had such ambitions for her." He lowered his voice. "Mrs Raynsford wanted to rise in society. She wanted me to stand for Parliament, had high hopes of my being awarded a knighthood. But I had no such ambition. And when she realized her hopes were to be dashed, her aspirations fastened on our daughter."

"I'm truly sorry, sir. But at least she must be thankful that Arabella had not yet married Delaney before he was found out. Surely that would have meant a greater scandal. As it is, only a few people know Bella Forde's real identity. I certainly will not reveal it to a soul."

Henry drained his glass, got up and refilled it. "I know I can trust you, Sloane," he said, looking shrewdly at the young engineer. "You are fond of my daughter, aren't you?"

Nat blushed. This was his opportunity. He looked Henry in the eye. "I love her, sir. I have from the moment I saw her. But when I heard of her betrothal I tried to forget her." He toyed with his glass and went on, "Out in Turkey I saw her devotion to the sick men in her care, heard her sweet voice lulling them to sleep. It was then I knew I could not forget her, that I truly loved her."

"Would you marry her — even knowing what you do about her?"

Nat's heart started to thump. He could hardly believe what he'd heard. "Yes — yes, I would," he gasped. But then his whole body sagged as he remembered Arabella tenderly cradling the dying Captain Wilson. Could he really believe what Henry had told him earlier — that James had been like a brother to her? Or was he anxious to get his daughter married off before there was any hint of scandal?

He stood up and spoke firmly. "It's true I love Arabella and want to marry her, but only if she is agreeable. I would not coerce her if she is grieving over the death of another man."

"Naturally, it would have to be with Arabella's consent."

Before Nat could reply, Caroline came into the room. She seemed unnaturally calm after the disturbance and merely inclined her head at Nat's greeting. "I thought we were dining alone," she said to Henry. "But since Mr Sloane is here —"

"I have already invited him to stay and informed the servants of the extra guest," Henry said.

"Nat realized that they were trying to maintain a semblance of normality and, playing along with them, asked if Miss Arabella would be joining them."

"She is unwell and will have a tray in her room," Caroline said.

Seated at the dining table, she continued to behave as if this was just an ordinary evening, talking about the weather, the setting up of the Nightingale Fund and her pleasure that Harry was home from the Crimea and unlikely to be sent out again.

Nat responded as best he could but his thoughts were on Arabella, hustled up to her room and, most likely, ordered to stay there until her mother had decided what to do with her. He wondered why Henry had not mentioned their earlier conversation to his wife. Surely she would agree that a marriage between him and their daughter would be the best solution to the problem.

He daren't broach the subject himself and decided to give them time to discuss it in private, concentrating on his food and only looking up when Caroline asked him how long he would be in London.

"I must return to Balaclava soon," he said. "I had almost finished my work there but I felt I must return to England to make sure that Delaney was exposed for the traitor he is. Now that he has been arrested I can go back."

"What about the trial?" Henry asked. "You'll be asked to give evidence."

270

"I'll be back for that. I believe that the war is almost over. There may be the odd skirmish or two but the Russians know they are beaten. They have withdrawn from Sebastopol —"

Caroline fluttered a hand. "No more talk of the war — please."

Nat apologized and Caroline asked him where his work would take him afterwards. "I do not have a project in mind as yet," he said. "My contract with the army has a few months to run. But I am thinking of going to America — it is a land of opportunity for men in my profession. Railways, bridges, new buildings going up in the cities." His voice rose with enthusiasm.

"But you will visit us before you leave?" Henry asked. "We still have much to discuss."

Nat reassured him but he was disappointed that, even after Caroline left the men to their port, the subject of Arabella was not raised again.

As he left Essex House, he glanced up at the windows overlooking the square, wondering which was her room. He thought he saw a shadow moving behind the drawn shades and tried to picture her there.

Turning away, he trudged through the rain to his lonely lodgings, wondering if Caroline Raynsford would agree to her husband's suggestion. Even more importantly, would Arabella agree? Whatever else happened though, he was determined to see her again before he embarked for the continent once more.

CHAPTER
TWENTY-ONE

Arabella sat in a chair by the window, gazing out at the murky afternoon, hoping that Charlotte would come to call. Mama would have to let her out then. She couldn't keep her locked up forever.

It had been three days since Oswald's arrest and she had spoken to no one except her mother's maid in that time. Burton had kept silent, depositing the tray on the bedside table and taking away the dirty crockery, her disapproval evident.

The older woman must have heard her quarrel with Mama and drawn her own conclusions. She could just imagine the gossip below stairs.

When the key turned in the lock, she didn't bother to turn round until her mother spoke.

"Make yourself presentable and come downstairs," she said, turning away before Arabella could ask any questions.

She tidied her hair, smoothed her dress and started down the stairs, her mouth dry with apprehension. Was she about to discover her punishment for deceiving her parents?

She sighed with relief when she saw Sergeant Keen standing in the hall, his hat tucked under his arm. He was accompanied by a stout, older man in a dark suit. "Good afternoon, Miss Raynsford. This is Inspector White from the special police section that I told you about. He is investigating the case of Mr Delaney. We need to take a statement from you."

Henry appeared in the doorway of the library. "I hope you are feeling better, my dear," he said, taking her hand. He turned to the two men. "I fear this dreadful business has taken its toll of my daughter's health. She has kept to her room since that man's arrest." He patted Arabella's hand. "They will not keep you long, my dear. Come through to the library, gentlemen; there is a good fire in there."

Arabella followed him, gasping as she saw who was already there.

Nat had been leaning against the mantel but he came towards her and greeted her formally. She managed a smile and hoped he would not notice how breathless she was. She had thought him long gone — back to Sebastopol or Constantinople.

His warm smile gave her hope. He had tried to protect her from Oswald's accusations and it seemed he did not find her actions so scandalous, or surely he would not be here.

She sat down and the two policemen sat opposite. Sergeant Keen took a small notebook from his pocket, licked his pencil and said, "Tell the inspector exactly what you told me, Miss."

She looked to her parents, not sure how to begin. Her mother stood behind her chair, tight-lipped. Her father nodded encouragement.

She started with Oswald's request that she should deliver a letter for him when she reached Constantinople. "I did not see any wrong in it," she said. "He assured me that the man was a business colleague and that since the post was so unreliable he wanted to be sure of the letter's safe arrival."

The inspector leaned forward in his chair. "I see — go on."

When it came to the encounter in the souk she began to falter. She glanced at Nat, unwilling to involve him. But he smiled and gave a small nod.

"Mr Sloane came to my rescue. It was a terrifying experience," she said.

"I'm sure it was. Mr Sloane has already told us his part in all this. Now we need you to corroborate his words." The inspector turned to Davie. "I hope you are getting all this down, sergeant."

"Yes, sir." Davie continued to scribble furiously, pausing occasionally to lick his pencil again.

There wasn't much more she could tell them. "When I returned to England, I told Davie — Sergeant Keen — what had happened and asked his advice. I tried to put it out of my mind but I knew Oswald would blame me if he was caught out. He threatened to tell —" Her voice faltered and in a whisper she confessed to her secret career on the stage of the Half Moon. It was easier now that her parents and Nat already knew about it. She was probably now the talk of London and she told herself she didn't care, but she still blushed when the inspector stared at her.

274

However, there was no condemnation in his eyes. "It was very courageous of you to stand up to Delaney. Many people would have given in to his blackmail."

"I almost did," Arabella confessed. "I knew how upset my mother would be when she found out —" Her voice faltered and she glanced round at her mother. "I'm truly sorry, Mama."

Caroline's face remained impassive but, as the inspector stood up and Davie replaced his notebook in his pocket, she said, "I hope you will not need to speak to my daughter again. This ordeal has taken its toll on her health and I am taking her to the country to give her time to recover."

"There will be a trial, no doubt, but I do not think Miss Raynsford will be called to give evidence." Inspector White turned to Arabella. "Thank you for your cooperation, Miss."

As the policemen turned to leave, Arabella said, "Davie, please tell Maisie I wish you both well and thank her for being such a good friend."

"I will, Miss."

Nat made his farewells at the same time, taking Arabella's hand and squeezing it as he said, with more formality than usual, "I am sorry for all your trouble. I must return to the Crimea soon, but I hope you will allow me to call on my return."

Had she imagined the look in his eyes — a look that spoke more than words? She smiled, unable to answer for the lump in her throat.

Henry said in his bluff way, "You're always welcome here, Sloane."

Caroline said nothing but when they'd gone, she turned to Arabella, her face white with fury. "I never knew such shame. Policemen in our house, all and sundry knowing our affairs. Why couldn't you be like Charlotte, settle down and marry a suitable man?"

Arabella could not stop herself retorting, "Like the suitable man you chose for me?"

Caroline raised her hand as if to slap her daughter's face, but Henry restrained her. "Now, my dear, we were taken in by Delaney too. And, as for this other business, well —" He turned to Arabella. "Go upstairs and stay there. And tell Burton to start packing. You and your mother leave for Whitstable early tomorrow."

Hands tightly clenched at her sides, Arabella left the room without answering.

Her heart beat faster as she mounted the stairs to her own room. She should have been feeling unhappy at the thought of Nat's departure, as well as the fact that she was to be whisked off to the country with no opportunity to see her friends before she left.

But clasped in her fist was the piece of paper that Nat had passed to her as he shook hands in a formal goodbye.

In her room, she sat at her dressing table and, with trembling hands, unfolded it. She gasped and could scarcely read on as the first words leapt out at her: "*My own dearest Bella,*"

"Dearest," she repeated, smiling. So he did love her.

She read on: "*I have spoken to your father and he is in favour of us marrying — but only if you are in agreement. Dare I hope that you are? Dearest, Bella,* do say yes. As I said, your father agrees but, unfortunately, your mother is adamant. I have a plan which may help to sway her. Can you wait until I return? I do hope so. I could see that you were longing to rebel when your mother said you were going to the country. But please do not let your impulsive nature lead you to do anything in haste. I know how much your singing means to you, but if you persist, your parents may take more drastic action. I will come to see you in Whitstable when I return from Sebastopol and then I will tell you of my plan. I am sure your adventurous spirit will delight in what I propose.

"I love you, my darling Bella, and have done since the first time I saw you. Your devoted and adoring, Nathaniel Sloane."

Arabella kissed the paper where he'd signed his name and clasped the letter to her bosom. She wanted to run, to dance, to sing.

The door opened abruptly and Burton stood there. "Mistress says I'm to pack," she said.

Carefully composing her features, Arabella turned round. "Yes. Mama and I are going down to the country tomorrow. Pack whatever you like. I don't care." She put on a sulky rebellious tone to match her face. She was sure that the maid reported to her mother and she didn't want her telling tales of sparkling eyes and light-hearted smiles.

The journey to the Raynsfords's country house on the hills above the little harbour town had been even more tedious than usual. This time there was no Nat to

277

relieve the boredom and Arabella passed the time reliving that earlier journey eighteen months ago. That was when she had begun to fall in love.

Nat was so different from the other young men she had met, treating her like a real person instead of just an empty-headed society girl. She had been captivated by his enthusiasm for his work, his interest in the world around him, and, not least, by the fact that he listened to her and seemed interested in her opinions.

His frequent visits to Whitstable during the lovely summer of 1854 had strengthened her feelings. But she had, from a sense of duty, stifled them as best she could. She was promised to Oswald Delaney and at first she had been almost sure she would honour that promise. It was only when she realized that the man was no better than a criminal that she had vowed that no amount of coercion — from her parents or from Delaney's threats — would force her to marry him.

So much had happened since then and there had been times when she had doubted Nat too. But now, as the coach rumbled through the bleak winter landscape of north Kent, she mentally re-read his letter and allowed herself to hope that she might have a future with him.

This time life at Mill House was different. There were no house parties or trips to the Assembly Rooms in Canterbury. Arabella mostly kept to her room, unable to face her mother's constant recriminations. She spent the time writing long letters to Nat — letters which were never sent.

For weeks there was no news from London — and no word from Nat either. The excitement of Oswald's arrest as well as Nat's revelation that he loved her might never have happened. Only his letter, much creased from constant re-reading, was a tangible reminder of his declaration of love.

Christmas passed quietly. Harry came down from London for a few days, accompanied by his father, and Arabella hoped that Charlotte would join them to liven things up. But she had remained at home with her mother who had been unwell. It was plain that Harry couldn't wait to return to his fiancée.

"I only had a few days' leave anyway," he apologized, as he said goodbye.

When he'd gone, Arabella, still in disgrace, relapsed into sulky silence. After a few days, her father said that he, too, must go back to London. Arabella begged him to allow her to go with him.

"No, my dear. It's best you stay here a little longer. Delaney's trial takes place in a couple of weeks and I fear he will try to implicate you. Down here, the scandal will not touch you. We'll think about your return when it's all over."

Caroline agreed with her husband, although it was clear she wasn't happy in the country either. She missed the social round of visits, balls and musical soirées. Blaming Arabella, she took her displeasure out on her daughter, losing no opportunity to point out her shortcomings.

Things might have continued in this way. But in late January a letter arrived from Henry. Arabella had reluctantly come down to breakfast and was picking at a plate of kedgeree, disappointed that once more there was no letter from Nat.

Caroline opened her own letter, gasping in dismay.

Arabella looked up, her interest piqued. "What is it?" she asked.

"It's from your father," she said.

"What does it say?" Arabella asked eagerly.

"There's been a verdict in Delaney's trial."

"Was he found guilty?"

Caroline skimmed the page and turned it over. "Oh no. I can't believe it. Your father says the case was dismissed."

"I don't understand. He must be guilty." Arabella's stomach churned and she pushed her plate away. Delaney was no longer in prison. Would he try to get his revenge on her for betraying him? For, in spite of the judge's decision, she knew that he was guilty.

Her mother finished reading the letter and sighed with relief. "There was insufficient evidence to convict him. But your father says that Inspector White has been to see him. He told him that, knowing there was a chance Delaney would go free, they agreed to dismiss the case on condition he returned to Ireland and never came back to England again. The inspector personally escorted him onto the boat."

"Thank goodness," Arabella said.

Caroline put the letter down and, for the first time in months, smiled at her daughter. "Perhaps now we can put this whole business behind us and start afresh. I have been so worried about you, wondering what the future holds for you. I thank the lord that your engagement to that awful man was never formalized. Now, we can set about bringing you into society again. I'm sure that before long you will meet an eligible young man. There are many such among your brother's fellow officers."

"No, Mama. I have said I do not want to marry."

"Don't talk such nonsense." The pursed lips were back. "I have tried to be patient with you. I have forgiven your disgraceful behaviour. Now, you must do as I say." She softened and leaned forward to touch Arabella's hand. "What other future is there for a girl of your station? I know I made a mistake about Delaney — but we were all taken in by him."

"I never was. I knew what he was like right from the start." It wasn't entirely true. Arabella remembered her first sight of him and his charming smile. But it hadn't taken long for her to recognize the cruelty behind the smile.

"I know you were reluctant," Caroline conceded. "It occurred to me that could have been the reason you acted as you did. Maybe you thought that he would not agree to marry you if he discovered you'd been singing in public. Of course, I blame that girl. She encouraged you to rebel."

"It wasn't Maisie's fault. Yes, she helped me. But it was all my idea. And I'm not sorry. I'd do it again —" Arabella almost began to cry.

Caroline pushed her chair back with an angry exclamation. "Well, you won't get the chance. You'll stay here until you come to your senses."

The brief moment of empathy was over and Arabella, knowing she'd never get her mother to understand, retreated to her room once more. But as the days lengthened, bringing bright sunny days, her mood lightened. Surely there would be word from Nat soon. The war in the Crimea was over although the peace treaty had not yet been signed, but at least the fighting was done.

Harry came down a couple of weeks later to say that all London was celebrating the end of the war and the imminent homecoming of the military.

"Thank goodness it was over before you had to return," Caroline said.

"I won't be home forever though. When you're a soldier you must be prepared to go anywhere," Harry said. "But I hope Charlotte and I can get married before my next posting abroad."

"A spring wedding," Caroline said smiling.

Already the daffodils were piercing the frosty grass under the apple trees and each day the sun had more warmth. While their mother corresponded with Charlotte's mother making plans for the wedding, Arabella strolled with her brother in the grounds of the house, looking down the hill towards the grey waters of the North Sea which today were sparkling in the sun.

"I'm so pleased you're here," she said. "I was so bored with just Mama for company. She hardly speaks to me and every time I look up from reading or sewing she is glaring at me with her lips pursed."

282

"Can you blame her?" Harry asked. "I warned you how it would be if they found out. Fortunately, the word has not spread."

"I suppose that pleases you, at any rate," Arabella said with a toss of her head. She was still smarting from her brother's inference that her actions could affect his army career.

"I confess I was worried. But it's you I'm thinking of, Bella. First there was your disastrous engagement to that man —" Harry almost spat the words. "You must see that any further scandal would ruin your chances of a good marriage."

"Marriage! That's all anyone thinks about. Mama is already talking of finding another suitor."

"I just want you to be happy."

"Singing makes me happy," Arabella said softly.

Harry took her hand. "Dear sister, no one is saying you cannot sing — merely that you should confine yourself to entertaining our guests."

"It's not the same."

Harry shook his head. It was no use; she'd never be able to make him understand. But Nat did. With the thought, her spirits rose and she fingered Nat's letter, which she always carried with her and which was now hidden in her muff.

With the war over, he would soon be home and they could start planning their future. She wondered what the plan was that he had referred to. Did he want them to elope? The thought was exhilarating but where would they go? And would he allow her to return to London and grace the stage of the Half Moon theatre once more? Nat had said he saw no shame in her singing in public. But it might be different once they were married.

As she returned to the house with Harry, their footsteps crunching on the frosty grass, they were both silent. Despite their closeness, Arabella knew that her brother would never reconcile himself to her rebellion against convention. She was sad at the thought. But it concerned her less than the fact that Nat might agree with him.

CHAPTER
TWENTY-TWO

Once Harry had returned to London, Arabella relapsed into boredom again. She wished she could escape the confines of the house. But Caroline, while not allowing her to go out alone, refused to accompany her when she wanted to go into town. Her mother was still coldly uncommunicative unless she was berating her with tears and recriminations.

"I cannot face the thought of running into any of our acquaintances," she said.

"But, since there was no trial, no one knows about Oswald — especially here —" Arabella protested.

"You know that is not what concerns me. People will ask why we have come down at this time of the year, and why we are not entertaining. They will want to know when you are getting married." Caroline held a handkerchief to her lips. "I cannot bear the thought of any hint of scandal."

"Mama, how many times must I say I'm sorry? Besides, if word had got out you may be sure our friends and neighbours would be calling just to get a glimpse of the notorious Bella."

"Do not mock, girl. I don't think you really understand how deeply this whole affair has hurt me. And then there's the worry over your father."

"What about father? Is he ill?" Arabella asked, already regretting her flippant words.

"He is worried about his business. Now that the copperas works has closed down —"

"But he still has the ships."

"Only one now. As you know, he mortgaged two of them to Delaney and another has been sold to pay debts. We may even lose this house and I couldn't bear that — for your father's sake. Mill House has been in the Raynsford family for over a hundred years. Losing his ships is bad enough but —"

It was unusual for her mother to talk about such matters and Arabella had had no idea that things were so bad. Business was discussed by men over brandy after the ladies had retired, or in their club. It wasn't done to involve their wives.

"I'm sure things can't be as bad as that," she said in an effort to comfort her mother. She didn't care for herself. She had always taken her comfortable life for granted — the servants, the London house, the place in the country, the generous dress allowance. But since those months at the hospital in Scutari, such things had ceased to be important. And when she'd returned to London to lodge with the Fentons she had seen that their way of life, though nothing like what she was used to, had much to commend it.

But for Caroline Raynsford, the loss of status would be devastating. When they were in the country she took

286

every opportunity to mention their "town house". And when in London, their place in the country featured often in conversation. By marrying Henry, Caroline had taken a step upwards and she'd had ambitions to rise even higher. Hadn't Arabella often heard her declare proudly that one day Henry would stand for Parliament, might even be awarded a knighthood?

Arabella began to think that if only she'd stayed at home and married Oswald as her parents wished, everything would have been all right — for her family at least. Her father would have got his ships back and been able to pay his debts. No one would ever have known of Oswald's perfidious behaviour and her own secret would have been safe.

Would it have been worth it for her parents' peace of mind? As Arabella was about to say so, she stopped herself. No, she had done the right thing in exposing him. It didn't matter what happened to her or her family, at least Delaney was no longer free to continue his treachery.

But she couldn't leave her mother worrying like this. It was time for one last confession. "Mother, will we really lose the house?" she asked.

"It's possible. Oh, I know you will say we still have Essex House, but I love this place. And to get away from London during the heat of summer —"

Arabella took a deep breath. "How much money does father need?" she asked, bracing herself for the expected outburst.

"It's nothing to do with you, girl. How dare you ask such a question?" Caroline's indignation evaporated and she sighed. "Besides, what difference does it make?"

"All the difference in the world," Arabella said quietly. "You see, I have some money of my own." Before her mother could ask, she rushed on. "I was paid for my work in the hospital, and I never spent a penny of it. There was no need since I had my allowance and my needs were few while I was out there."

Caroline gave a short laugh. "I hardly think the pittance you were paid would be enough to cover your father's debts."

"You're right, of course. But, you see, I asked Sam — Mr Fenton — to invest the money for me and it has increased in value considerably."

Caroline sniffed at the mention of the theatre proprietor's name. "I suppose you think such an offer will repay us for all the trouble you have caused." She squared her shoulders. "Well, you must speak to your father about it."

Arabella was about to confess more but she judged it wasn't the right moment. Mother would be outraged at the idea of her being paid to sing — and even more scandalized if she knew precisely how much her performances at the Half Moon had brought her, for Sam had insisted that it was only fair she take a share of the profits. While not exactly rich, she had, thanks to Sam's wise investments, secured a measure of financial independence. But she would give it all up to help her father out of his present difficulty.

Now that the decision had been made, she felt happier. Despite the fact that she'd never regretted the act of defiance that had led to her singing career, she was truly sorry for the pain she had caused her family. Maybe this would make up for it.

Arabella's buoyant mood didn't last long. The brief promise of spring hadn't lasted either, and a bitter wind coming in from the North Sea flattened the burgeoning daffodils and tore the blackthorn blossom from the hedgerows. Confined to the house, Arabella didn't even have the heart to play the piano, let alone to practice her singing. What was the point, anyway?

Every morning and afternoon when the post boy toiled up the lane from the village, she was there waiting. A letter from Nat was the only thing that could cheer her up.

But there was no word. Sometimes she thought she must have dreamt those few moments in the drawing room at Essex House when he had looked into her eyes so lovingly and pressed the letter into her hand. If it wasn't for that she would hardly be able to believe that he really wanted to marry her.

She read it once more, his loving words bringing a smile to her lips. "Oh, Nat, why don't you come?" she murmured. She smoothed the paper on her lap, pondering his talk of a plan. Surely it could only mean that he wanted them to elope. But how would that sway her mother into accepting their marriage? She sighed and looked out of the window again at the trees tossing their heads in the wind, the white caps of the waves on the distant sea. She prayed Nat wasn't on his way home in this weather, remembering the terrifying storms they had encountered on the way to Constantinople.

Nat was back in London. He had met Harry at his club and learned the latest news about Delaney. He doubted that banishing him from the country would do any good. But British justice demanded evidence acceptable to a jury before a man could be punished.

"I must say I'm not happy about it, but I have to admit it would have been hard to get a conviction," he said.

Harry agreed. "At least my sister is free of him." He sighed. "Of course, if she hadn't behaved so badly he would have had nothing to hold over her."

Without thinking, Nat leapt to Arabella's defence. "If the man wasn't such a scoundrel he would never have threatened her with exposure. Besides, was her behaviour so reprehensible?"

"Can you doubt it — singing in a public place, a music hall at that, exposed to all sorts of low characters —" Harry almost spluttered into his brandy.

Nat grinned. "Low characters? I believe I saw you and Captain Wilson at the Half Moon more than once."

"All the chaps from the regiment went, all smitten with the 'beautiful Bella.' If only I'd known earlier, I'd have put a stop to it."

"But you didn't know. None of them recognized her, so where was the harm?" Nat shrugged. "It made her happy."

"Well, she was bound to get found out in the end. Was it worth upsetting her whole family just for a few moments of enjoyment?"

"I think she would say that it was. She is a truly talented performer. And I, for one, don't see any difference between entertaining a few friends and singing to a multitude. Others have done it. What about Jenny Lind, the Swedish Nightingale? She has just returned to London from America. She is fêted wherever she goes and has even been befriended by the royal family? Where is the difference?"

"I suppose when you put it like that —" Harry stared moodily into his glass. "I can't see my mother taking the same view. Can you imagine her going along to the Half Moon to hear Arabella sing?" he gave a short laugh. "It was hard enough persuading her that a visit to the Princess's Theatre was respectable — even with the Queen herself in attendance."

Nat laughed too, remembering that theatre visit two years ago when he had first met Arabella. He had fallen in love with her right from the start and had spent many sleepless nights tormented by the thought that she was to marry Delaney. Now, he clung to the hope that things might turn out right for them, after all. Dare he confess his hopes and plans to her brother?

As he was about to speak, Harry said, "They're still down in the country you know. Poor Bella's bored silly, but Mama insists she stays there until all possibility of a scandal is passed. They will be back next week though."

Nat's heart leapt. His work had prevented him from paying the promised visit to Kent and he had been reluctant to put his proposed plan to Arabella in writing in case her mother intercepted the letter. Harry had asked him to stand as best man in place of James

Wilson, but he had hardly dared hope that Arabella would be allowed to attend the wedding. Her mother had already spread the story that she was ill to account for her daughter's absence.

"She will be there?" he asked, holding his breath for the answer.

"Of course, she is to be Charlotte's bridesmaid."

Next week — just a few days away, Nat thought.

Arabella gave a final twitch to Charlotte's veil and looked over her friend's shoulder into the mirror while Tilly, the maid, hovered behind them, hairbrush in one hand, pins in the other.

"You look lovely — Harry is a lucky man," she said, suppressing a twinge of envy. If things had been different she would have been the one preparing for her wedding. But then, Charlotte was marrying a man she truly loved whereas Arabella still had no idea if she would ever be so lucky.

Although Nat was to be Harry's best man, she still hadn't heard from him personally. She had gone direct to Charlotte's home from Kent in order to prepare her friend for the coming ceremony. She was to be bridesmaid and still had to finish dressing.

Charlotte stood up to allow Arabella to take her place so that Tilly could do her hair and fasten the circlet of flowers onto the elaborate coiffeur. She stood for a moment watching, then began to flit around the room, prey to a sudden attack of nerves. "Where did I put my gloves?" she wailed. "And will the carriage get here on time?"

Arabella tried to reassure her while Tilly struggled to fix the pins in her hair.

"Do keep still, miss," the maid said. "And you, Miss Charlotte, sit down and take a deep breath. Everything is under control. Your gloves are here on the dressing table. Your uncle and mama are waiting downstairs." She pushed a final pin into Arabella's hair and straightened the coronet on her head. "There, that's both of you ready. Now, if you don't mind, Miss, I must make myself presentable and join the other servants."

"Of course, Tilly. You go on now." Charlotte smiled and impulsively squeezed the girl's hand. "Arabella will take care of me now. Thank you for all you've done."

"It was a pleasure, Miss," the maid said, bobbing a curtsey before she left the room.

Arabella stood up. "If we're both ready, we should go down."

The girls linked arms and went out on to the landing, looking like sisters in their white organdie and lace dresses, with fitted bodices and full skirts over several petticoats. Thank goodness the hooped skirts had gone out of fashion a few years ago, Arabella thought. In her present costume she looked a little too much like Bella Forde but for the piled-up chestnut hair in place of blonde ringlets. A crinoline would have completed the picture of the famous singer and, with so many of Harry's fellow officers in church, the danger of recognition was always present. Her thoughts were interrupted by her friend's deep sigh and she berated herself for her selfishness on this day of all days.

"I do wish my papa were here," Charlotte said. "I always dreamed he would give me away. And James too — he was to be Harry's best man."

Arabella squeezed her arm. "I know how you feel. But they wouldn't want you to be sad — not on this happy day."

The trace of a smile appeared and Charlotte said, "A happy day for you too, Bella. It was good of Nat Sloane to step in. I have arranged for you to sit next to him at the wedding breakfast."

It was hard to appear unconcerned as her heart started to beat faster. She had hoped there would be an opportunity to speak to him but she had feared it might be impossible in the crush of guests back at the house.

At the foot of the stairs, Charlotte's mother gave a little cry as her daughter descended into the hall. She clutched her brother's arm and held a handkerchief to her eyes.

"Now, Mama, no tears, please," Charlotte said with a little laugh.

"I'm sorry, my love. You look so beautiful in white. Both of you do." She turned to her brother. "Don't you agree, Jack?"

"A real picture, my dear," said Charlotte's uncle, kissing her cheek.

The church was just round the corner from the Wilsons's house on the opposite side of Essex Square so Arabella and Mrs Wilson walked, accompanied by friends and neighbours of the couple who had been invited to the ceremony.

294

Outside the house an open carriage drew up, pulled by a magnificent grey. As they turned the corner Arabella looked back to see Charlotte's uncle handing her up into the carriage. Her steps quickened. In a few moments she would see Nat.

One of Harry's fellow officers who was acting as usher waited in the porch of St Stephen's Church. Bidding Arabella wait until the bride arrived, he escorted Mrs Wilson down the aisle to her place in the front pew.

As Arabella craned her neck for a glimpse of Nat, she heard the carriage pull up. She hurried outside and adjusted her friend's veil, handed her the bouquet of cream roses and kissed her cheek, just as the organ started to play. As they entered the church, Harry turned round, resplendent in his Captain's uniform.

"Doesn't he look handsome?" Charlotte whispered.

Arabella nodded but her eyes were on Nat in his lavender trousers and darker frock coat. Her heart thundered in competition with the organ as she walked slowly behind her friend, wishing with all her heart that she and Nat could change places with Charlotte and Harry.

The wedding breakfast was almost over, the speeches made and Charlotte was cutting the cake into small squares to present to each guest as they departed, yet still Arabella had not managed a private word with Nat. They had sat beside each other after exchanging formal greetings, they had drunk toasts and sampled the array of dishes set before them. But Arabella had only nibbled at the refreshments and she noticed that Nat had not eaten either. From time to time he turned to her and smiled, a smile which told her his feelings hadn't changed since they'd been apart. But when would they get the chance to be together?

When Arabella came downstairs again after helping Charlotte to change into travelling clothes, she discovered to her dismay that Nat had gone. In the flurry of farewells to the couple there was no chance to wonder why he had left so suddenly until Harry, bending to kiss her goodbye, whispered, "Don't worry, little sister. He'll be back. He is performing one last duty as best man — he has gone to the railway station to see to our luggage."

As her brother and her best friend climbed into the carriage that was to take them to the station and on to their secret honeymoon destination, Arabella threw rice and lucky slippers with enthusiasm. In return Charlotte threw her bouquet, making sure her friend caught it, and Arabella laughed with the rest of the guests, blushing as they congratulated her on the omen that meant she would be the next bride.

She caught her mother's speculative glance and her stomach churned. Would she ever accept Nat as a suitable match or was she already lining up a more advantageous prospect for her rebellious daughter? Arabella didn't care. Nat had said he had a plan and he would soon be sharing it with her.

Charlotte's mother dried her tears, her brother comforted her and the guests began to disperse.

Arabella strolled across the square with her parents, anxiously glancing around to see if Nat had returned.

Back at the house her father seemed restless, glancing at the clock over the mantel. "I wonder where Mr Sloane has got to," he said. "I asked him to come and take supper with us. But he had some business to attend to first."

Arabella gave a sigh of relief. At least he was expected to return. But as the day wore on into evening there was no sign of him.

CHAPTER
TWENTY-THREE

Arabella spent a sleepless night, her thoughts constantly veering between elation and doubt. Nat had smiled, had taken her hand and tried to speak before his duties as best man had taken him away from her side. But Henry had said he was to return. At the time she'd been sure that he was coming back to speak to her father, to ask permission to marry her. Now, she wasn't so sure. It had probably been some business they wanted to discuss which could just as well be done at Henry's club the next day. Besides, she was sure that nothing Nat could say would sway her mother in his favour.

They must elope — that was the only answer. And if elopement was Nat's plan, why hadn't he seized the chance while she was down in the country? Being so close to the coast, they could have taken a ship and been in France before the day was out.

As she tossed and turned she tried not to think about Charlotte who, at this moment, was sleeping in the arms of the man she loved. She should be happy for her. But all she could feel was a burning envy, coupled with the despairing thought that it was most unlikely she'd ever share her friend's good fortune.

When she did eventually fall asleep it seemed only minutes before she was woken up by her mother's sharp voice. "Come along, Arabella. You cannot stay in bed all day simply because you overindulged yourself at the wedding. Get up and dress at once. We have visitors," she said, roughly shaking her shoulder.

Sleep fled at once, replaced by a flare of joy, and she sat up quickly. "Nat," she said. "He's here."

"Nonsense, child. Why would Mr Sloane be asking for you?"

Arabella sank back on her pillow. "Who is it then?"

For once Caroline seemed unsure of herself. Her eyes burned with excitement and she fluttered her hands. "You'll find out soon enough."

Arabella swung her legs over the side of the bed. Who could have caused her mother's agitation?

"Hurry up, we mustn't keep them waiting," said Caroline. "Burton will help you to dress, and make sure you are presentable before you come down."

Now in a fever of curiosity, Arabella went to the wash stand and hastily completed her toilet before allowing Burton to help her on with her day dress. Her fingers fumbled with the tiny buttons on the bodice and she sighed and gave in to the maid's ministrations.

As she sat to have her hair brushed and pinned into place she wondered who could have called so early and got her mother in such a state. It couldn't be another suitor surely. If her mother had set her sights on someone he would have been invited to the wedding and she would have been forced to dance with him. Maybe it was something to do with Oswald. Had that police inspector come to warn them that he had sneaked back into the country — perhaps to seek his revenge?

The little shiver of apprehension was quickly brushed away. Mama would surely have said so and besides, that would hardly account for the sparkle in her eyes. Impatiently, she pushed Burton's hand away and stood up. Hurrying downstairs she heard a murmur of voices from the library's half open door. Recognizing one of them, she entered the room, her mouth open in astonishment.

"Sam, what on earth are you doing here?" She clapped a hand to her mouth. "Is it Maisie? Has something happened to her?"

But Sam was smiling — that broad grin she was so familiar with. And, to her astonishment, her mother and father were smiling too.

Only then did Arabella notice the other occupant of the room and it took a moment for it to sink in. The man was wearing the livery of the royal household.

"What is it?" she asked faintly.

"Sit down, my dear," said Henry. "Mr Fenton has a proposition for you."

Arabella took her seat in a daze. She could not believe that Sam had even been allowed into the house, let alone invited into the library to meet her parents and speak to her about singing — for it could only be her singing that had brought him here. And, glancing at the liveried servant who so far had said nothing, she felt her heart begin to pound with excitement as it dawned on her what his presence could mean. No wonder her mother was looking so smug.

She could hardly take in what Sam was saying as the thoughts whirled in her head. He leaned forward in his seat, his hands clasped between his knees. "It's not me as is proposing anything, Bella me dear, but this feller here. He's come with a summons from Her Majesty."

That made her sit up and open her eyes wide. "The Queen —?" She noticed that her mother was wide-eyed too and, strangely, had not seemed to take offence at Sam's familiarity.

"Yes, me dear. Queen Victoria herself has heard tales of a songster to rival the Swedish Nightingale and wants to judge for herself." He gestured to the servant. "Tell her, Hopkins."

Hopkins coughed and hesitated. "As you know, Her Majesty is interested in all the arts — theatre, opera and such. All London is talking about Miss Bella Forde and Her Majesty is curious to know if her reputation is a deserved one." He nodded at Arabella's wide-eyed look. "Yes, Miss Raynsford, Queen Victoria wants to hear you sing."

Arabella couldn't stop herself from interrupting. "You mean, she's going to attend a performance at the Half Moon?"

Hopkins pursed his lips in affront and Sam gave a hearty chuckle.

"Course not, me dear. Can't expect Her Majesty to mix with some of the types we get there."

"It is Her Majesty's birthday in two weeks' time. She will be at Windsor for the celebration. You are

301

commanded to attend as one of the entertainers," said Hopkins.

"I'm to sing for the Queen — at Windsor?" Arabella said faintly.

"Yes, Miss. She wants you to sing two songs." He held out an envelope. "Here is your invitation. There is also a list of Her Majesty's favourite songs — you may choose which ones you like." He coughed. "Just a hint, Miss. She is very fond of Mendelssohn."

Arabella found her voice. "Thank you. Please give Her Majesty my kindest regards and say that it will be an honour to entertain her. I shall write a formal reply at once."

Hopkins gave a small bow and turned to leave the room but Arabella detained him. "May I ask if Mr Fenton will be allowed to accompany me, to play for me? I would feel less nervous with a familiar pianist."

"Of course, Miss." Hopkins left the room and Sam made to follow, but Arabella put her hand on his arm. Ignoring her mother's sharp intake of breath, she said, "Please don't go yet. Stay and have some refreshment. I wish to hear what has been happening at the theatre in my absence. And how are Vi and Maisie?"

Recovering quickly, Caroline nodded. "Yes, please do stay, Mr Fenton. Let us go into the morning room. It is more comfortable there." She rang the bell for the maid and turned to her husband. "Will you join us, Henry?"

He had hardly spoken since Arabella had come into the room, but now he smiled at her and kissed her cheek. "Well done, my dear. It seems that Mr Sloane was right when he said your voice deserved a wider

302

audience — royalty no less." Beaming, he turned to his wife. "How lucky we are to have such a clever daughter, my dear." He waved a hand. "You go on. I am expecting another visitor — business you know." As he turned away, Arabella was sure he had winked at her.

In the morning room, as Arabella dispensed coffee and macaroons, she wondered if she had imagined it. Everyone seemed to be behaving strangely today.

She turned to Sam, eager to hear how her summons to the castle had come about. But Caroline forestalled her, saying, "So you are the man who led my daughter into deceiving her family? I should be angry with you but it seems the situation has changed."

"Your pardon, madam. I regret causing distress to Bella's family. However —"

Before he could go on, Arabella interrupted. "Sam did not lead me, Mama. He was most reluctant but I begged him to let me go on stage just once, for the excitement of it. And when I proved such a success, he in turn was reluctant to let me go." She leaned towards her mother and took her hands. "I wish I could make you understand. Up there, with the audience holding its breath, it was like magic. I was in another world."

"I don't suppose I will ever understand. But it seems I must accept the situation now — especially in the light of recent events. But how you could have even contemplated entering such a low establishment is beyond me."

Sam put down his cup with a bang and Arabella quickly intervened. "The Half Moon is *not* a low establishment, Mama. How could you insult Sam to his face like this? It is a perfectly respectable theatre."

Caroline had the grace to look a little shame-faced. "I did not mean to insult you, Mr Fenton. I apologize."

"Never mind, Madam. Many of your class make the same mistake. I admit that some of the music halls are a bit rowdy and attract the lower classes but I have tried my best to rise above that."

Caroline sniffed. "Whatever the case may be, you must realize, Mr Fenton, that my daughter will not be appearing there again. Once she has appeared before the Queen, she will be fêted everywhere. They will be clamouring for her to sing at the Royal Italian Opera before long."

"No doubt, Madam, but they will have to wait until the rebuilding is complete since the theatre burned down a couple of months ago." Sam gave a little cough. "Besides, surely it is for Bella to decide for herself. She is of age, after all."

Unable to keep silent any longer, Arabella said, "I do wish you would not discuss me as if I weren't here."

"I'm sorry, but whatever Mr Fenton says, you must see it is impossible for you to carry on at his place. Besides, you will soon marry and I am quite certain your future husband will forbid any such display in public."

The argument was threatening to become more heated but, as Arabella was about to retort, she realized that her father had re-entered the room. And, as she saw who was behind him, she leapt to her feet, her eyes shining, the disagreement forgotten.

Before she could greet him, Nat came towards her and took her hands. He turned to her mother. "Mrs Raynsford, forgive me, but I'm afraid I must contradict your last remark. Bella's future husband would be delighted to hear his wife sing — in public or wherever she chooses."

Ignoring Caroline's shocked gaze, he leaned towards Arabella and whispered. "I do sincerely hope, though, that she will sometimes sing just for her husband's pleasure."

Henry was beaming as he leaned over to kiss his daughter's cheek. She gave him a hug and whispered. "Thank you, Papa."

With his arm around her, Henry turned to his wife. "Mr Sloane has asked for our daughter's hand, my dear — and I have given my consent."

Caroline, still reeling from Nat's earlier remark, managed a faint smile. "I suppose congratulations are in order then," she said. She lowered her voice but Arabella heard her say, "Henry, are you sure he is suitable?"

Nat had heard too and Arabella smiled as he took her mother's hand and bowed over it, brushing her fingers with his lips. "Madam, I may not be rich or have estates in Ireland but I am honest and a hard worker. What's more, I love your daughter. I will make her happy, I swear."

Caroline winced at the jibe but she was still not convinced. "But, he's an engineer — he builds things," she said faintly, clutching her husband's arm.

"No, he designs things for others to build. Your future son-in-law is a very clever man — somewhat like your own father, my dear."

Caroline had the grace to blush at this oblique reference to her own origins which, since her marriage to Henry, she had tried so hard to forget. "Well, since you put it like that —" She turned to Nat and Arabella, who were now standing by the window, hands clasped and gazing into each other's eyes as if there were no one else in the room. "I hope you'll both be very happy," she said. "And you, young man, take care of my daughter, do you hear?"

Sam, who had sat quietly throughout this exchange, now stood up and pumped Nat's hand. "I told you it would all turn out right, didn't I," he said and, ignoring Caroline's scandalized gasp, he grasped Arabella's shoulders and planted a noisy kiss on her cheek.

At the door he turned and his normally cheery face was sombre. "Looks like this is the end of our association, me dear. But it was fun while it lasted. Goodbye — and good luck."

"But Sam —" Arabella gasped. But it was too late. He had gone. When she made to call him back, her mother gently detained her. "It's for the best, Arabella," she said. "Now that your talent has been recognized, you must see that it would not be wise to continue your association with Mr Fenton."

Anger boiled in her. "You've certainly changed your tune, Mama. It isn't so long ago you were berating me for bringing shame on the family." She hastily swallowed her angry tears. "I don't care what you say

306

— I must have Sam to play for me, otherwise I won't go."

"Don't be silly, dear," her mother said and Arabella almost stamped her foot in frustration. Why did they still treat her like a child?

She suddenly became aware of Nat smiling at her and immediately felt ashamed as she realized that she was indeed behaving like a child. Besides, as Sam had said, she was of age. She could make her own decisions. She would write to Sam immediately and remind him of his promise to play for her at the castle.

Grudgingly, she apologized to her mother who accepted readily. "It's the excitement, I expect, dear," she said. "Now, come along, we have much to do — the preparations, a date to be set, and so soon after Harry's wedding. Dressmakers, caterers —" She began to pace the room. "The Queen, Windsor, oh my goodness —"

Henry took her arm. "Hush, my dear. There is plenty of time. Why don't you go to your room and rest? Too much excitement, you know —" He led her out of the room, turning to smile at Nat and his daughter. "It is a little warm today. Perhaps you two would enjoy a turn in the garden?"

Nat took Arabella's hand. "An excellent idea." They went out through the French windows, descended the terrace steps and, hand in hand, crossed the lawn to a secluded arbour.

When they were seated, Arabella started to speak but Nat's arms came round her and he silenced her with a kiss that seemed to go on forever. It was all she had dreamed of and she willingly gave herself up to his embrace. At last he drew away from her and said, a little breathlessly, "You don't know how long I've been wanting to do that."

She smiled mischievously. "As long as I've been waiting for it?" she asked.

"The day we met, I felt I'd found my destiny but there was so much in the way."

"I felt the same but I thought I owed a duty to my parents. And then there was my career." She gazed at him earnestly. "It means a lot to me, you know. Did you mean what you said about letting me carry on?"

"Yes, but not at the Half Moon. Now that your mother seems to have accepted us marrying, it wouldn't be fair to hurt her any further."

Arabella loved him for his sensitivity. Even when she had been most at odds with her mother, she had always loved her. "I really never meant to hurt her, you know — she had such aspirations for me. But if I want to keep on singing, what can we do?"

"I have a plan."

Arabella laughed. "Oh, the famous plan you referred to in your letter. I thought I'd never get to hear it."

He silenced her with another kiss. A little later he murmured, "Do you want to hear my plan or not, you shameless hussy?"

"I'd rather carry on as we are but I cannot have my future husband thinking me shameless." Arabella giggled. "Go on then — your plan?"

"We have Sam to thank for this, actually. His cousin, who runs a theatre in New York, had heard of you and wanted you to perform there. Sam kept quiet about it

— afraid of losing you to a rival, but I think his conscience was pricking him."

"New York? How exciting." She frowned. "But I couldn't possibly go — not if we are to be married. Nat, my darling, you mean far more to me than a singing career."

He grinned at her. "I'm very pleased to hear it. But you shall not give up your singing. I'll go to America with you, of course." He stifled Arabella's gasp with another kiss. "If you're out of the country, your mother will be spared the shame, as she calls it. And who knows, some day she may even be proud of you."

"She'll still be upset." She frowned again. "What would we have done if she had not accepted our marriage?"

"Then we should have to elope," Nat said with a grin.

Arabella laughed. "When I read your letter I thought that was what you meant but I couldn't see how it would sway Mama into accepting our marriage."

Nat laughed too. "Fortunately that wasn't necessary."

He kissed her again and she snuggled up to him, inhaling the scent of his cologne, wanting more of him. But, now that their future together was assured, she could be patient. She allowed herself to picture the long sea voyage to America — days and nights aboard ship where they could express their love for each other in ways she could only dream of. Blushing at her thoughts, she pushed away from Nat and became practical.

"What will you do in America?"

"I can design bridges and buildings anywhere and New York is an exciting place to be right now — a growing city with lots of potential."

"I can't wait," Arabella said.

"But we can't go too soon. There is your command performance to prepare for."

She gasped. "I could never have imagined myself saying this but the prospect of our marriage had quite put it out of my mind."

In the hectic days that followed, Arabella hardly saw Nat but there was no time to miss him — except at night when she fell asleep reliving those tender moments in the garden and anticipating their future together.

The house was in an uproar. Despite Arabella's constant pleas to keep the arrangements simple, Caroline was not to be thwarted. Her son's wedding had of necessity been a quieter occasion due to the Wilsons's recent bereavement and their grief at the death of Charlotte's brother.

This wedding would be as lavish as they could afford with so many bridesmaids, ushers and guests that, as Arabella said in a letter to Charlotte, she was sure they would never fit into St Stephen's Church let alone into Essex House for the reception afterwards. Her friend was enjoying her honeymoon in St Tropez but had written that she would be home for the wedding to act as her friend's matron of honour.

As she was constantly harried with lists and menus, hustled here and there for fittings for her wedding gown and the trousseau that her mother deemed only fitting for her daughter, Arabella came close to losing her temper more than once.

At such times she wished she and Nat *had* eloped and once even sat down to write him a note begging him to come and take her away. Of course she didn't send it, realizing that accepting her mother's arrangements was the least she could do after all the trouble she had caused her. Besides, she had never seen Caroline so happy. This was what she had dreamed of for years — a grand society wedding for her only daughter. And, if it wasn't quite what she had envisioned, if the groom wasn't quite out of the top drawer as she had wished, there was the consolation of knowing that in a few days she and her daughter would attend the Queen's birthday celebrations. Seeing Arabella perform for Her Majesty would more than compensate for all the upsets she had suffered recently.

When friends came to call, Arabella sat quietly in a corner, smiling as her mother boasted of her daughter's achievements. One would never guess how horrified she had been, how many tears of shame had been shed when the secret of her singing career had come out.

"Of course, we all knew Arabella had a wonderful voice. I said so when she was just a tiny tot. We always knew she would be recognized one day," she said.

And the ladies smiled and nodded over their teacups. Arabella guessed there would be gossip among themselves later but for the moment it seemed as if a summons to perform before royalty completely wiped out the shame of treading the music hall boards or being sent home from the Crimea in disgrace for entertaining the common soldiery.

Despite her irritation at the conflicting standards, she couldn't help being amused. At the same time, she wished it could all be over and that she and Nat could escape to their new life. Even the prospect of her attendance on the Queen did not excite her as it once would have done.

At last the day came and when it was over there would be only a week to get through before the moment she was really waiting for — stepping on board the steam ship *Persia* at Liverpool docks. At last she would be alone with Nat and her new life would begin.

How she missed Nat and longed to see him. But he was busy winding up his business affairs in preparation for their departure. He would not even be able to hear her sing this time but, as he said, he would have the privilege soon of being able to hear her any time he wished.

In a way, it was a relief that he would not be accompanying her to Windsor, for as the time drew near, Arabella began to experience the butterflies in her stomach that had always plagued her before a performance. This time they were worse than ever. Nat would have been a distraction when she needed all her concentration to get through what was rapidly beginning to feel like an ordeal.

She wished her mother were not coming too but her parents had been included in the invitation. After all,

Arabella must have a chaperone on the long drive to Windsor — never mind that she had travelled alone to Turkey and witnessed scenes such as her mother — and the Queen herself — could never dream of.

When she was finally ready, Caroline surveyed her with approval. "That russet colour is perfect for you, my dear. It complements your hair and eyes so well and the gold trimming sets it off."

Arabella looked at herself in the mirror, reflecting that this "Bella Forde" was as unlike the fêted music hall singer as it was possible to be. She took a deep breath, mentally rehearsing the songs she was to sing and wishing once more that it was all over.

The butterflies refused to settle down and Arabella closed her eyes, willing herself not to be sick and letting her mother's voluble chatter wash over her as the coach rumbled out of London towards the castle. Afterwards, she could not remember their arrival, the long walk through corridors hung with sumptuous tapestries, the great hall where the Queen and her guests were assembled.

She scarcely recognized Sam when he appeared in his finery until he smiled and gripped her hand. "Everything will be all right, Bella me dear. Here's your music. Just remember what I taught you." He put his hand on his abdomen. "Breathe from here and just let it all come out."

He sat down at the piano and she stood alongside, her hand resting lightly on the polished lid, the other pressed to her diaphragm. Sam played the introductory chords and, as always when the music started, she was transported to another world. The pure notes rang out.

"*On wings of song I'll bear thee, My loved one far beyond —*"

And she too, was borne away on wings of song, as she always was by the music and the poetry. The lovely words of Heinrich Heine's poem filled her with a great yearning as she pictured herself with Nat, wandering in that beautiful garden to "*drink of love and peacefulness, to dream our blessed dream.*" As the last notes died away there was a sudden hush and then the applause began.

As it died down, Sam played the opening bars for her second rendering — "Home Sweet Home", another of her favourites. Tears came to her eyes as she sang, realizing that she would soon be leaving her old home behind for a new world. Would it be all she dreamed of? Would Nat keep his promise to allow her to carry on singing? At this moment it didn't matter. Even if she never sang again, this would be her moment of triumph, a fitting swansong. The applause rang out again and then Sam was leading her forward to make her curtsey to Her Majesty and the assembled household. It was a moment to treasure as Queen Victoria murmured her sincere appreciation.

Three weeks later, Arabella had other moments to treasure. As she leaned on the ship's rail looking towards the new land that was to be her home, she felt that she was the happiest girl alive. They had been at

314

sea for thirteen days and the voyage was almost over. If only it could go on forever, she thought.

The weeks until their departure had been hectic and Arabella had given in to all her mother's demands. It was the least she could do after everything that had happened. Her performance at Windsor, which at one time would have been the high point of her life, faded into insignificance as she walked with her father down the aisle of St Stephen's a few days later and took Nat's hand.

The ceremony, the wedding breakfast, the leave taking, and the journey to Liverpool had passed in a blur. At her insistence, Maisie, together with Sam and Vi, had been invited to the wedding. The hardest thing of all had been saying goodbye to her faithful friends.

"We'll meet again, Bella me dear," Sam said. "Who knows — we may even fetch up in New York ourselves one day."

"And you'll be back to visit your family from time to time," Maisie said. "Just don't forget your old friends." She wiped a tear from her cheek. "I just wish you could have seen me and Davie wed."

"Me too," Arabella said, giving her friend a final hug. Then there was a chorus of goodbyes from the rest of their friends and relations and it was time to leave for the railway station and the train to Liverpool.

Henry and Caroline had accompanied them and it wasn't until they had boarded the steam ship *Persia* that the newly married couple had a chance to be alone.

Arabella had said a tearful goodbye to her parents but the tears had soon dried in the excitement of the crowds, the scurrying sailors casting off huge ropes and hawsers, the shouted commands from aloft and the belching smoke from the *Persia*'s two funnels.

The noise and smoke had sent most of the passengers scuttling below but Arabella, entranced by it all, had begged Nat to stay and watch as the great ship's screws began to turn and the vessel made its stately way out of the harbour and into the Irish Sea.

Nat did not need much persuading. His engineer's heart was exhilarated at travelling in one of the new passenger liners which, although it still bore its sails, relied on steam as the predominant force propelling it across the ocean.

Arabella in turn was enchanted by the romance of it all despite Nat's laughing warning that when they reached mid-Atlantic she would probably succumb, as most of the passengers already had, to seasickness.

But today, the sky was blue, the little wavelets capped with white, sparkled in the sun and Arabella felt she was the happiest girl alive. She turned and smiled at Nat and he squeezed her hand with an answering smile.

"Are you cold, my love?" he said. "Perhaps we should go below?"

She nodded and a warm glow encompassed her body at the thought of what would follow once they were ensconced in their cabin. Yes, if only the voyage could last forever, she thought, as they descended the steps. On the way they passed a crew member and he gave them a knowing smile. Everyone on board knew they were newly married although they had not mixed very much with their fellow passengers. They had asked for their meals to be served in their cabin and spent their time either there or on deck, high up in the bows, sheltered from the gaze of others.

Her time alone with Nat was all she had dreamt it would be. His lovemaking, tender and patient at first, had become more passionate as she became accustomed to his touch. Each time it seemed to get better. And so it was again, Arabella reflected much later as a discreet knock came at their cabin door.

She giggled as Nat scrambled into his clothes. "What is it?" he asked, waving a hand at her to be quiet. She giggled all the harder and buried her head under the sheet.

"I thought you would like to know, sir, that land has been sighted. Most of the passengers have gone up on deck."

"Land? Already? Thank you for letting us know."

Arabella sat up, her eyes shining. "Land. Oh, Nat, let's go up and look."

"I'd rather stay here," he said with a mock frown.

She threw a pillow at him and scrambled off the bunk, grabbing for her skirt and bodice.

On deck, she and Nat crowded the rail with the other passengers, searching the horizon. And there it was — a smudge of darker colour where the sky met the sea. As she looked up into the face of the man she loved, a huge white bird, the first they had seen for days, flew over the ship. Her heart soared with it and her head was filled with music as she followed its flight towards the new world.

Nat's arm came round her shoulders and he bent to kiss her. "Welcome home, my darling. You see, I have borne you away on wings of song to an enchanted land where all is bliss and joy — just like your song."

Arabella felt like singing but, as she responded to Nat's kiss, she began to realize that there were some things in life more exciting than music.

Also available in ISIS Large Print:

The Girl at the Farmhouse Gate

Julia Stoneham

An evocative story of love, loss and the tragedy of war.

It is early spring in 1944 and Allied troops will soon invade northern France. Alice Todd is beginning her second year as warden of a Land Army hostel located in the wilds of Devonshire. Here she has won the affection and confidence of the girls in her charge and found herself caught up in lives which are complex, humorous and sometimes tragic.

ISBN 978-0-7531-8616-9 (hb)
ISBN 978-0-7531-8617-6 (pb)

Facing the World

Grace Thompson

Sally Travis appeared to have been badly let down by Rhys Martin, who had gone away when under suspicion of burglary. Sally knew he was at college and secretly supported him. She had faced the gossips alone when their baby was born, and ignored the worrying rumours about him.

Rhys's father, Gwilym Martin, had lost a leg in an accident but whereas Sally held her head high under difficulties, Gwilym, who had been a popular sportsman and athlete, hid away, unable to face being seen in a wheelchair. But Sally ignored unkind remarks and helped others, especially Jimmy, a young boy put in danger by his parents' neglect during their marital difficulties.

But doubts about Rhys begin to grow. When Rhys finally returned, would she still be waiting? Or had too much happened for things to be the same?

ISBN 978-0-7531-8586-5 (hb)
ISBN 978-0-7531-8587-2 (pb)

Back Home

Bethan Darwin

Ellie has fallen in love with a high-flying city lawyer, but when her heart gets broken there's not much choice but to decamp from their illicit 5 star love-nest in Primrose Hill to the rather more humdrum confines of her granddad Trevor's house in Clapham.

Finding herself back home isn't all bad. Ellie can always hit the backpacker trail again, or maybe find a job she enjoys enough to stick at. And it's lovely spending time with Trevor, drinking tea from real china cups, swapping wine tips with her mum, or sorting out her best friend Gina's torrid love life. That is until she meets handsome Gabriel . . .

But just when it looks like everything is shaping up "tickety-boo" there's a knock on the door that turns Trevor's world upside down and takes them all back to the Welsh Valleys in wartime . . .

ISBN 978-0-7531-8568-1 (hb)
ISBN 978-0-7531-8569-8 (pb)

Legacy

Tamara McKinley

Following in the pioneering footsteps of the women who have gone before her, Ruby and her new husband James brave a long and treacherous journey to start their new life together. However, they soon discover that there are many more dangers than just those that meet the eye. When James is tempted away by the gold rush, Ruby must join forces with the Aborigine girl Kumali and learn to adapt, if they're going to survive.

Meanwhile there are other new arrivals to Australian shores: a Tahitian with a mysterious past, a naïve young schoolmistress, and an English aristocrat, all unaware that their destinies are irrevocably intertwined. As fortunes are made and lives are lost, many secrets will be uncovered. But those torn apart by feuds, greed, hatred and circumstance, will ultimately find they have to unite under the same flag . . .

ISBN 978-0-7531-8540-7 (hb)
ISBN 978-0-7531-8541-4 (pb)

No Sin to Love

Roberta Grieve

Young Dolly Dixon is determined to overcome her illegitimate background and lead a respectable life, attending evening classes in an attempt to better herself. But when her mother runs off with a lover, she is forced to leave her office job to look after her unappreciative stepfamily.

Her life of drudgery is brightened by her love for handsome market trader Tom Marchant. It is not just his good looks and devastating smile that have won her heart. He is ambitious too and longs to escape his youthful involvement with the criminal Rose brothers. Dolly believes him and at the start of World War II they get married and leave London to open a shop in a Sussex village. But have they really seen the last of the brothers? And what is the other secret that Tom is hiding?

ISBN 978-0-7531-8364-9 (hb)
ISBN 978-0-7531-8365-6 (pb)

ISIS publish a wide range of books in large print, from fiction to biography. Any suggestions for books you would like to see in large print or audio are always welcome. Please send to the Editorial Department at:

ISIS Publishing Limited
7 Centremead
Osney Mead
Oxford OX2 0ES

A full list of titles is available free of charge from:

Ulverscroft Large Print Books Limited

(UK)
The Green
Bradgate Road, Anstey
Leicester LE7 7FU
Tel: (0116) 236 4325

(Australia)
P.O. Box 314
St Leonards
NSW 1590
Tel: (02) 9436 2622

(USA)
P.O. Box 1230
West Seneca
N.Y. 14224-1230
Tel: (716) 674 4270

(Canada)
P.O. Box 80038
Burlington
Ontario L7L 6B1
Tel: (905) 637 8734

(New Zealand)
P.O. Box 456
Feilding
Tel: (06) 323 6828

Details of **ISIS** complete and unabridged audio books are also available from these offices. Alternatively, contact your local library for details of their collection of **ISIS** large print and unabridged audio books.